Also by Sam J. Miller

The *Art* of Starving

DESTROY
ALL
MONSTERS

SAM J. MILLER

HARPER TEEN
An imprint of HarperCollins Publishers

For Juancy,
my husband, my hero, my heart

I always thought of photography as a naughty thing to do—that was one of my favorite things about it, and when I first did it, I felt very perverse.

—DIANE ARBUS

The best and most beautiful things in the world cannot be seen or even touched. They must be felt with the heart.

—HELEN KELLER

ONE

ASH

"He's sleeping on the front porch again," my mom said, her voice sounding sad the way only Solomon can make it. "Do you want me to have your father talk to him this time, Ash?"

I did not want that. Dad would scare the shit out of Solomon. Our front porch was probably the last safe place Solomon had, and I could never let Dad take that away from him.

"I'll go," I said, getting out of bed even though it was 2:00 a.m.

Not that the time mattered. I hadn't been asleep. I stopped by the kitchen, fished two sodas out of the fridge. Diet Coke for me, vanilla Coke for him. I always made sure we had vanilla Cokes cold and ready.

When I stepped out onto the porch, I was almost ashamed to wake him. There was a cold edge to the night, and he was wearing a tank top and what looked like boxer shorts. He seemed so small, in spite of the bulk of his biceps. The sturdiness of his shoulders.

Another reason I didn't want to disturb him: he was smiling. I only ever saw him smile when he was asleep.

Someone at Solomon's aunt's house—or was it his mother's friend Sioux he was staying with these days?— might have been wondering where he was. Might have been worried about him. But that was a big, unlikely "might." If Solomon had anyone else who cared what happened to him, he probably wouldn't have been sleeping on my porch in October in the first place.

"Hey," I said, sitting down on the porch swing. I noticed he was curled up just right to leave enough space for me to sit.

He mumbled something, curled up tighter. I grabbed one of his feet and squeezed it.

"Ash, hey," he said, like it was nothing, like this was totally normal. The night smelled like rain and smoke and a little bit of skunk.

"Everything okay?"

He didn't answer me right away, and I knew he was weighing his words. Wondering how much to tell me. The stories he told—they were part of why everyone was afraid of him. Crazy stuff he didn't seem to understand was crazy. A city full of monsters and magic and vicious police officers.

And dinosaurs. With Solomon it was always dinosaurs.

But he didn't talk about any of that. Not this time. He sat up, rubbed his eyes. "Skunk," he said, wrinkling his nose, and all of a sudden he's a little boy and we're ten years old and the world is so big and full of wonderful, terrible things.

I put my arm around his shoulder and he leaned into me so fast and gratefully that it made my throat hurt.

"You're okay," I said. "We're okay."

"We're not," he whispered.

I knew he was right, so I didn't say anything. His breathing slowed down. Solomon was safe, now. We were both safe, so long as we stayed there. Stayed still. Every awful thing was asleep. The night protected us, a deep black star-studded security blanket. I gave him his soda and he guzzled it greedily.

Anything could happen once he stepped down off my porch. Returned to the real world with all its terrors and uncertainties. But in that moment, we had each other.

"You'll be up all night if you drink that," he said, taking the Diet Coke away from me when I popped the top.

"That was already the way things were going."

His eyes were huge, and wouldn't move away from mine. I tried not to look into them, but they were unrelenting. "Why?"

I started to say, *It's the meds,* but decided against it. The last thing Solomon needed was another reason to be afraid of medication.

I'd gotten on antidepressants three weeks before. They were just starting to take effect. And they worked . . . mostly. The ground I walked on was feeling less and less like thin ice that might crack open at any moment and plunge me into the dark freezing water where I'd sink like a stone. Any side effects seemed slight when compared to that.

"It's this photo project," I said hastily. "It's a ton of work."

"What's it going to be about?"

"That's the work. Figuring out exactly what I want to focus on." Then I said, "Connor was asking about you."

Solomon stiffened. Sat up. "You two are still a . . . thing?"

"You sound like him," I said. "Always wanting to put a label on it."

"But you still see him. Still hook up."

"Yeah," I said. "Is that a problem?"

"Of course not," he said, leaning forward, holding his head in his hands. So, yeah, This Was Very Definitely a Problem.

I didn't know what his deal was with Connor. Less than a year younger than us, he'd always been Solomon's adoring little stepbrother. If something went wrong between them, I couldn't imagine what it was.

"I should go," Solomon groaned.

"Don't," I said. "Sleep here tonight. You can crash on my floor."

"Your father would murder us both."

"Not *both*," I said. "Probably just you."

"Very comforting."

"Hey, is everything okay?" I asked. "Why'd you come here tonight?"

He rubbed the back of his head. "I don't know. It seemed important at the time. Had to tell you something. Warn you. I don't remember what about."

"Ah," I said. "Well. You can message me, if you remember."

Solomon nodded. His face looked like it was about to crack open.

I wondered: What was it like, losing your mind? Being unable to tell the difference between dreams and the waking world? Not knowing what's real and what's not?

"Later, Ash," he said eventually, standing up. Which is when I noticed he had no shoes. Six-foot-plus, muscular like most guys wish they could be, and he'd always look like a helpless little boy to me.

I watched him lope off, into the darkness. The smell of smoke was stronger now. The cold weather was upon us. Summer was officially over, and I should have been in bed. I stayed on the porch until my soda was finished, and then headed inside to browse through 150 years' worth of photography on the internet until sleep snuck up on me.

TWO

SOLOMON

I shouldn't have gotten involved. They were police officers, and there were three of them, and they were in a bad mood.

It was a cold night, and the streets smelled like a hundred different kinds of smoke. Burning plastic, wood, paper, garbage—all the things people were lighting up to keep warm. Summer was officially over, and I should have been in bed.

My stomach grumbled. I wanted to eat a piece of apple pie and fall asleep for the next several days. I didn't want to save anybody. And chances were pretty good the cops just wanted to scare the old woman pushing the shopping cart. She had a velociraptor on a leash. I wondered if they'd hassled her for its license. Dirty cops harassing othersiders was nothing new; it happened a thousand times a day in Darkside. But once in a while they picked on the wrong person or pushed someone too far, someone who wasn't shy about summoning up fire or ice shards—which meant the cops were legally within their rights to respond with deadly force.

Which, I suspected, was what they wanted in the first place.

But the old lady's face was kindly. So I did the dumb thing. I started trouble.

"Come on, girl," I said, kicking gently at Maraud's sides. My allosaurus flexed her nostrils, which is how she smiles. She doesn't like bullies any more than I do. Her claws opened and closed and she stepped out of the alley and into the street.

"Hey. Leave her alone," I called.

They looked up at me. Astride Maraud—her mouth open and dripping hot, hungry saliva—I must have been an imposing sight. For a split second, they were afraid. Then they remembered their guns, their power, the city that supported their abuse, and the fear melted away.

"What's it to you?" said one of them. The woman pushed her shopping cart off and hurried down the street, turning only once to mouth *Thank you* at me. Her velociraptor, scuttling beside her, made a guttural noise that Maraud echoed back.

I didn't have a good answer for him. So I did what I

tend to do in stressful situations: I took a picture.

It's an instinct. If you stop to think, you'll miss the shot. And since selling a photo to the *Clarion* often meant the difference between eating and starving, I tended to take the shot.

Problem is, cops hate having their pictures taken.

"Hands up!" they hollered.

My hands went up.

"Drop it!" they said.

"It's not a weapon!" I called, bending my knees, holding up the camera. "It'll break if I drop it, and I can't afford to replace it. So I'm going to put it down very slowly, okay?"

"I said drop it, you—" And they called me a whole bunch of superhorrific names. Fine. It gave me time to set the camera gently on the ground the instant before they walked up and punched me in the stomach. And kept on doing so, until I fell to the ground beside my camera.

"Somebody needs to learn to mind their own damn business," the shortest cop said, picking up my camera. He inspected it, deciding it probably wasn't a weapon after all. He held it out to me, but when I reached for it, he pulled it back and let it drop. Something cracked. I bit my lip to keep from exploding with a string of curses. Maraud huffed and stamped her foot, sharing my anger.

"What's your ability, punk? You a watersider? You have something to do with that robbery last week, down by the docks?"

There was no use trying to deny that I was an othersider. Nobody else would be walking around this part of town at night . . . with an allosaurus. It's why they call us *monsters*, because we're not afraid of the creatures that walk the streets of the city. "I don't know what my ability is," I mumbled.

Lady cop laughed. "You expect us to believe that?"

"I don't expect anything from the fine upstanding police officers of Darkside," I said. "Not when law-abiding othersiders get jumped every day by goons, and you never do a damn thing about it. Not when those attacks are on the rise and y'all never seem to notice."

Unfazed by my attitude, dude cop continued, "We run your name, we gonna find anything? Prior offenses, associations with illegal organizations?"

"I don't have any *current* offenses," I said. "Let alone priors. I'm not doing anything wrong. I just don't think it's right for you to harass helpless old women."

"This punk," lady cop said, and came at me fast.

"Shit," I whispered, closing my eyes and bracing myself for the inevitable assault.

Instead, an explosion rocked the street.

I opened my eyes to see two of the cops running down the street. One was on his radio. Flames swirled up from a scorched hole in the side of a building around the corner.

"What about this guy?" asked the woman, lingering with her hand in the air in front of me, like she was aching to get in one last punch.

"Don't be an idiot," short cop said.

Then they were gone. I breathed a sigh of relief. Exhaustion washed over me. I needed to be in bed beneath the bridge.

"You're welcome," called a voice from a doorway across the street.

I squinted into the shadows. "Who's there?"

He strolled into the street with a smile on his face and his hands full of lightning. A single bolt spun in a beautiful sphere, dozens of strands of it intricately coiled together. It was beautiful—almost as perfect as his face, which looked like summer even though summer was gone.

"Hi, Niv," I said. "I take it that's your handiwork burning a hole in that building over there?"

"Hey, Solomon. You looked like you could use a bit of help."

"Thanks," I said.

He clasped his hands together and the lightning shrank down to nothing. I felt so happy to see him, and I hated how happy I felt.

Niv was the personal bodyguard for my best friend,

Ash. Yes, *that* Ash—the Refugee Princess, living in hiding in the very same city where her mother was queen.

Niv's job was to move her from safe house to safe house. Because Ash was an othersider, and the queen's advisers assured her that if the bigoted citizens of Darkside ever found out that her daughter was part of that hated and feared community of so-called criminals and parasites, there'd be a full-scale uprising.

So Ash and Niv were on the run, in the city she'd rule one day. If she lived long enough—and the city didn't tear itself apart before then.

"Cops have been getting even crazier lately," he said. He smelled like burning sage—a clear, cleansing smell.

I've never trusted him. I don't know why. Maybe because he's so beautiful? Pretty people can't be relied upon. They have too many options.

"Can't you talk to her mother about that?" I asked.

"You know as well as I do that the police are a law unto themselves. They don't even listen to the queen."

"She could fire the commissioner, hire somebody who isn't such a bigot."

Niv laughed. "You think she's in a hurry to trigger a coup? They'd take her out in a second if they thought she was trying to change the way they do things."

"I guess," I said begrudgingly. Cass, the editor in chief at the *Clarion*, Darkside's scrappy opposition paper, had said the same thing to me not so long ago. "How's Ash?"

"She's . . . the same."

I winced, remembering Ash staring out the window at the snow, not even seeing it. Playing our favorite songs for her and seeing that she felt nothing. "Can't the doctors . . ."

"She's seen dozens of them, and they all say the same thing. The only way to bring her out of this . . . whatever it is . . . is to lift the spell the court sorcerers put on her."

"Shit," I said. We both knew her mother would never allow that. The spell kept Ash's powers in check, buried them deep. Since the age of twelve, Ash had been childlike on the best of days, and semicatatonic on the others.

"She's fighting it. Wherever she is in there, she's working hard to break the spell. That's why they have to keep making it stronger. She's nobody's victim."

"Of course she's not."

"Come see her," Niv said, and named an address in Raptor Heights. A rough-and-tumble working-class neighborhood where lots of othersiders could afford to live, because its bad reputation kept the rents down.

"Should you be telling me that?" I asked. "Isn't her location supposed to be a huge secret?"

He looked hurt, and I didn't feel bad about it. Protecting Ash was my primary purpose in life. This pretty boy I'd been crushing on since I was ten didn't matter, in the grand scheme. "She loves you, Solomon. There's no secrets from you."

"But if you'd tell *me*, who else would you tell?"

Niv frowned, and his face flashed red. "Good to see you, Maraud," he said, patting her side. She blinked slowly, in happiness. Then he turned and left.

Maraud took two steps to follow him. When I pressed my hand to her neck to stop her, she turned to look at me in confusion.

"Sorry, girl," I said, climbing on board. "Let's head for the bridge."

As we went, she kept trying to turn. Still following Niv's scent—and Ash's, on him.

"Ash is going to be okay," I said, knowing she could hear the lie in my voice. "We're all going to be okay."

A ship's horn sounded in the distance, low and lonesome, arriving from the Spice Islands. We hurried home through streets that stunk of cinnamon.

THREE

ASH

The morning hallway stunk of cinnamon, which meant that autumn was here, and Dunkin' Donuts was selling Pumpkin Spice Everything, which meant that Hudson High would be full of hot, milky beverages. The smell, I didn't mind. What bothered me was the herd mentality. The mandatory nature of the pumpkin spice latte. The way it was a status symbol, a way to say, *Look at me, I have a car and drive myself to school and I can go out of my way to Dunkin' Donuts and get a four-dollar coffee every morning.*

Sure, it's strange, but something that stupid could let the old darkness loose, tightening my chest and making it hard to breathe.

Hudson High is jam-packed with terrible triggers for my depression. Seeing all those unhappy kids crowded together. Watching the hundred different ways some people just couldn't help but make others miserable, if not with their fists then with their words, or their clothes or their too-strong perfume or their costly caffeinated beverages.

Too many ways to end up less than.

Another hallway trigger: Solomon. Or rather, the lack of him. Looking for him and not finding him. He didn't come to school every day. And when he did, he didn't always stay.

The medication was helping me. I knew it. I felt it. I was already so much better. But the darkness was still there, a black frigid ocean I was precariously balanced above, and there was nothing like the halls of Hudson High to plunge me back in.

So I did what I do whenever I feel that way: I took out my camera. When the world feels like too much, looking through the lens helps me break it down into manageable pieces.

Reality is messy. Reality is horrible. My camera allows me to make something out of that chaos. Something beautiful.

I took a couple pictures of people with their Styrofoam cups. Then I swung by the cafeteria, where they were still serving breakfast for five more minutes. I took a couple pictures of the cafeteria workers, one of whom flashed the most beautiful smile you ever saw.

Then the bell for first period rang.

"Thanks." I waved to them, then made my way to homeroom.

People are what inspire me, as a photographer. I'm not so into landscapes or pretty geometry or action shots. Every time I took a picture of someone, I could feel it, sense it, just out of reach—the *things* I needed to capture. The story I needed to tell.

The project that would get me the hell out of Hudson.

Outside the cafeteria, I saw a girl standing against a wall. I didn't know her. She looked barely old enough to be in high school. Based on who she was hanging out with, I figured she was from one of the trailer parks along Joslen Boulevard. Four piercings framed her face: one on each eyebrow, one in each nostril. She was gorgeous, and sad. I raised my camera.

There's no noncrazy way to say this. Through the lens, I could see her damage. I saw it billow in the air around her, like clouds of black ink. I saw it scuttle across her skin: tiny shadow crabs. The longer I looked, the more I could see. Shapes appeared in the darkness behind her—the things she'd seen, the people she was afraid of.

Shivers went up my spine. They would not stop.

What the hell was going on?

The girl looked up. Locked eyes with me. "Is it okay?" I asked, tapping the camera with one finger.

She shrugged, then nodded. Did her best to smile.

I took the picture.

A tiny glimmer of light. I saw her, and she saw me. I was sad, but so was she.

It was nothing, but it mattered.

"Thanks," I said.

"Sure," she told me.

Shivering, I lowered the camera. My spine still tingled. I shut my eyes, hard, as if I could unsee what I'd seen.

Just when I thought I was getting better, something else goes wrong with my brain. Something a little pill might not be able to fix.

"Hey, Ash," Jewel Gomez said when I joined her at her locker.

"Hey," I said. "I'm halfway through that book. It's so fucking—sorry—it's so good."

Being around Jewel made me curse more than normal, because she never ever said even the mildest swear word.

"Isn't it!! I'm so glad people don't *actually* know the day they're going to die. Can you imagine?"

I remembered when Jewel came to Hudson High in ninth grade. All anyone knew about her was that she was super-Christian. So much so that she made people nervous. I'd assumed because of her religion that she'd be homophobic or something, but she was actually the sweetest thing on Earth. To everyone. Which just made people even more nervous around her.

Everyone but me. We both loved books and movies, and loved talking about them—but on a deeper level than most people did.

A voice from behind us cheered, "Hey, ladies."

"Hey, Sheffield," I said, without turning around, because no one else in school was ever that happy about anything. And because my heart hadn't slowed down, and my spine still shivered.

"Where are your blue baseball caps?"

"Oh shit," I said as insincerely as I could. "Did I forget mine *again?*"

During baseball and football seasons, pretty much everyone wore a blue baseball cap. It was to show support for the team, they said, although really it was because if you *didn't* wear one, you were likely to get bullied, yelled at, or otherwise interrogated by a slick, smiling button-nosed jock who looked like he was already planning his presidential campaign.

"You know you make people uncomfortable," he said. "When you don't wear one. Like you think you're better than us."

"That sounds like an 'other people' problem, rather than a 'me' problem," I said.

Sheffield scoffed. "Later, Ash. Jewel, may the Lord bless and keep you."

Sheffield shuffled off. Jewel and I rolled our eyes, and headed in opposite directions to get to our homerooms.

Someone ran past me, sobbing.

And then the hallway erupted. Talking, pointing, laughing. I could feel the gossip move through the air like a thunderclap. Phones were passed around. A photo, sent to a bunch of people, each of whom passed it on to a bunch more. Someone shoved it in front of me, without asking if I wanted to see it. And, like an idiot, I looked.

Six swastikas, spray-painted onto the side of Judy Saperstein's house.

The bell rang, but the crowd barely budged. Everyone had something to say on the subject, and they were all saying it at the same time. Most of them were angry, afraid, pissed off—but more than a few people seemed to find it hilarious.

I went to the window and tried to catch my breath. Outside I saw the same old boring landscape as always: the sloping soccer fields, Hudson's rotted city sprawl, the mountains across the river beyond.

But then I raised the camera to my eye, and looked again. I saw the dark fog, the billowing black clouds. The longer I looked, the more they took on shape. Became something real. Something terrifying. Buildings rose up into the sky. Shapes flew through the air, flapping wings too big to belong to birds.

Another city. The one that Solomon saw, where monsters walk harmlessly through the streets beside hordes of delicious humans.

The city where I, supposedly, was a princess.

Except it couldn't be. Because that city wasn't real. It was all in Solomon's mind.

"No," I whispered. The shivering in my spine had become so pronounced I could feel my fingers shaking.

This can't be real.

This can't be happening to me.

People say Solomon is suffering from a serious mental illness, the kind that will inevitably lead to his inability to function as an independent human in the world.

It's because of his other world. His delusions.

But if he sees this—and now I'm seeing it—maybe I'm sick too. Sick with something more serious than depression.

And then the thought came like a whisper into my mind.

The treehouse.

Back when Solomon and I were twelve, something happened in that treehouse in his stepfather's backyard. Something neither one of us could remember. I ended up in the hospital, with a crack in my skull around my left eye. And Solomon was never the same.

So what if whatever happened to Solomon and me

was making us both go crazy?

What if we were both destined to break down, further and further, until there was nothing left?

Because neither of us knew what happened.

And you can't fight a monster you can't see.

FOUR

SOLOMON

"Good morning," Radha said, when I came out of my room. A cup of hot, sweet milk tea waited for me on the table.

I hugged her. My landlady, my auntie. My foster mother. My friend.

Immense and unstoppable.

She'd taken me in four years ago, when Ash had fallen sick and her mother, the queen, had kicked me out of the Palace. Traumatic at the time, but in some ways it was the best thing that had ever happened to me.

"Sit," Radha said.

"Can't. I need to get going."

"You need to sit."

I sat. I sipped my tea as fast as I could, and watched

the Underbridge come awake. The shantytown beneath Dragon Pagoda Bridge was at its quietest now, before the night shift workers trudged home and the day shift ones marched out. The wind was right, so we got the breeze from the river instead of the swamps to the north. I kissed Radha on the cheek, then crossed the square to the shower stalls.

Shacks were piled ten stories high, dilapidated but stable on their scaffolding. Narrow streets and alleys and garden plots ran between them. Everyone paid a tiny bit into a common fund every month, to pay for repairs and maintenance and security. And feed for the monsters, of course, who slept in a big pen to ensure they didn't get hold of someone's chickens.

That's how it was. Poor people knew that all they had was each other.

Migrants had been living under the bridge for decades when the police started cracking down—arresting people for trespassing, burning shacks when people refused to get out. To her credit, and everyone's surprise, the queen had intervened. Granted royal permission to live under the bridge to anyone who wanted to. Ordered the cops to stop messing with people. Which pissed the cops off immeasurably.

Ten years later, we're still here. Five thousand of us. It's overcrowded and everyone is always up in your business and sometimes it smells bad, but I love it. Walking back, fresh and clean and hungry, I looked up in time to see a pod of sky whales heading east. Their massive tails shattered clouds with each swing.

"Connor still asleep?" I asked, when I got back.

"Enjoy it while it lasts," she said, and chuckled.

I debated waking him up, before I headed for the *Clarion*'s office. Radha's six-year-old son had entirely too much energy, and was way too much work, but I adored him. He was smarter than most kids twice his age—and he was a prodigy with his abilities, able to control fire from the age of four, while most othersiders don't come into their abilities until they hit puberty.

Or, in my case, later. Or possibly never.

There is magic in me. I feel it all through my arms and legs, shivering in my stomach, burning in my brain. But when I try to access it—I freak out. Sometimes it's like a seizure, other times I black out. Sometimes I start smashing stuff up.

But it's there. I've always known it's there. I've also known I need to keep it a secret, in a city that hates my kind so much.

I opened the door to the room we shared and watched Connor sleep.

I loved him—but sometimes, in my darkest, most self-pitying moments, I couldn't help but envy him.

Sure, he was dirt-poor like me, but he had a mother and he'd grown up surrounded by people who loved him. They'd valued him, nurtured him, encouraged him. The light in his deep brown eyes had never dimmed. Spend thirty seconds with Connor and you could see that the fire he could summon was part of his very soul.

Someone ran past the window, sobbing. Someone else laughed.

And then the shouting started.

"Stay here," I told Radha. I grabbed my camera and ran outside. Random jerks routinely came around the Underbridge, looking to beat up on some othersiders. They tended to regret it pretty quickly and run like hell. But hopefully I could get off a couple of good photos for my editor, Cass, first.

A crowd had gathered in the dusty alley, so thick I couldn't get anywhere near the action. I could see what was happening, though. These were not random jerks. These people were *together*. They were *organized*.

They all wore ultramarine armbands. I don't know why that worried me so much. Maybe it was the idea that someone, somewhere, had sewed them. That these people were part of something bigger.

My feet slid into horse stance, one of the few things I remembered from the self-defense classes that Ash's trainer let me sit in on. My hands made fists. I may not have known yet what my ability was, but I would fight with all of my regular human strength before I let anything happen to Radha and Connor.

An armbanded man walked right up to me.

Now, I'm pretty tall, and muscular, so people tended to assume I knew how to fight. What frightened me was the confidence on his face. Like he'd marched right into a lion's den and didn't believe the lions could hurt him. It enraged me.

"You lost?" I asked him.

"I'm exactly where I need to be," he said. "It's you who aren't supposed to be here. You aren't supposed to be anywhere. You're an abomination. All of you."

I laughed. I couldn't help it. "You really believe that?"

"We haven't forgotten the Night of Red Diamonds," he hissed.

"Neither have we."

Just a few years back, the simmering tension between people with magic and people without it boiled over. A big bloody brawl in the streets; each side said the other was to blame. And whatever the real story was, at the end of the night there was a whole lot of blood and a whole lot of broken glass in the street. Glittering like red diamonds.

That was when street gangs started targeting us. Othersider businesses were burned down. People began calling on the queen to make our magic illegal, or to drive us out of Darkside altogether.

"There will be a reckoning," he whispered, stepping closer.

A rock struck him, in the head. Not too big, and not too hard. He knelt there, his face reddening, one hand holding himself up and the other clenched into the tightest fist I'd ever seen. I dropped to my knees, to be eye level with him, to capture the chaos in the background, the blurry crowd and the flames, and took a photograph.

He stood up, breathing heavy. Ran off. I remained on my knees. My friend Shoshana waved, from the window of a shack across the way. She held her hand out in front of her, and rocks rose up into the air, waiting for the next jerk who came along looking for trouble.

It wasn't long before we had the armbands in retreat.

I glanced down at my camera. What I had captured— if it came out— It was powerful. The best picture I'd ever taken. Cass would be proud.

I headed for the dinosaur paddock.

"Come on, girl," I said, when I got to Maraud, and kissed the smooth pebbled texture of her purple skin.

The streets smelled like patchouli oil and cigarette smoke. On my way out, for the first time I saw the graffiti. An ultramarine silhouette, life-size, on one of the pillars that held up the bridge. A man, broad-shouldered, legs apart, hands clasped behind his back.

Spray-painted underneath: "He Is the Answer."

But who was "he"?

And if he was the answer, what the hell was the question?

FIVE

ASH

I shut the door behind me as carefully as I could, which wasn't carefully enough, because a whole pack of crazed dogs came pouring down the stairs, barking like wild animals. Cass's house smelled like patchouli incense and cigarette smoke, and was so bright it seemed like her whole ceiling was made of glass.

"It's you," she said from the top of stairs. "I thought maybe it was a serial killer."

"Then you should lock your doors," I said.

Cass shrugged. "You don't have to pay off your debts if you're murdered. Or worry about really anything anymore."

If a serial killer did come, they'd have very little resistance from her dogs, who were excitedly rubbing their faces against my legs and jumping up to lick my face.

"Come upstairs if and when you succeed in fighting them off," Cass called, and turned to go. She wore a long black hooded gown, something I am sure sold for thousands of dollars and was gifted to her for free. Cass treated it with utter carelessness, as evidenced by the stains on the wrists from her photo chemicals.

I didn't know why I'd come. It wasn't like Cass could help me through the trauma of suddenly being able to see another world. Or, worse, suddenly discovering that I was way more messed up in the head than I had previously believed.

But if there was anywhere I could go to get out from under the weight of all that, to feel better about humanity, to feel less helpless about swastika graffiti and Solomon's madness, it was here.

Once upon a time, and for many years, Cass had been the editor in chief of *Strut* magazine, which for most of the seventies made *Vogue* look like *Highlights*. The most artistic and innovative photography; the most edgy-looking and diverse models. *Vogue* didn't put a Black woman on the cover until 1974, but in 1972, *Strut* did a whole issue featuring exclusively Black models and designers. Every photographer and designer and model and celebrity were dying to be in its pages, but Cass had the final call, and if she didn't think you were *It*, she couldn't be convinced by fame or love or money.

Before that, she had been the assistant to—and protégée of—my favorite photographer, Diane Arbus. Somewhere along the line Cass'd gotten obscenely rich—maybe through marriage, maybe through savvy real estate investments—and bought this huge house far away from New York City. She was our town's only Recluse, which is to say, the only person with enough money to be listed separately from all the other shut-ins, who are Just Crazy.

"Coffee in the kitchen," she called from upstairs. So I headed that way.

When I was fourteen, and deeply obsessed with Diane Arbus, I saw Cass mentioned in a footnote in an Arbus biography. I knew the name, from hearing my parents talk—Cass was the closest thing Hudson had to a celebrity. I rode my bike to her house and went up to the door and knocked. She was pretty impressed by my fourteen-year-old chutzpah, and the camera around my neck (a battered barely working vintage Leica I'd bought cheap online), and she took me on a tour of her house. Her walls were covered in exquisite, priceless framed photographs by the greatest artists of a century and a half, carelessly hung in chaotic jumbles. Haunting sculptures crowded shelves and tables. She also agreed to look at my photos, if I brought some back, and give me her honest—brutal—opinions. That was the beginning of our awkward awesome relationship.

I poured myself a cup of (cold) coffee and went up to see her. Her work desk was heaped with old photos and she was inspecting them with all the intensity of someone who still had a job. I picked up a photograph and then immediately dropped it. An Avedon; I could tell at once, from his signature minimalism and the almost-invisible expression on the model's face. I felt like I'd just committed a grave sin. Like accidentally getting my greasy dirty fingerprints on a Rembrandt.

"Calm down," she said. "He's dead; he can't yell at you. Although he definitely would, if he saw that." She tsked. "Such a little bastard." She shuffled pictures from one pile to another. I noticed that she was wearing thin white gloves. "So, Ash, how is your project coming? What have you figured out?"

"I'm stumped," I said. "I want to create something that *means* something. Tells a story that needs to be told. If I'm going to get into a decent art school—and get the kind of scholarship I'd need to actually be able to go there—I need to create something . . . important."

I'd stopped at home, after school, to develop the pictures I'd taken and round up a bunch of other recent prints. I handed them to her, nervous as hell, the same as always.

"This is shit," she said of the first one, a photo of Jewel.

"What's wrong with it?" Jewel was smiling, in her

living room. Hard focus on her, background blurry. Nothing special, but I hadn't thought it was shit.

"There's nothing there. You can't see that?"

Now that she said it, I saw it. And I cringed as she shuffled through the next ten images, saying *Shit* for each one.

"I think they're very competent," I said, struggling to keep my voice from breaking. I worshipped Cass, and she was forever putting my fondness for her to the test.

"Precisely!" she said, and stabbed one finger at me, like I'd fallen into the trap she'd set for me. "Lovely. Well composed. *Competent*."

"Then what's the problem?"

"Competence is the enemy of genius," she said, lighting another cigarette. Dogs barked in the hallway. "You can capture reality. Bravo! That's the easy part. You need to go deeper. You need to capture something *else*."

She stared at a photo of a handsome boy in a T-shirt. "This one is a tiny bit interesting. There's something naked in his expression. A hunger. A desperation. Very small. I don't think you noticed it yourself."

I hadn't noticed it.

"I totally noticed it," I said.

Connor. Solomon's stepbrother. Son of Mr. Barrett, the vice principal and football coach of Hudson High School.

"Is that your boyfriend?"

"Not really. Just . . ."

"Someone you're fucking," she said.

I nearly swallowed my tongue. "You know that from looking at the photo?"

She shrugged. "I *know* it from what you just said. But yes, the photo made me think that. At any rate. I don't believe you saw it, because if you saw it, you would have dug it out of him. Exposed it. That expression, that thing he's hiding. *That's* what photographers do."

I wondered how I would have done that. What could I have said, or done, to coax it out of him, the thing he was trying to hide from me?

Photographing Connor, I had gotten stuck on his handsome face, on how he looked like a younger, softer version of his father. How to get past that? Beneath the surface? Sometimes Cass said things that filled me up with excitement and confidence, tips and insights that opened doors and made me feel like I could do anything, and sometimes she said things that made me feel like the most talentless hack in the entire world.

"Now *this!*" she said, startling me back to reality. "This is something special."

It was the girl from that morning. The trailer park girl in the hallway, moments before all hell broke loose.

No swirling ink clouds. No monsters. What I had seen through the lens, it didn't come through in the final image.

"Who is she?"

"No idea," I said.

"Well. You've come very close, with this one. Her face is a marvel. You can see how much she's been through."

"So what's missing?"

"Her smile. It's practiced."

"I asked her permission before I took it. So, she smiled. You always told me it's wrong to take pictures without someone's consent."

"You could have paused, for a second. Two, three, maybe five. Wait for her smile to falter just the slightest bit. You could have taken one right away, and when she heard the click, she would have dropped the smile, and you could have taken a second one that she wasn't expecting."

I looked out the window and across the street, to the abandoned factories with brontosauruses spray-painted onto their brick walls. Past that were the cow fields. The air smelled like dung.

"Seems shady to me," I said. "Like I'm trying to trick people."

"You're a photographer, not a friend. Being an artist sometimes means breaking the rules of civilized human behavior. Do you have the courage to do that?"

I nodded, but I wasn't sure if I did. And Cass's words had reminded me that I hadn't been a very good friend.

Solomon. He had been hiding from the world. From what was wrong with him. I'd been letting him, because I was too frightened to go where he needed me to go. It wasn't enough to bring him a vanilla Coke once in a while, and let him talk to me for an hour about whatever cartoon he was obsessed with that week. If I was going to help him, I had to follow him into whatever weird world he was living in lately.

And then another thought occurred. Maybe I could get the honesty that Cass wanted. Maybe I could get to the soul of my subject—if that subject was Solomon.

But first, I'd have to find him.

SIX

SOLOMON

The whole block of the *Clarion*'s offices smelled like brontosaurus dung. I could hear them groaning in the massive factories where they were shackled and marched in a circle, turning giant wheels to generate power to work the machines. Cass had kept the paper in the factory district, in the same building as the printing presses, long after all the other newspapers moved their editorial operations to the ritzier part of town.

And of course Cass was hard at work when I got there, alone in the immense old building, except for the ink-splattered men working the print machines down on the ground floor. But they were the night shift, and their day was ending, whereas Cass's workdays had no shifts; no endings and no beginnings. She slept at her desk, most nights. She was an addict, hooked on the never-ending stream of news that washed across her desk. The murders and the intrigue, the politics and the scandals. The backroom deals that would lead to a thousand people getting evicted. The movie star divorces no one could shut the hell up about, even though they made not a damn bit of difference in the lives of anyone.

She stood there, tall and bone-thin and ancient, peering through thin glasses at stacks of clippings. Chain-smoking, like she always did. I wondered if printer's ink was flammable, and decided it must not be, or she would have burned up decades ago.

"Solomon!" she called, snapping her fingers like she'd summoned me. "Excellent. What have you brought today?"

I handed her the picture of the thug at the Underbridge. It had come out as powerfully as I'd hoped it would. High contrast, the background full of energy and motion, his expression complex, equal parts rage and shock and even a little bit of shame, like on some level he knew what he was doing was wrong. Not because he was a decent person, but because the camera scared him. The thought of someone *seeing* what he was doing made him think twice, and I caught that single instant of self-doubt.

"This is breathtaking," she said. "I'm proud of you. When was this?"

I told her the details. She picked up the phone, barked at whoever answered: "Gang attack on the Underbridge today. Head down there, get some eyewitness accounts, write it up for page three. Play up the angle that this was an organized effort; something is going on. Go talk to the precinct captain to see what they're doing to protect people. No, you don't need to bring a photographer. We got the shot already."

She slammed the phone down, and frowned, and then looked up and smiled at me. "Right place at the right time, or you went looking for this?"

"The first one."

"Well. Luck is half of catching the shot. The other half is being prepared—having a good eye and ear so you know it when it's coming."

She handed me two twenty-ruble bills, and rubbed my head. I nodded gratefully. I didn't know why the great Cass Otterby had decided to take an impoverished othersider gutter kid under her wing, but she had, and I was damn lucky.

My parents had moved to Darkside from the Waterlands during the plague called the Great Rot, back when I was just a baby, but like a lot of people who flooded into the city during those years, they got the Rot and died on the way. Before that they'd fallen in with a caravan of migrants, which included two men, a couple, who'd befriended them and taken care of them while they were sick. I was an infant and I had no one to take care of me, and the choice was either leave me by the roadside or raise me as their own. Luckily for me they did the latter.

Pop was beaten to death by thugs who hated other-siders, when I was three. Da was arrested a year later, allegedly for using an illegal magical ability, and died in a camp. I don't even know their real names. I was so little. They were only Da and Pop to me. The faces I see, when I think of them . . . I'm not even sure if they're really theirs. I only know I still have the warm, safe, loved feeling I had when I was with them.

That, and a camera. Pop had been a photographer, back in the Waterlands, and I'd inherited his battered old knockoff "Leika." So when I was ten years old, that's how I started. I took pictures for tourists in front of landmarks and I took pictures for street gangs of the graffiti in rival territory. Kind of like a spy. I didn't know what I was doing; I just knew I needed to eat. I was small and quick and I didn't ask for very much money. Pretty soon I was getting hired by jealous lovers, and taking pictures for business owners, of their competition's price lists.

One of them thought I had a good eye, and told me to talk to Cass. She often bought shots off street urchins. She took a liking to me. Bought my pictures even when they weren't very good. Gave me advice. Sent me out on assignments with her actual photographers, so I could see how it was done.

The rest, I guess, is history.

"Have you seen this?" she asked, handing me an eight-by-ten glossy photo. Black and white: a bare white wall with "Destroy All Monsters" spray-painted across it.

"No," I said. "Where was this taken?"

"Back of the Darkside Cinema Palace," she said. "But it's been popping up all over. The same tag—but lots of different handwritings and styles. I think it's evidence of something new—a movement, a degree of organization that we haven't seen before. It's not just a bunch of random assholes anymore. Something scary is on the horizon."

I remembered the ultramarine armbands in the Underbridge attack. "I think you're right."

"Keep an eye out, will you? Anywhere you see this tag, take a picture? And remember where you took it"—she crossed to the giant map of the city on her wall—"because I want to map out the places where this pops up. I'd be in your debt."

A thousand times Cass had helped me eat when I would have gone hungry, so I was pretty sure she'd never be the one in my debt.

"I'll do what I can," I said. "Thanks, Cass."

And it was then, just when I was starting to feel okay about everything, that I noticed the top item on one of her piles of folders. Attached to the front was a blurry old newspaper photo . . . of Ash.

"What's this?" I said softly. My heartbeat was so, so loud.

She shrugged. "We don't know yet. A reporter was holed up down at the docks, in a bar known to be popular among nativists, just listening, trying to see what we could find out. This one guy was drunk, saying a lot of nasty stuff, but like he knew something. *A reckoning is coming; he's got something up his sleeve; he's going to change everything.* Like he was in on whatever was going on. My reporter waited till he was half-passed out, then stole the guy's satchel."

"You teach your journalists to be thieves?" I said, laughing. "Seems dangerous."

"I teach my journalists to get the story. Anyway, there wasn't much in the satchel to tell us what's going on with 'destroy all monsters,' but there was a lot of information about the Refugee Princess."

"Really," I said, and it was hard to keep my voice neutral. "Do you think she's a—a target of whatever's going on?"

"Could be," she said. "Nobody knows anything about her."

"Wow." I wanted desperately to open the folder and see what was there, but I couldn't risk Cass wondering why I was so curious about it.

Because that was my big secret. My friendship with Ash. A refugee; a princess; an othersider. She was the biggest news story of the year, maybe the decade, and I'd been holding out on Cass. Hiding what I knew. I told myself Cass would understand, even appreciate my loyalty to my friend—but I also knew that she was a newswoman before anything else. Her first allegiance was always to The Story. So she wouldn't be able to keep from acting on anything I shared.

To distract her, I told her about the graffiti I'd seen on one of the bridge pillars. The big blue man; the barely legible scribble underneath it: "He Is the Answer."

"Might be the same person," I said. "The one that guy was talking about. 'He's got something up his sleeve.'"

Cass didn't know who he was, or what *he* might be the answer to.

But Niv might. He had access to the Palace intelligence officers.

I just needed to swallow my pride and ask for his help.

SEVEN

ASH

A big blue man, spray-painted onto the side of the abandoned elementary school. An illegible scribble underneath it. The smell of swamp water and soggy marijuana joints. Broken glass. Discarded condoms. Rain-bleached jelly beans all over the ground.

I should have loved this place. Desolation is photogenic. Graffiti makes for great pictures. I raised my camera, aimed it at the tags. Bright blue smears. But I couldn't stop thinking about those swastikas spray-painted on the side of Judy Saperstein's house. The thought of them made everything uglier. Scarier.

I wondered if Solomon had heard. If not, I sure as hell wasn't about to be the one to tell a Jewish boy who already thought the world was against him that there were swastika tags going up.

Greenport School had been closed and empty for three years. It was isolated enough, across from the abandoned match factory and up against the woods that ran along the railroad tracks, that you could hang out there and hardly anyone would ever mess with you. Cops never came around. Guys who were really up to no good had better places to go do that. Mostly the people who hung out here were teenagers nostalgic for the innocent kids they had been when they were elementary school students inside that building.

Those kids and, I hoped, Solomon.

I parked my car and made my way around the long single-story building. Past the playground, where the swings had all broken or been stolen so their chains hung loose in the wind. I took pictures of them, but I knew they wouldn't come out right. I wasn't skilled enough to capture their sadness.

And every time I looked through the lens, I saw some new impossible, awful thing. Skeletons sitting on the monkey bars; bees as big as vultures wobbling through the air.

My spine would not stop shivering.

When I went around the corner, I saw him, exactly where I'd thought he'd be. Asleep on the rusty old purple dinosaur seesaw he'd loved so much when he was in first grade.

What a happy kid Solomon had been. Back before his mind began to betray him.

He was smiling now, at something in a dream. Flakes of paint were stuck to his face. At his feet was a battered old library book: *Illegal Identities: A History of Homophobic Police Practices Around the World.* I thought about taking his picture, but it seemed wrong. Like I'd be taking advantage of him. Cass's words echoed in my head. *Being an artist sometimes means breaking the rules of civilized human behavior.* But before I could debate it internally any further, Solomon opened his eyes and reached out to touch my face.

"Ash," he said. "I was just going to go see you and Niv."

"And here I am," I said, settling down on the soggy gravel, deciding not to ask who or what Niv was. "Your tyrannosaur is looking rough," I said, pointing to the places where the metal was worn thin, bent, broken.

"Her name is Maraud. She's been through a lot. And she's an allosaurus. T. rexes have two fingers; she has three. See?"

"Right," I said, because I was pretty sure he'd explained this to me more than once before. "So where are you living these days?"

He shrugged. "Who lives?"

"Don't you quote Natalie Wood at me," I said, mock-punching his muscular shoulder. "I'm the one who showed you *Rebel Without a Cause*, remember?"

"And where would I be without it?" he said. "James Dean was how I knew I was gay."

I paused. Best to jump right into it. "You're not with your aunt anymore?"

He shrugged. "Her son got evicted. He's crashing with her, so I don't have a room. She says I'm welcome to sleep on their couch, but the place is pretty crowded."

Solomon's father had never been in the picture. His mother had gotten locked up, right around the time she divorced Connor's father, Solomon's stepdad. He'd offered to let Solomon stay with them, but Solomon refused. Ran off. Got caught, brought back. Ran off again.

"I did something stupid," he said, looking at his hands.

"What's that?"

"There were three guys, and they were picking on this old lady, and I just lost it. One second I was talking to them normally, the next I was just yelling gibberish into the air. And I couldn't stop. Like I could see myself, from the outside, and I couldn't control what was happening."

"Oh my god," I said. "Where was this?"

"Fairview Plaza."

"Jesus." That strip mall was as close as Hudson came to an actual mall. And usually it was full of people. Any one of them could have called the police.

And the police didn't tend to respond well to emotionally disturbed young men who were six feet tall.

"What did they do?" I asked. "The three guys?"

"They ran. I don't know if they were scared of me or just didn't like all the commotion I was causing. By the time I calmed down, they were gone. So was the old lady, for that matter."

"Did anyone . . . I don't know, try to help you? Try to talk to you?"

He shook his head, then lowered it into his hands. I reached out to take his hands in my own. "We need to get you some help," I said.

"No one can help me," he said. "Not the way I need to be helped."

"How do you need to be helped?"

Again he shook his head, pulled his hands away from me.

I wanted to tell him about myself. About the meds, how they were helping. How I was trying. How *he* needed to try.

But whatever was going on with him, it was way worse than what was happening to me. The treatment options for him could be extreme. Plus, Solomon didn't want to be medicated. He'd said so over and over again.

But I hadn't either, at first. It was a journey, getting to the place where you could admit how you need help.

"You need to talk to someone, at least," I said. "Figure out what's going on, and what kind of treatment options are available. I used to think—"

And then, with a nakedness and need that made me shiver, Solomon interrupted me and said: "I need you to remember."

"Remember what?" I asked, and waited, but he never answered.

"Help me, Solomon," I said. "I want to remember. Help me to remember."

He looked off into the distance.

"It's getting worse," I asked. "Isn't it? I saw—I think I saw something. . . ."

Solomon nodded. "Something is coming. Something that will upset the balance. Change everything."

I waited for more, but there was none. Eventually, he shut his eyes. Smiled. Whispered something.

He was gone. Back into that dream world of his.

A tiny part of me envied him his ability to escape to a better reality so easily.

The rest of me felt sick.

I remembered the first time I ever saw a homeless person, on a trip to New York City with my family to go to a Broadway show. A woman was sitting on the sidewalk, hugging herself. Her clothes were filthy. Her skin looked awful. And I got so sad and nauseous that

I couldn't enjoy the show, and I was miserable for the next several days.

I kept seeing her in my mind's eye. I wanted to help her, but what could I do? My mother and father had kept on walking, and so, so had I.

I kept wondering: What had happened? Where had her life gone wrong? Why hadn't someone taken better care of her? Who had evicted her, kicked her out of her home?

Sitting there next to Solomon, shivering in the chilly air of the abandoned playground, surrounded by fallen jelly beans and shattered bottles, I wondered if I wasn't watching the exact moment where his life went wrong.

EIGHT

SOLOMON

Jellybeans, everywhere. Jellybeans and broken glass, like someone had dropped a hundred jars full of them. Maraud dipped her head, attracted by the sweet smell, but I pulled back on the reins.

It wasn't a completely unusual sight. Raptor Heights was kinda like that. Crazy characters lived out here. One time I came through and there were thousands of balloons, tied to every lamppost and street sign and fire escape and tree branch. . . . Anything you could tie a balloon to, there were balloons tied to it.

I wondered if that was someone's othersider ability; the power to summon up inflated balloons. If so, it seemed like a pretty useless ability. If not, a whole lot of people spent a hell of a long time affixing helium balloons for reasons unknown.

We'd been wandering the streets for hours, looking for "Destroy All Monsters" tags. We found plenty. Bright blue smears. And every one made me a little bit sicker. More scared. *Monsters* meant us. Othersiders. We were what people wanted to destroy.

I'd imagined that they'd be concentrated in the neighborhoods where anti-othersider sentiment was highest, but the opposite was true. They were targeting us. The tags were emblazoned on the walls and doors of known othersiders, and the stables where our dinos were kept. Like a warning; like a threat.

Slowly, I steered us toward the address Niv had given me. I tied up Maraud a block away. No sense drawing attention to the place, especially if Ash really was there.

When I knocked on the front door, I heard a lot of whispered conversation happening on the other side.

"Hey!" Niv said, opening up for me. Beautiful dimples bloomed in his cheeks.

"Hey," I said as sullenly as I could.

"So happy you came. It'll do her so much good to see you."

"I brought pie," I said, holding up the box I'd bought at Momma's Bakery. "Apple. Ash's favorite."

He ushered me into a big, desolate building. Palace guards eyed me uneasily. They knew me, of course.

"We're only here for another day or two. We try to

move every five days. Just in case, you know?"

"Yeah," I said. The Refugee Princess; the greatest mystery in Darkside. Everyone knew about the assassination attempts; everyone had their own theory about what was behind them. Everyone wanted to know where she *really* was.

Niv led me into a bright, bare, sunny room. "Were you followed?" asked a grumpy old man. It was Ed. Part of Ash's security detail since she was born—he had never liked me.

"Nobody knows who the hell I am," I said.

Ed harrumphed. I wondered how he felt, this wise old soldier, obeying a head of security as young as Niv.

Ash sat in a chair by the window, looking out. The sunlight made her seem fragile, like paper. Her hair was cut boy-short. She wore black leather pants and a coarse workingman's shirt. I wondered who dressed her. I figured it must have been Niv. Someone who cared for her; someone who remembered who she had been, back before the queen made her mostly catatonic.

I was eight, when she found me. She literally pulled me out of the gutter. Some boys had been pushing me around; she'd watched the whole thing from her royal carriage. Ordered it to stay, even when her mother the queen demanded they move on. She saw them calling me names, saw me call them names right back . . . and then she saw the three of them kick me to the ground and stomp me like a bug. Her footmen picked me up and carried my stinking, bloody little self into the carriage.

Her mother was not amused.

This behavior was not unusual; Ash felt from a very young age that it wasn't right for her to have so much when so many people had so little, and she tried her damnedest to feed every hungry person she saw—but when she found out I had no parents, no one to take care of me, she refused to let her mother's servants put me out at the end of the day.

Neither the queen nor anyone else could talk Ash out of taking care of me. For four years I lived in the Palace like I was an actual nobleman. For four years we explored the catacombs and turrets and libraries and kitchens and pterodactyl rookeries of the imperial residence. When we got bored with the building, soldiers escorted us to whatever part of Darkside we wished.

"Ash. Hey, can you hear me, Ash?"

No answer. I leaned closer, spoke softer.

"Your city needs you, Princess. Something is up. Something big."

So. We had a good four years. But when we turned twelve, something terrible took place. I don't know what. I wasn't there when it happened, but the story was that her othersider ability had revealed itself in a horrible way. People were hurt; some said people died. The Palace hushed it up. But after that traumatic incident, her mother put the first of many magic spells on her. It prevented future accidents . . . but it also made Ash lose her train of thought, struggle to form sentences, suffer from headaches that kept her in bed all day.

By the time the Palace staff put me out like so much garbage, Ash was in no position to defend me any further.

"I need you, Princess."

Niv appeared beside me. "In my monthly report to her mother, I asked her to consider lifting some of the wards they put on her."

I was impressed. That couldn't have been an easy thing to say to the famously volatile queen. But I wasn't going to give Niv the satisfaction of a pat on the back. "And?"

"She said it's a dangerous time. When things calm down, maybe."

"Things will never calm down," I said.

"No, but there *is* something new to be afraid of. There's a force in this city. Palace intelligence hasn't come up with much, but they know it's big, and well-resourced."

"Any connection to Destroy All Monsters?"

Niv nodded.

"And the ultramarine armbands?"

He shrugged. "I'm lucky to get the little scraps of intelligence that I have, and most of that is just whispers in corridors. All I know is, something is coming. Something that will upset the balance. The fragile peace between othersiders and everybody else. Seeds that were planted long ago are beginning to bloom."

"What about sending Ash out of the city? She could go into exile, somewhere it wouldn't matter if her magic was exposed. We could go with her. We could take care of her."

"According to Queen Carmen, there's nowhere on Earth that's safe from her enemies."

"Do me a favor? Ask around. Somebody in the Palace might have some intel on this ultramarine graffiti, and whatever anti-othersider activity is happening. Cass thinks—" But I didn't know what Cass thought. Just that she was scared, and she was *never* scared.

"I will," he said. "I promise."

"Do you remember?" I asked. "What happened to her?"

Niv shook his head. "That whole week was so crazy, it's a total blur."

"Crazy how?"

He laughed. "You don't remember? It was right around the same time as the Night of Red Diamonds!"

I looked at Ash. Something about that coincidence felt wrong. My spine shivered.

I took out the pie, cut us each a slice. Niv got plates, forks. Then he said: "Look!"

Ash's eyes were on my camera. She turned her head and then leaned forward.

"I haven't seen her respond to something like that in months," Niv said, rubbing his hands together. I loved him for how much he clearly loved her. It still didn't mean I trusted him.

Ash reached out to touch the camera, and smiled. Then, very slowly, she took a forkful of pie and ate it.

"That's amazing!" Niv said, and even old Ed's face softened, like maybe there was a halfway decent human in there somewhere. "She's fighting hard. I told you she was a warrior."

We ate pie together. Ash chewed slowly. And then she looked right at me, like somewhere deep inside her a door had been unlocked, and very definitely smiled.

"It's okay," I said. "We're okay."

Her smile faltered. Went away. Came back—but sadder, now, like she knew it wasn't true, but appreciated the fact that I'd lie to her, to try to make her feel better.

NINE

ASH

I watched them for a while. Five football players in the morning hallway, clearly up to no good. Standing around looking suspicious.

"What are y'all whispering about?" I asked, after sneaking up on them.

No one said a word. Then Sheffield spoke up. "Someone vandalized Marcy Brockelmeyer's house," he said, and held up his phone. The screen was cracked. Marcy's white house was covered in black splatters.

They all looked at him, waiting for what would come next. Here's the weird thing about Sheffield. He's popular in a way only jocks are, normally. But he's not on any sports team. Used to be a football player, but now he's not. The whole team loves him, though. He's at every practice. Every game. He's their ringleader, even from outside the ring.

"That's awful," I said, and looked from jock to jock. "And none of you had anything to do with it, I suppose?"

"What a truly terrible accusation," Sheffield said, and his smile implied *we* were complicit, him and me—that we were in on a secret. "Clever prank, though, don't you think? Most vandals use spray-paint, or feces, if they're especially juvenile. Easy to wash off, or paint over. But this prankster used *tar*. The only way to fix it is to scrape it all off and paint the whole thing over. Job like that could cost thousands."

I scanned his face. There was something there, but I couldn't tell if he was genuinely just impressed with the vandal's ingenuity. This was doubtless part of Sheffield's appeal to the other boys: the lack of fear; his utter absence of morality. He could half confess this crime to me—whether or not he actually had anything to do with it—because he knew I couldn't prove he was involved, so I couldn't do anything about it.

Solomon's words echoed in my head. *Something is coming. Something that will change everything.*

I stepped back. "This is probably connected with what happened to Judy Saperstein's house, don't you think?"

"I doubt it," he said, all innocence. "What makes you say that?"

"You don't think it's weird that all this vandalism is happening? All of a sudden?"

Sheffield shrugged, and walked away. He didn't hurry, just sauntered down the hall. I wanted to punch him right in his button nose.

I could feel it: darkness, bubbling up inside me. Felt the way the ground beneath me did not seem so solid anymore. The sea was there, and the ice I stood on was getting thin again.

I shut my eyes, took ten deep breaths. I was stronger than them, these goons that surrounded me, and I would not let them push me into a full depressive episode.

The bell rang, and I was grateful for it. On my way to homeroom, I passed by Solomon's room. He wasn't there, but maybe that didn't mean anything. After all, I wasn't in mine either.

At lunch, I went to the guidance counselor's office.

"Ash!" Mr. Taglia said, gesturing for me to take a seat. He was young, as school employees went. Thirty at the oldest. Thin, bearded, wearing suspenders that I think were ironic.

"It's about Solomon."

"Yes," he said. "You're worried about him." I didn't like Mr. Taglia, but I trusted him. If that makes any sense.

I nodded. "You said you thought he was schizophrenic."

"That's one possibility."

"But you're not a psychiatrist. So you're not qualified to make that diagnosis."

"No," he said. "But something *is* clearly going on. And he needs to be assessed by a professional to determine his condition and figure out the best way to treat it—whatever it is. But the bottom line, Ash, is that he has to *want* to get help, and right now he doesn't."

"I know. I need to help him, but I don't know how."

"He trusts you. He doesn't trust any of us."

I nodded again. I already knew that.

"I've been reading up on it, though," Mr. Taglia said, "and here's the thing about severe mental illness. It's like a physical illness, in that the sooner you catch it, the better your chances of recovery. The sooner someone starts treatment, the better their chances at having a normal life. At not being disabled. If this is indeed schizophrenia, it's in what's called the *prodromal phase*. Damage is being done, and you can't reverse the damage, but if you act early you can minimize it. If not . . ."

He didn't finish the sentence. He didn't need to.

"What . . . causes it? Triggers it?"

"It's hard to say," he said. "But we do know that the greatest risk factor for developing schizophrenia is having a relative who has it, so there's obviously a genetic component."

I didn't want this answer, but I needed it. "What

about if . . . something happens. Something really bad. Can that . . . ?"

"Well, yes. Trauma is often a trigger."

I thought of Solomon's words: *I need you to remember.*

Something *had* happened. To both of us. How much of it did he remember? And why couldn't I? And did it have anything to do with my own depression, the feeling like a hole had opened up in my chest that would suck me into myself forever? If we could get at the truth of it, together, it might save us both.

"Thanks, Mr. Taglia," I said, standing up.

I called up Connor, because he hates phone calls. As Solomon's stepbrother, he might have some information or insight that I lacked, into what had happened around the time I fell out of his treehouse. He didn't answer, but I got three text messages in quick succession:

I'm trying to learn here.

Jerk

Why can't you text people like normal people do?

The last one came with a winky face.

After school he found me in the parking lot, sitting on my car's fender, watching seagulls and sparrows squabble over scattered popcorn.

"Hey, Ash," he said, standing right in front of me.

My motives had been pure when I called him up. But now that he was so close, with the familiar clean-clothes smell of him filling up my nostrils, I weakened. When

I was down, when I was stressed, when the hole inside me was at its deepest—I won't mince words, sex with Connor straightened me out.

"Hey," I said. I could have grabbed him by the hips and kissed his stomach, snatched a handful of T-shirt and pulled him down to kiss me, but I didn't do any of those things. When we're alone he has no shame whatsoever, but he's weird about doing stuff that other people will see. Probably because we're not technically A Thing.

"What's going on?"

"I wanted to talk to you about Solomon," I said.

His smile wilted, faded. "Did something happen?"

"Not really," I said. "But I've been thinking a lot about when we were kids. I'm afraid something happened to him, some traumatic thing he's blocking out. That can happen, with . . . mentally ill people. And I was thinking that maybe helping him remember . . ."

Connor nodded, and sat on the fender beside me.

"Do *you* remember anything? Something I didn't know about, or forgot after my accident? Something you saw, something your father might have said?"

"About Solomon? No. It's a sore subject around the house. My dad tried hard to help him, after his mother got locked up, but Solomon pushed him away. So I guess he feels like he failed him? I know I do."

I smirked. "People Who Failed Solomon. We could form a club."

The wind picked up, and started me shivering.

"You're cold," Connor said matter-of-factly.

"You're not?" I tapped at his arms, bare below his T-shirt sleeves.

"Nah," he said, and inched closer so I could leach heat off him.

"Want to come over to my house?"

He smiled, knowing what I meant. "Sounds great," he said, after a second, but not like a guy excited to sleep with somebody—like somebody doing a favor for a friend. Because Connor was a really good friend.

We got in. I started up the car and pulled out of the parking lot.

"The night of the accident. That was the last night Solomon ever spent in our house," he said, halfway to my house. "I just remembered that. My dad was at the hospital until late—he felt so bad that you'd gotten hurt on our property—and Solomon slept in the basement. In the morning he ran off."

"Wow," I said. "I hadn't realized. Thanks."

I reached out my hand, and he took it. "At your service, my lady. Always."

With his crew cut, with his air of perpetual positivity, Connor seemed to be a creature out of time, a refugee from some other, less-fucked age. Some fictional 1950s of wholesome wood-paneled station wagons piled high with surfboards and poodle-skirt girls and Coke-bottle-brandishing boys.

I knew none of that was real. I knew the 1950s was a pretty shitty time for most people. But I got it, why folks wanted to pretend like those were the good old days. Because Connor seemed to exist in that alternate reality where the world wasn't a wretched place full of awful people. It made me happy just to be close to it.

And then I pulled up in front of my house, and the bubble popped.

Because there was Solomon, sitting on my front porch, strumming a guitar. And as happy as I was to see him, I was also superworried. Because Connor tended to freak Solomon out.

"I didn't know he played the guitar," Connor said, his voice so much smaller already.

I nodded. "Writes songs, too. He's pretty good."

I parked. Got out.

"Ash, hey!" Solomon said, waving, standing up, and I saw the precise second when his smile cracked, when he caught sight of Connor.

"Solomon!" Connor cheered, waving, and it hurt my heart, to see him run toward his stepbrother, to see how Solomon stiffened, to see Connor give him a big, hard hug anyway, and to see Solomon finally relent, soften, hug him back. Shut his eyes. Smile.

They're both big boys. But standing next to Solomon made Connor seem like a little boy again.

"Missed you, man," Connor said. "You never come to see me."

"Sorry," Solomon said. "I know how busy you are. With the team and all."

Team or not, Solomon had always felt weird around Connor. I'd tried to get to the bottom of it before. Was it guilt? Jealousy? Inadequacy? Whatever it was, it was deep, and it was getting worse. They used to be able to have an actual conversation, but now Solomon was already shambling down the walkway, saying how he had to head down to the docks, and Connor and I exchanged a quick, weird glance because there are no docks in Hudson, nor anywhere near Hudson.

"Solomon!" Connor called.

His stepbrother stopped. Turned around. Showed us all the pain that was on his face, so that as soon as Connor spoke again I wished I could snap my fingers, stop the words from ever having been said.

"I feel like you hate me," Connor said, his voice sounding as low and small as a six-year-old's. "And I don't know why."

Solomon didn't answer, not right away. Stared at his hands like he couldn't get his head around what he'd done.

"Neither do I," he said, and turned and ran.

We watched him go, and we didn't speak for a long time after that. Sex was the furthest thing from my mind.

"You want a ride home?" I asked.

"Yeah," Connor said. "I'm sorry."

"Don't be," I said, and hugged him. He turned his face into my neck. I could feel his wet eyelids fluttering against my skin. He didn't make a sound, but when he pulled away, my collar was damp.

TEN

SOLOMON

Down at the docks, seagulls and tiny harpies squabbled in the air overhead. A plesiosaur rose from the water, its head as big as me and full of long snake-sharp teeth. I leaped back, but I had nothing to fear from this one: it was muzzled and harnessed to a transport raft, bringing crates from a ship docked out in the river. It kept rising and rising until its neck extended two stories up, and I could see the armor plating on its side, painted with the complex circular glyphs of the Sea Peoples.

The Underbridge docks were busy, like they always were, with a hundred kinds of commerce, both legal and illegal, but right away I could see that something had changed. The volume level had been turned way down. The normal shouting and banging and crashing and stomping just—wasn't. No racket of machines chugging in the background either. This could mean lots of things. Police crackdowns happened from time to time. War between smugglers. People also tended to be pretty somber, right after a big shipwreck or dockside accident, but I hadn't heard about any of those things happening out here.

Out on the plains, I've read, all the dinosaurs go silent when a new one comes along. When they don't know whether or not they should be afraid.

I had the sense there was a new dinosaur here in town, and I was pretty sure that dinosaur was the man I'd seen spray-painted on the bridge pillar.

Radha was hard at work—doing laundry for her neighbors was one of the many ways she made ends meet—but she'd told me Connor was being babysat at the Mammoth Narwhal, so that's where I went.

My mind hadn't been right, ever since leaving Ash. Seeing her smile had been magnificent, but it had also reminded me how far gone she was. How much we were up against. And spending time with my foster brother was the best way I knew how to make myself feel better.

A mammoth tusk and a narwhal horn hung in the window. Built on a floating platform, it was a shabby, glorious restaurant with good noodles, strong coffee, and cheap drinks. Sailors and merchants and dockhands all frequented it, alongside the folks who made their living illegally—smugglers, pickpockets, sex workers, drug dealers selling spiderwebbing or manticore scales or phoenix feathers.

"Solomon!" Connor said. He caught sight of me as I walked in the door, before my own eyes had adjusted to the gloom. The restaurant smelled like heaven, like smoked ham and brown sugar. Shouts from the kitchen echoed off the low ceiling. He came running, and gave me a big, hard hug.

"Hey, Solomon," said Quang, who owned the restaurant. "You come to take this little troublemaker off my hands?"

That was when I noticed smoke pouring out of the kitchen.

"What did you do, you little monster?" I asked, hoisting Connor up.

He screamed in delight, mock-struggling, as I carried him.

"I just wanted to show him a way to cook the noodles faster! It was taking too long."

"You practically cooked the whole kitchen," Quang said, laughing. We sat down at a table, beside a window with green river water rippling right outside.

Quang was an othersider, with the ability to transport any object over any distance. Power like that, most people would go crazy with. Steal money out of cash registers, build an empire on thievery, but Quang just wanted to live a simple life. He had a sea wyvern tattoo on his forearm, and rumor had it that he was telepathically linked to a monster as big as a battleship, dwelling deep in the sea. He did a good, honest business—although, allegedly, when a local tough guy did something terrible to one of his waitresses, he teleported the guy clear to the far side of the Waterlands. Never to be seen again.

"Solomon," said Evvy, one of the cooks. A big, beautiful butch woman, she shook my hand so hard I had to wince. Which made her laugh.

I handed Connor a paper place mat, and sat him down on my lap. He began to draw, using his finger—focusing a tiny flame, burning black lines onto the white surface, slowly sketching out Maraud's familiar outline.

"You've gotten so good at that," I said.

"Shhh," he said, lips tight with concentration. Under the faint scent of smoke, I could smell the laundry soap of Connor's clothes.

I turned to Quang and Evvy. "You guys know anything about this 'Destroy All Monsters' nonsense popping up all over the city?"

A long pause. They looked at each other. Then they burst out laughing.

"What?" I asked.

"Tough subject," Quang said. "We been arguing about this all week."

"Not arguing," she said. "Discussing."

"Evvy is a sympathizer."

"Shut up," she said, and turned to me, alarmed. "I'm not, I swear. I just think Quang is wrong to write them off."

"Write . . . who off?"

"The nativists. The anti-othersider mob," Quang said. "The ones behind 'Abolish All Magic' and 'Destroy All Monsters' and all that sh—" He looked at Connor, chose another word. "Nonsense."

I asked Evvy, "How could you *sympathize* with creeps like that?"

"I told you, I don't. But my brother does, and my dad, and so do lots of this-siders. People who are scared of what this city has become. We shouldn't have to live in fear all the time."

I'd heard this a million times before. People actually believed that othersiders were violent—or more violent than this-siders, just by nature. They believed that their powers were weapons, and that they'd use them against a this-sider whenever they felt like it. Just for fun.

Idiotic. But lots of people swallowed that nonsense. And if someone was stoking those idiotic beliefs, I could see them gaining a lot of power.

"I'm sure their message resonates with a lot of people," I said diplomatically.

Connor looked up. "Are they going to get us?"

"Shhh," I said, and kissed the top of his head. Feeling

awful, for saying stuff that had scared him. "No one's going to get anybody."

"But they hate us."

"They're just scared," Evvy said.

This was all so new. Seemed like just a little while ago, Connor tuned out every grown-up conversation and never had an idea what any of us were saying.

"I got you, kid," Quang said, and picked up a spoon from the table. "Anybody tries to hurt you, I'll do this to them."

The spoon vanished, and then reappeared outside the window. Plummeted into the river; sank like a stone. Connor laughed, and clapped.

"My boys," Radha said, walking in.

"Look at Connor's latest," I said, holding up the place mat.

"Such an artist," she said, pulling up a chair. She reached out, took Connor's hand in one of hers and mine in the other. I could feel the cracks in her skin.

Stout and sturdy and fearless as she was, I could see the weariness in her face.

"Noodles?" Evvy asked, and at our enthusiastic nods she headed for the kitchen. Connor hopped off my lap, began to run through the mostly empty restaurant.

"You shouldn't encourage this," Radha said, pointing to the place mat.

"Why not?"

She released my hand. "Are you blind? Don't you see what's happening in this city? You haven't heard that people are *disappearing* now? All over, dozens of othersiders—not coming home from work, vanishing on the way to school. It is not safe for him to use his power out in the open where anyone can see."

I knew that people were being targeted—harassed. I hadn't heard that people were disappearing. Certainly not by the dozens. I'd have to ask Cass about that one. See what she'd learned. Because of course the Darkside Police Department wouldn't be doing a damn thing to rescue abducted othersiders.

"Mama, look!" Connor called.

A bird made of fire flapped its wings in the air in front of us. Quang and I clapped, but Radha leaped up from her seat and grabbed Connor by the arm.

"Stop. Stop it right now. You must never, *never* do that again," she hissed.

She yelled at Connor from time to time. You had to, with a kid so energetic and loud.

But she wasn't yelling now. Her voice was dead calm. And that made the blood in my veins turn to freezing-cold river water.

The bird blew away in a wisp of black smoke. Connor began to cry.

"I need you to understand. Do you understand?" she whispered. She had to say it a couple more times, before he nodded.

Connor sat down, crying hard now. I rubbed his shoulder, and he got up and sat on my lap. Buried his head in my chest.

"Shhhh," I said. "It's okay."

He sniffled, and nodded again. I felt glad that he still believed me.

Radha turned her head away so he wouldn't see her tears. We sat there in silence and waited for our noodles. I wished there was something I could say.

Here's what I think: my magic has something to do with emotion. I don't know what it is, exactly, but sometimes, when I feel a strong emotion, I get the kind of tingly sensation that some othersiders describe when their powers are starting to trigger.

I felt that tingle then. It made me wonder if maybe I *could* help Radha and Connor. Make them less afraid, less sad.

I shut my eyes, tried to access it. Focused on my spine, the way the Palace trainers had taught us—felt energy running along it, coursing through my body. Breathed deep. Felt the tingling get stronger. Tried to think happy, positive, peaceful thoughts.

But something was wrong. I tried to move my arms,

and couldn't. I opened my mouth to ask for help, but no words emerged. Just like always, before a freak-out.

"Solomon?" Radha said, but her voice sounded very, very far away.

ELEVEN

ASH

What makes a photograph great?

Taking pictures is easy. I take dozens, every day. With my camera, with my phone. I post them to Instagram. Facebook. People like them. But I still don't know what I'm doing.

Every night I'm on the internet, or flipping through books, stalking the images of famous artists and social media nobodies, trying to figure it out. Which photographs move me, and why? Face after face slides past me, each one full of unreadable emotion. Whole lives I will never know anything about.

Look up Richard Avedon's photo of Marilyn Monroe. Look at her face. See how much pain is there, how lost she is. Compare that to the tens of thousands of other photographs that were taken of her, the smiling happy sex symbol, and you know that Avedon caught something special. Something haunting.

How? Cass told me the story about that one. How Avedon spent all night photographing her, in his studio, with props and backdrops and costumes, in motion and standing still, hundreds of exposures as he tried to get at the truth of her. Country girl Norma Jeane, who created a fictional creature to hide behind, and made her into the most famous woman in the world. He couldn't break through that facade. Finally, he told her he was all finished with the shoot. She relaxed. Let her guard down. All the exhaustion she'd been hiding flowed into her face. In that instant, he took a photograph. And that's the one.

On the one hand, it's kind of a dick move. To trick a woman into revealing something she tried her hardest to keep hidden. To steal her secret, and tell everyone. On the other hand, there's a truth here, a story Hollywood didn't want to hear, about a lonely person who was tired of being exploited and crying out for help. If more people had heard that story, maybe she wouldn't have taken her own life at thirty-six.

Being an artist sometimes means breaking the rules of civilized human behavior.

I shut my laptop. I counted to ten.

That evening, I'd gotten a call from Solomon's aunt.

His mother's sister; his legal guardian. A sweet woman, overwhelmed by everything the world had thrown at her. She'd been crying. And when I hung up, so was I.

I had to, she said, and *I had no choice,* and *They would have charged me with neglect.*

She'd reported Solomon missing, to the Hudson Department of Child Protective Services. She'd spent weeks trying not to. Reaching out to him, trying to get him to come home. She'd covered for him for as long as she could. But now they'd be looking for him. They might even send cops.

Once I stopped crying, I went online and started staring at photographs. It helped, for a little while. And then it didn't.

I tried my hardest not to call Connor. I hated myself when I did it: for exploiting him, for resorting to sex with no strings attached as a way of feeling better. Especially since he'd been so upset by seeing Solomon, the last time we were about to hook up. But the darkness was getting stronger. The hole in my chest was getting wider. I needed contact, distraction.

I went over to his house.

"What happened?" he asked, opening the door. "Are you okay?"

"Of course," I said. "Why?"

"You only come by when you're stressed out about something. Or upset, or sad, or whatever."

"That's not true," I said.

Connor shrugged, and bit his lower lip. His body had definitely become a man's, even if he still seemed so much like a boy sometimes.

He was right, of course.

"I can go, if you want. I don't want to make you feel . . ."

"I don't want you to go." He summoned up a sweet, sad smile. "Come on in."

"Evening, Ash," said Connor's father, when we walked past the kitchen. He stood at the counter, reading a newspaper.

"Hey, Mr. Barrett."

Solomon and I had both been crushed out on Connor's dad, back in the day. He'd had the same broad shoulders and bright brown eyes as Connor, the same fair hair and unblemished skin.

We walked past the room that had been Solomon's, before he ran away. The door was shut. It was always shut. Like they were trying to lock the memory of him away.

Connor's room was superclean. The kind of clean that makes you feel bad about yourself, because you look like a slob by comparison. Like the guy had an undiagnosed disorder. He sat down on the bed with a helpless look on his face and I sat down beside him, feeling like I was taking advantage. Which I guess I was, except that

Connor enjoyed it as much as I did.

"What've you been up to?" I asked, because it felt rude to cut right to the part where we made out.

"Football practice, football practice, and, sometimes, when I have free time, more football practice." He tugged off the T-shirt he wore, which fit him disturbingly well. "You?"

"Trying to figure out what I'm gonna do for my photography project."

He sat there, shirtless. Defenseless.

"Is there something going on, with the football team?" I asked. "I talked to Sheffield, and he seemed real weird. Even for him. Especially about the graffiti stuff that's been going on. Do you—"

"I don't want to talk about Sheffield or any of them," he said, and it was only the kiss that made me ignore my curiosity about the look that flashed on his face. A look that wasn't guilt exactly, but was certainly something like it.

Afterward, we spooned. I'm taller than him, but his arms felt so strong around me. Out the window, I could see the treehouse. Solomon's favorite place, when he lived here. Connor never had much love for it.

"What can we do for him?" Connor asked. "For Solomon?"

"That's what I'm trying to figure out. Did you talk

to your dad about him? He's gotta know some people. Maybe—"

"Solomon's mom really fucked my dad over. He's still super–pissed off about it. So, whenever I bring up Solomon, he's not in too much of a hurry to discuss it."

"Solomon's not responsible for what his mom did." I scowled.

"No, but it goes both ways. Solomon's just as angry. He's not rushing over to sit down and have a heart-to-heart with my dad, either."

"Keep trying, will you?" I said. "He's a kid, just like us. And he's in danger. Your dad's a grown-up. Vice principal. Football coach. Pillar of the community. Everybody loves and respects him. If he can help Solomon, he should."

"I know," Connor said, and kissed the back of my neck again. I reached back, and he took my hand. We spent an hour like that, not talking, not moving. Time with Connor was like meditation. It cleared my head, calmed me down.

I didn't sleep long in Connor's arms, but I did sleep deep. Plunging from dream to dream to memory to fantasy, until I couldn't tell where one ended and the next began, or where the real world was in relation to all that.

A floating restaurant. A mammoth tusk.

A boy who could summon up birds made of fire.

And then—something else, something so sharp and

real I knew it had to be a memory.

Deep inside me, a door had been unlocked.

Connor's house, the same place I was presently sleeping, except back then I thought of it as Solomon's stepfather's house, and Connor was just this scrawny short kid who idolized his stepbrother.

The house is bigger, now, because I am smaller. Dark polished wood floors. Framed photographs of faraway cities and strangers in black and white. A basement big enough to hold all the monsters in my imagination.

Solomon and I are exploring. We're eleven, maybe twelve. His mother and stepfather are at Connor's Little League game. I wonder why they don't take Solomon to watch those anymore. He's big for his age, and strong, but he has absolutely no interest in sports.

He takes us out back. The treehouse his stepfather built for Connor. We climb up.

"This is my favorite place in the whole Palace," he says. "Sixty stories high. It's where the war pterodactyls launch from."

The thing I love most about Solomon is his imagination. How he sees the world. How full of wonder it is.

"Do I have magic?" I ask.

"Yes," he says solemnly. "But some magic doesn't manifest until later. Whatever it is, it'll be incredible."

I wonder what video game or fantasy novel he got all this out of.

"Take my picture," he says.

I raise the camera. It's cheap and digital. This is long before the Leica.

Through the lens, he looks like a normal boy. Wearing a shirt that is maybe a tiny bit too small for him.

Solomon smiles. I push the button. The camera clicks.

TWELVE

SOLOMON

A camera clicked.

I opened my eyes to total darkness. My arms and legs were still tingling.

I had been plunging from dream to dream to memory to fantasy, until I couldn't tell where one ended and the next began, or where the real world was in relation to all that.

A house, high in a tree.

Ash, carrying a camera.

"You're awake," Connor said. Just a voice in the dark; small and fragile.

"Are you playing with my camera?" I asked, struggling to sit up. The camera clicked again. "You can't take pictures in the dark, silly. Light striking the film is what makes a photograph. No light, no picture."

He sat down on the bed beside me. Put his hand on my forehead. "Are you still sick?"

"I'm okay," I said, feeling so tired that every word was an effort. "What happened?"

"You had a fit," he said. "At the restaurant. Quang snapped you straight into bed, though. You're lucky, because me and Mama would never have been able to carry you."

"I'm superlucky," I said.

He kissed my forehead, which is what Radha always did. The best medicine, as far as he knew.

"Thanks, brother," I said. "I need to sleep, now."

"Mama told me not to bother you," he said.

"I'm glad you disobeyed her."

And I was out, quick as that. Swallowed up by a dream. A memory. Something I blocked out.

Me and Ash, down at the train tracks. The nine women soldiers in her personal guard following at a careful distance. Armored stegosauruses on either side of us; mammoth-sized jaguars ahead of and behind us.

Storm clouds are piled up like black cliffs in the distance. They've been there for days. They'll be there for days, like the storm is stalking us. Watching. Waiting.

"I've been feeling it more and more lately," she says. "A tingle up my spine. I focus on it; I can feel it getting bigger and bigger—I just don't know how to release it."

"Your nine guards can't help you?"

"They're trying. It's just a block I have, I guess."

We are twelve. At breakfast, as I was spooning diced dragon fruit over a really very modest serving of yogurt, the queen had announced to the whole crowded room full of courtiers and servants: "The way that boy eats, you'd think he just came in off the street this morning." And all of them giggled. And I'd spent most of the rest of the day crying. I was better now, but not by much.

"In two days, my guards are going to try something new," Ash says, and I can hear the fear in her voice. Those nine soldiers love Ash to death and would gladly die for her, but they push her hard.

But I can't feel pity for the princess's problems. Not today. My own hurt feelings are echoing too loudly in my ears. Hurt feelings, and fear. Memories of hunger. Of how horrible the city could be.

Also, I'm superhungry, because I wasn't about to eat that food after the queen made fun of me. So I'm not thinking straight. So please forgive me.

"What's with you?" Ash asks.

"You really don't know?"

She makes a *psssh* noise. "You're still thinking about what my mom said? Don't pay any attention to her."

I stop walking. Try to make myself calm down.

I know Ash can't help it. She is what she is. All her

needs were met; she never had to worry about anything except for when her magic would start to work.

"You'd never understand," I say. My voice is hard, mean, and I know that's not me, not us, but I can't stop myself. "How could you? You've never been hungry. Never been assaulted on the street, while a police officer looks the other way."

"But you're not out there anymore, are you? Because I saved you. Because I know how ugly this city is, even if I never had to live with that ugliness."

This is Ash. The princess. My friend. Who picked me up out of the gutter. Who I love so fiercely and owe so much to that sometimes I resent her.

But it sucks, loving someone. It means you're not in control of what you do anymore. It means you're helpless. That's what I'm angry about, when I open my mouth and say:

"While you're sitting up in the Palace, safe and sound, or out here surrounded by war jaguars as big as houses, people are living lives and dying deaths you could never imagine. So don't ever *pssssh* at me."

The look she gives me in response is hard, and full of things she chooses not to share.

We don't say another word, but we spend a long time walking. Sometimes the silence feels almost comfortable, like it normally does, and sometimes it prickles like a thick, thorny hedge between us.

What we don't realize is that we only have two more days together.

In less than a week, I'll get kicked out on the street and Ash won't be the same.

I don't know why I remember that now, in the safe warm dark of Radha's home. I blocked out the memory because I was ashamed of what I'd said. And now that I could remember it, I could connect the dots. Ash's words. *In two days, my guards are going to try something new.* And the fact that two days after that conversation, everything went wrong.

THIRTEEN

ASH

The high school parking lot had become a minefield. Students and teachers alike stood around, gawking.

In the middle of the night, someone had spread a bucket of tar on the pavement of the student parking lot, then sprinkled a sackful of broken bottles on it, and nails and screws and other random, sharp metal things, so that in the morning when people started pulling in, their tires all got shredded. By the time I pulled up for school, the parking lot was closed and there was a line of tow trucks trying to figure out how to get everyone's car to safety so the tires could be changed.

I took pictures. People's faces. More than one person was crying. Everyone was somber. They looked at each other with suspicion; with fear. This wasn't some little prank. This was destructive, aggressive—scary.

The student parking lot. Whoever did this knew that the people who came first would get it the worst. So it had been set up to target the nerds, the good students.

I thought of the ultramarine swastikas. Marcy Brockelmeyer's house, vandalized. And now this. They couldn't be unrelated. Something was up. Someone was responsible.

Solomon was picking up pennies from the train tracks, when I got there at four o'clock. He must have laid them down on the rails the night before, to be run over by a freight train, because they were huge and flat and thin—lopsided metal ovals.

"I call them trained pennies," he said, holding one out to me. "Get it? Trained? Like they got run over by a train?"

"Awesome," I said, taking it. It was still hot from the autumn sun on the rails. He'd called me up, the night before. From a bar. One a.m., and my seventeen-year-old best friend was hanging out in a bar. But at least he'd called.

I wanted to see him, because I had something to say to him. Something he wasn't going to like. I had to convince him to get help. Because at this point, with his aunt having reported him missing, it was just a matter of time before someone put a hand on his shoulder and said, "Come with me, son"—or someone from Child Protective Services recognized him, which was pretty likely in a town as small as ours. And I didn't think Solomon would respond well to "Come with me, son."

But I had to work up my courage to get to all that. "What do you do with your trained pennies?" I asked.

"It's a kind of currency," he said. "Certain transactions, you can't use regular money for."

"So you use these."

He nodded.

You see my dilemma, with shit like this. I had a lot of questions, but ask too many of them and he might pick up on my skepticism, or think that I was trying to diagnose him. Which, yeah, I kind of was. "What kind of transactions?"

"Lots of groups don't trust the queen or her government, or they don't want to pay taxes that support the police. They have their own economies."

The queen. Her government. Secret economies.

Paranoid. Tinfoil hat kind of stuff.

When he was done picking up pennies, he walked along the train tracks and I followed him.

Solomon did not smell good. His clothes were sour with cigarettes and scotch—someone else's; Solomon didn't drink or smoke. There was also definitely body odor—his own.

"Do you want to come over to my house?" I asked,

after a while. "Hang out, eat some food, take a shower?"

He laughed. "I stink, don't I?"

"How long has it been since the last time you bathed?" *And did you know that lapses in physical hygiene are a common symptom of mental illness?*

He shrugged. "Couple days. There's a brakeman's hut up ahead, where I sleep sometimes. Doesn't exactly have the amenities of a four-star hotel."

We walked. I tried out about a hundred questions, in my head, before saying, "Tell me about the queen."

"She's an asshole," he said, then laughed. "But she's in a difficult position. Half the city is afraid of the other half, and vice versa, and she has to make both sides as happy as possible, even though most of the time they're at each other's throats. She still wears all black, even though her wife died six years ago. She rides a white tyrannosaur—the only tyrannosaur allowed in the city. It's a nod to the othersiders—the people with powers—that she cares for them, too."

He stopped.

"Sometimes I can see it so clearly—what's real and what's not. Like right now, this all sounds crazy, and I know it's not real. But then something will happen, I'll hear a bell, or see the color blue, or I'll doze off, and it's all of *this* that seems crazy—these train tracks, this town, these people. You . . . talking to me like nothing's wrong. That's what's not real."

His make-believe world was getting stronger. He was sick. But maybe he was also . . . special? Able to see things other people couldn't? What if something real was happening—to me, to the world around us—and he had insight into it?

"You said something was coming," I said. "What kind of something?"

"Seeds that were planted long ago are beginning to bloom. People are afraid; people are angry. Fear and anger don't stay silent. They become action."

I thought of Sheffield. The wave of vandalism.

"Do you remember?" I asked, and this time the question came out without my thinking about it. "Do you know what happened to us? When we were twelve?"

"Some of it," he said. "But I can't tell which memories to trust. Which ones are real. That's why I need you. To figure this out for both of us."

"It happened at Connor's house," I said. "Tell me what you remember. All of it. Real or not. We can figure it out together."

He didn't say anything. His face was tight, and reddening fast. I knew I was hurting him, but I had to press forward.

"Your mother," I said. "She got locked up— It was right around the same time. Right?"

He didn't move. Didn't nod, didn't say anything. But I knew that much was true.

"Did something happen with her?" I whispered. "Did we see something? Something she did?"

"I can't," he said, and held up both hands so I could see how they shook. "When I try, I get—I don't know, sick. Nauseous. And then I space out. And then bad things happen."

His arm twitched. His leg jerked. Solomon was struggling with the fight-or-flight response, and I knew that in a minute, maybe two, he'd turn and run. I might not see him again for a while. And I might not get the chance to warn him.

"Solomon, your aunt called Child Protective Services to report you as missing."

His eyes opened, wide with sudden startling fear.

"She had to— Otherwise she could get charged with child negligence. She could go to *jail*, Solomon. She protected you for as long as she could."

Solomon nodded, but the terror did not go out of his eyes.

"This doesn't have to be a bad thing," I said. "Come home with me tonight, shower and eat and get some rest and feel better, and then tomorrow we can go to the department of social services and talk to them. Would you do that?"

He looked at his feet for a long, long time. "I can't," he said finally.

"Why not?"

"What if they want to lock me up?" he whispered.

"They're not going to lock you up after one visit!" I said, almost laughing.

"They wouldn't lock *you* up, Ash."

They'd locked up Solomon's mother, hadn't they? Why would he think it would be any different for him?

I took his hand. Took his other hand. Held them both, hard. Waited for them to stop shaking, but they would not. I breathed slow and deep, trying my best to be calm, to clear my mind, to find some peace and send it Solomon's way.

"Solomon, you need to see a doctor," I said. "Would you do that? For me? Please? I'm scared for you— They say the sooner you get treated, the better your chances are."

He pulled his hands away from mine, turned away. Took a step, then another.

And then . . . Solomon screamed. Howled. The force of it doubled him over, and when he screamed again, he fell to his knees. He kept screaming. I'd never imagined a sound so big coming out of him.

"Hey," I said, reaching out to touch his shoulder.

Solomon reacted on raw, unthinking instinct. When he felt my hand, he flinched. Twisted his body and pushed me away.

I fell. My butt hit the ground, hard.

He wasn't trying to hurt me. I know that.

FOURTEEN

SOLOMON

Connor and I sat on the floor of Radha's hut, drawing. He burned shapes and images into pieces of paper with his finger-fire, and I colored them in.

"The flames should be blue," Connor said.

"Of course," I said.

Physically, I felt fully recovered from my latest freak-out. My throat hurt, like I'd been screaming, which was weird because Radha swore up and down that I never made a sound, but otherwise I was fine. Physically.

Mentally, not so much. I remembered all the awful things I said to Ash before everything went bad, and that was painful enough, but I couldn't ignore the suspicious timing of it all. Ash's nine soldier-guards were going to use some scary, painful method to shock Ash's power out into the open—and the very next day, Ash was sedated. Magically restrained. Subdued into a near-coma.

Coincidence, I told myself, but I was unconvincing.

"You're outside the lines," Connor said, snatching the crayon out of my hand.

"Sorry, brother."

Normally, Connor would have been at the Narwhal . . . but the place was locked up tight, and no one had seen Quang. Radha had asked me to stick around, help watch Connor, and I'd been very happy to agree—especially when I saw how worried she clearly was about the possibility that Quang had disappeared, among so many others.

A knock from outside. Radha was in the kitchen making dinner, so I went to answer the door.

"Hello, Solomon," said Niv.

"What the hell," I said. "What are you doing here?"

"We need a place to hide," he said, his smile embarrassed and adorable. And that's when I noticed the woman behind him, wearing a hijab, who I'd initially assumed to be another Underbridge loiterer.

"Ash," I said, even before she turned around and I saw her face.

"Solomon," she said, her eyes unfocused, her voice tiny and far away.

I pushed past Niv, to hug her. Her arms stayed at her

sides. Part of her was still somewhere else. Somewhere terrifying.

I glanced past the two of them. They were alone. "You're alone?"

"Had to get out fast." Niv's eyes darted left and right, scanning for threat in his periphery.

I tried my best to smile for Ash, but fear froze my mouth in a frown. This was so, so bad. Niv's sense of duty to the Crown was all-consuming. To abandon his post, to essentially kidnap Ash—when we all knew that putting a member of the royal family in danger was treason? What could have happened, to push Niv to such drastic action?

"I'm sorry," he said. "I didn't know where else to go. Can we come in?"

"What happened?" I asked.

Ash looked up at me. Made eye contact. Handed me something. Like a coin, but flatter. And misshapen. Like a penny that had been stomped on by a titanosaur.

"I found that in her hand," Niv said. "It wasn't in there before. She said you gave it to her. After it was run over by a train. She said the two of you were down by the train tracks today. You were screaming."

And when he said that? I *did* remember. I remembered handing it to her. How it held the heat of the sun and warmed my palm. A whole host of other memories seemed to glimmer ahead of me, just out of reach. She could help me unlock them. I could help her. We could make each other whole again.

"The spell they have her under, she's been fighting it more and more," Niv said. "And if they don't know where she is, it'll be a lot harder for them to strengthen the spell, and sedate her all over again." His eyes told me he had more to say, but didn't want to say it in front of Ash. I nodded, to show that I got it, that we could talk about it soon.

"They're going to lose their minds, when they find out she's gone," I said. "They'll pull out all the stops to try to find her. Turn this city upside down."

He nodded. "I know. If I had any sense, I'd bring her back now. But this feels . . . important."

"You're right," I said. "Of course, you're right. Come inside, I'll see if Radha can put you up. It's crowded, but she's a miracle worker."

Radha emerged from the kitchen with water dripping from her hands. Connor came running to see the strangers.

"This is Niv," I said. "He's . . . my colleague at the *Clarion*. And this—"

I was scrambling for a story, about to say that she was his sister, Ananka. But Radha had already dropped to her knees. "Your Highness," she said.

I was surprised, and impressed, that she could recognize Ash without her royal trappings. But Radha adored the queen, and maybe she recognized some of Ash's mother's face and regal bearing in the young woman who stood before her. Ash inclined her head slightly and I swear I never saw Radha smile so deeply.

Niv stepped forward, stuck out his hand. "I'm deeply sorry to have brought her here. I know that it comes with a great risk. And I promise you, it will be a very short stay. We need to find a safer place where our presence doesn't put anyone else in danger."

"This is the safest place in the city for the othersider princess," Radha said. She looked like she was about to cry from happiness. "I'll protect her with my life, and so will everyone else in the Underbridge."

"Thank you, Radha," I said.

She bowed again, and went to prepare a pallet on the floor of the bedroom where Connor and I slept.

"Look what I can do!" Connor said, extending his fingers in front of him, until a ball of fire began to burn in the air. Ash laughed, and then he laughed, and the ball became a long, coiled dragon made of flame.

Ash smiled, held out her palm. It balanced above it, inches away, close enough to warm her without risking burning her.

The flames made her features seem so fierce, so solid. The old Ash was in there, all right. The angry, beautiful princess who would defy her mother and half the city if she thought it was the right thing to do.

Politics and pragmatism be damned. I grabbed my camera off the table and took a picture. The burning dragon, the smiling princess.

"Can I talk to you?" Niv asked.

I nodded, and we stepped into the kitchen. "You asked me to find out what I could, about the ultramarine graffiti? About the armbands? Turns out, Palace intelligence is spooked. This is big, Solomon. These people—they call themselves the Destroyers—"

"As in, 'Destroy All Monsters.' Except *monsters* doesn't just mean monsters. It means othersiders, too. It means us."

"Exactly. They want to eradicate magic from Darkside altogether. Their leader calls himself the Shield, says he's here to protect Darkside's citizens from the menace of the othersiders. But the big thing, the thing that has the queen really scared, is that he's got the support of the whole Darkside Police Department on the down low. Half of the cops are members of the Destroyers. Including Commissioner Bahrr himself."

I stared at him, my mouth hanging open. Every othersider knew the cops weren't friends. But this was something organized, something aggressive, something much, much worse.

"Police Commissioner Bahrr made the Shield into what he is. For years, he's been funneling weapons and intel to the Shield. The movement's grown ever since the Night of Red Diamonds."

I thought of Cass, the questions she would ask. "Is there anyone who will go on the record about all this?"

"You know there's not."

I nodded. "It's helpful, though. Thank you."

"I know you don't like me," he said, apparently out of nowhere. "I just don't know why."

Well. I gave him credit, at least, for not being afraid to say the difficult thing.

My camera was still around my neck. I raised it, and he smiled. The shadows danced across his face. I took the picture.

"I can't explain it," I said to him. "I've just always been suspicious of you. Like . . . I've always felt like you had an agenda I didn't understand. I—I'm sorry."

He smiled. Kindly, sadly. Looked into the fire. "Everybody has an agenda."

"Tell me about yours."

"Some other time," he said.

His face looked so sad. I wanted to kiss him, but I would not let myself.

FIFTEEN

ASH

"My throat hurts," Solomon said.

"Of course it does. You were screaming for what felt like forever."

"I'm sorry, about that freak-out."

"I know. It's okay. We're okay."

We walked. It was almost all the way dark, already. Without my realizing it, we'd followed the train tracks back into town. We made our way to my house, through the twilight streets. The evening smelled like woodsmoke.

"You fell," he said, when we got to my front door. "I remembered. That day. You fell."

"Out of your treehouse," I said, because suddenly I was remembering too.

"Connor's," he said.

"You were living there too, then."

We waited for more to come, but none did. We went inside.

The walk had taken longer than I'd thought it would. Dad would be home soon. I couldn't say that to Solomon, or he'd leave.

And go where? And do what? Hungry, still smelling, would he head back for that bar or the bridge he sometimes slept under? I led him upstairs. We would take our chances. If my dad had something to say, he could take it up with me.

Solomon took a long time showering. I didn't blame him. He had always loved how hot our water got. When he came out, towel around his waist and wet hair dripping, I couldn't help but smile. From pride. Admiration. He had become such a beautiful man.

He turned on my radio. Ms. Jackson, our favorite DJ. *The Graveyard Shift: Weird Songs for Weird Wonderful People.*

"One day she's going to be playing my songs," he said, and smiled, and I knew with complete certainty that he was right.

Then he picked up his dirty T-shirt and I snatched it out of his hand.

"You can't put this filthy thing back on, idiot," I said. "I'll wash it for you."

"What am I supposed to wear in the meantime?"

"Not that towel," I said. "It wouldn't be safe for you to walk down the street. Everyone would want a piece of you."

He smiled. Blushed. I pulled a backpack out from under my bed and tossed it to him.

"These are my clothes," he said. "Where did you get these?"

"From your aunt," I said. "She dropped them off a couple months ago. Said you would probably come by here more often than there. And anyway, she had bought a bunch of new stuff for you, in case you did come by her place. Those might be a little small."

He dressed in front of me, utterly unashamed.

"She's worried about you," I said.

"I know. It's just so crowded there, and she works so much so she's hardly ever even home. And her boyfriend is . . . not so fond of gay people."

"Sounds like she needs a new boyfriend."

He smiled, like he wished it was that simple.

Downstairs, the door slammed. Solomon flinched. "Your dad?"

"Probably," I said.

But it was both of them. I could hear my mother and father heading for the kitchen, arguing about something.

"It's okay," I said, seeing how Solomon's breathing had sped up.

"I want to go," he said.

"Wait. I know you're hungry," I said. "Stay for dinner. He won't say anything. I'll make sure of it."

"I want to go," he said, and his voice sounded smaller this time.

"Okay," I said. "I'll go downstairs first, and make sure the coast is clear."

I tiptoed down the stairs, and checked to make sure Dad was in the kitchen. I beckoned to Solomon, and he descended.

I knew we were caught by the way Solomon came down the stairs. His tread was so heavy, and the steps were old creaky wood.

"Solomon?" my father said, coming fast out of the kitchen.

"Sir," Solomon said, without turning around.

"Ash, you know you're not allowed to have boys over when no one is home," he said.

"Solomon is my friend, Dad." *You fucking idiot*, I added, in-brain only.

"Have a good night, Solomon," my father said. He moved to open the front door.

They hadn't always been like this. Dad had no problem with Solomon, back when we were little. I couldn't understand what had changed.

"Wait! Stay for dinner, Solomon!" Mom called from

behind Dad. "We brought home spaghetti from the church fund-raiser over at Grace Abounding. There's plenty!"

"No," Solomon said, and hurried outside.

"Solomon, wait," I called out the door. I grabbed one of the Styrofoam spaghetti containers, and a metal fork, and some napkins, and brought them outside and handed them to him. My dad reached out his hand to stop me, but I swatted it away.

"Thanks," Solomon said, standing there awkwardly in clothes that were slightly too small for him. He shifted the food into one hand, to wave goodbye. I tried not to think about him eating it by himself in the dark somewhere, down by the train tracks or on the bumper of someone's pickup truck.

There's a photograph of the two of us. Taken when we were ten. It's on the table by my bed. Two frowning kids, fully clothed, in a bathtub. Look at it and you'll think you're seeing a pair of miserable refugees. You can't see the adventure Solomon was taking us on, narrating a whole complicated, amazing story where we were infiltrating an evil kingdom, and defeating their army of ghosts. You can't see that this is the happiest we'll ever be. All of that is unphotographable.

Going back in, I closed the door behind me as quietly as I could. Mom was using her soothing voice on

Dad, which, like always, was having no effect.

"You can't be mad at that poor boy for what his mother did," she said.

"George is a friend of mine," Dad argued. George, aka Mr. Barrett; Solomon's stepfather and Connor's father. "He's a good man. And the awful things that woman did . . ."

He trailed off when he saw me.

"What did she do?" I asked, stepping into the kitchen.

Mom turned toward me, deer-in-headlights style. Dad turned away. "Nothing, sweetheart. Nothing you need to worry about."

"What did Solomon's mother do to Connor's dad?" I asked.

"You're too young to know the details," Dad said, his voice firm in that way that meant he would not be changing his mind.

"Anyway, what does it matter what she did? It has nothing to do with Solomon. What do you have against *him*?" I asked. "He's not my boyfriend. And I mean, you know he's gay, right?"

"Solomon is confused," Dad said. "And he's sick. Who's to say *what* he is?"

I groaned. "He's my best friend. You can't seriously believe he would hurt me."

"I'm not saying he would hurt you on purpose."

"This isn't *Of Mice and Men*, Dad," I said.

"Ash, he's delusional. And he has persecution fantasies. So who's to say he won't suddenly decide that *you're* the one persecuting him, and do something terrible to *you?*"

I stared at him, the silence stretching between us. "What makes you say that?" I asked.

"I'm eating dinner in my office," he said, taking his plate and going.

I skipped dinner altogether. Instead, I paced back and forth in my room. I read old interviews with Diane Arbus, on the internet. I did laundry.

I did not wash Solomon's T-shirt. I put it in a pillowcase under my bed. It smelled bad, but it smelled like him.

Ms. Jackson was still playing in my room. Her cigarette-scratchy voice sounded ancient, impossibly wise.

"Temperature's dropping tonight, beloveds," she said. "Better find a good book or a warm body to curl up with by the fire."

I put my headphones on, tuned out everything else. But no matter how loud I turned up my music, I couldn't drown out the remembered sound of Solomon screaming.

My father was only looking out for me. I knew this. To him, Solomon wasn't the sweet, shy little boy he had been. He was a big, strong, scary man. In my head, in the abstract, I understood my father.

But in my heart, in that moment, I hated him.

Because it had never occurred to me to be afraid of Solomon before. Not even when he shoved me down a few hours before.

I had never been afraid.

And now, a little part of me was.

SIXTEEN

SOLOMON

Now that I was looking for it, I saw the danger everywhere. Men on corners handing off notes, women watching from high windows. The scared, angry thissiders. The voice on the radio: *We will win in the end.*

I saw them, the blue armbands and the suspicious eyes, and I shot them.

For me, photography had always been about money. A means to secure my next meal. Its contents were irrelevant. Zeppelin fire, othersider fight, the latest victim of spontaneous human petrification. I was like a messenger who didn't care whether she was carrying narcotic spiderwebbing, illegal sky whale oil, or last quarter's financial reports—long as she got paid when she got where she was going.

But now, I had a purpose. I was a spy. I went looking for what no one knew was there. I took pictures not because I wanted to sell them to Cass, but because I wanted to stop the Shield and his Destroyers.

I wanted to save myself, and Ash, and my whole city full of magnificent monsters and magic that they wanted to destroy.

I turned on the battered, old battery-powered radio that hung from Maraud's neck. Ms. Jackson; Ash and my favorite DJ. *The Graveyard Shift: Weird Songs for Weird Wonderful People.* Her cigarette-scratchy voice sounded ancient, impossibly wise.

"Temperature's dropping tonight, beloveds," she said, and I felt safer already. "Better find a good book or a warm body to curl up with by the fire."

This was my city. As far back as I could remember I'd been walking its streets at night. Never looking for anything, or anyone. Wanting nothing, and fearing no one.

Now, for the first time, I had something to look for. And for the first time, I was afraid.

"Is this what I think it is?" Cass said, finding me in the *Clarion* archives later that day. "Is Solomon doing research? Are you transforming into an actual journalist?"

"Something like that," I said.

She lit a cigarette, sat down on the table in front of

me. Picked up a couple of papers. "The Night of Red Diamonds."

"Yeah," I said. "I realized I don't know much about what really happened."

"You and most of the city," she said, and picked up a glossy photo. A crowd, soaking wet in the pouring-down rain. Storm clouds piled up like black cliffs, moving in. The storm had been stalking us, and now it pounced.

Turns out, there were two very different narratives of what happened that night. The official version, the one that was reported in the *Darkside Post* and most other mainstream papers goes like this: a bunch of peaceful demonstrators were leading a march, calling on the queen to curb othersider magic, which they claimed was being used to gain an unfair advantage over people without magic. The demonstration went through a neighborhood heavily populated with othersiders. And those poor, helpless, peaceful demonstrators were attacked, and massacred, and two dozen people died in the streets, all law-abiding this-siders, the pavement covered in their blood and broken glass.

The other version, the one the *Clarion* reported, goes like this: a big gang of goons came looking for trouble. Happens all the time, but this one was bigger than most. And instead of turning the other cheek, letting them flip a few fruit carts and break a few windows of othersider-owned businesses, people fought back. And it got ugly. And two dozen people died in the streets, othersiders and this-siders alike, the pavement covered in blood and broken glass.

The photographs are stark, vivid, terrifying. Flames, corpses, a wounded velociraptor. But those pictures could support either story.

"Why the interest?" Cass asked.

"No reason," I said, the gears of my brain straining. Suddenly, the subconscious suspicion I hadn't even let myself suspect had become very, very conscious.

Ash's explosion—the thing that got her put into a magical coma—it happened the same day as the Night of Red Diamonds. What if they weren't separate?

"There must be a reason," she said.

Because I think my best friend, the Refugee Princess, might somehow have been responsible for this. Also, she's hiding at my house.

"Seems important," I said. "With so much hate on the rise, and people pointing to this night as the spark that lit the fire."

"Don't you believe that lie they tell. This fire has been burning for decades."

"Were you there?" I asked. "Do you remember anything that isn't in the papers?"

"They were a mob, no question about it," she said. "Came to hurt and intimidate people, got more than they bargained for. They were led by a woman, dressed

116

all in blue— She died that night."

"Yeah," I said. "Dressed in blue ... as in, ultramarine?"

Cass chuckled. "Maybe, kid. It was pretty dark that night."

She stood, tall and thin and all in black, and then she put her hand to her stomach—and I saw something strange in her face. Pain. She was old, and she was human. It was easy to forget those things with someone as strong as Cass. I reached out to take her hand and she blinked, startled back to the present moment.

"Are you okay, Cass?"

"Of course," she said, looking away from me too fast. "Just working too hard, lately."

Cass had dedicated her whole life to the Truth; to exposing secrets and bringing darkness to light. So of course she was a terrible liar. But I let her have the lie, because if she was sick or something, I didn't want the truth.

I left on foot; I'd kept Maraud in the paddock at the Underbridge all day. I didn't like all the nasty stares she got, lately. The Shield's "Destroy All Monsters" tags were having the desired effect—people were more and more hostile toward othersiders and the beasts they shared the city with. Maraud would snap the head off of anybody who started real trouble with me, but that was exactly the point. Decapitation, even if it were justified, would be a whole big mess I just didn't need.

Angry faces were everywhere. Ultramarine arm-bands. Every one of them made my heart sink a little, and chilled the blood in my veins a couple degrees. A teen-aged girl held a baseball bat with nails driven through it; two little boys clutched broken beer bottles by the necks and stared at me with cold, fearless hostility.

I took pictures of it all, because I didn't know what else to do with the fear I felt.

I stumbled onto the rally by purblind dumb chance. In a park in Riversea Terrace: a rough, crime-ridden neighborhood where hardly any othersiders lived. I saw a crowd, and I headed for it.

Signs said "Destroy All Monsters" and "Abolish All Magic" and "Down with the Queen" and "We Will Not Live in Fear."

It was not a huge rally. A couple hundred people. No podium, no microphone. Just a man, up front, barely fifty feet away from me, standing on the steps to a fountain that had run dry a decade ago, featuring a dragon that had long since been decapitated. Spray-painted blue, now.

"I am your Shield," he said. *"I will protect you from them."*

No mask. No uniform. I'd been imagining something from a nightmare, from a myth. A perfectly sculpted image. Perhaps wearing an anarchist's mask. This guy's hair was a mess, and his button nose and rosy cheeks and arrogant smile could have belonged to anyone. He could have *been* anyone. And here he stood, in a public park, out in the open, unafraid of the Palace or the police or the wrath of any othersider.

"We're one hundred thousand strong!" he said, the voice bigger and louder than I'd imagined would come from such a cherubic-looking face. *"The time for waiting is over."*

I took a picture. He was framed with the blue dragon directly behind him, its jagged wings looking like they could be his. Had he done that on purpose? An angel with ugly wings.

"We've been afraid for too long. Of the othersiders, and their powers, and their monsters. But I am here to tell you today that those days are over. Their powers don't matter. Not anymore."

Through the lens, magnified, he looked possessed. Inspired. The hairs along my spine stood up, and shivered. I took pictures blindly. Helplessly.

Then I was noticed. They came at me from behind, one on either side. So fast I didn't have time to struggle. Rough strong hands, picking me up off the ground.

"He's got a camera!"

"A spy!" someone called, as they carried me to the front.

No, I wanted to shout, but I had no voice.

They had me by the arms but my legs were free. I could have kicked, fought, struggled to free myself. Maybe I wouldn't get away, but at least I'd hurt them. So why couldn't I move? Fear had frozen me solid.

Their powers don't matter. Not anymore.

"He's a photographer!" someone said.

"Perfect," said the Shield, and they put me down. "Let him see. Let the whole city see."

He clapped. From behind the old dragon statue, men and women in ultramarine led out a long line of people whose hands were chained, with sacks over their heads. They shoved them into two rows on the steps behind the Shield, like a choir of hostages.

"Our days of being afraid are over."

The filthy burlap sacks were removed. Gasps went through the crowd—some of the captives were famous—crime bosses, entertainers, athletes.

The ones I recognized had unimaginable power. So why were they just standing there?

And then I saw Quang, standing in the back row, and at first I felt relief. He could blink and whisk all these Destroyers into a cornfield or the middle of the riversea or a Palace dungeon.

But Quang did not do any of that. He stood there, pale and shivering, his whole face wet with tears.

And I knew, somehow. What the Shield was going to say, before he said it. Because there was only one possible explanation for this.

"It is the othersiders who must be afraid, now. They can't hide behind their unfair advantages any longer. Because I have

been given a great gift. I have the ability to strip othersiders of their magical powers."

He turned, looked straight at me, into my camera. My finger flinched. The shutter clicked.

"*I can destroy them all.*"

SEVENTEEN

ASH

Now that I was looking for it, I saw the evidence every-where.

Something important was up. Boys at school stood in little groups, looking around nervously like the ama-teur criminals that they were. I watched them in the hallway, under the giant mural of the blue hawk, our high school mascot, a crude and ugly painting that had been freaking kids out since probably the 1970s.

"It's got to be him, right?"

Jewel looked up from her book. "Hmm?"

"Sheffield," I said.

We leaned against our lockers, waiting for the home-room bell to ring. Listening to worried laughter, uneasy conjecture about who would be next.

"He does look guilty," she said. "Then again, that's his default mode."

Sheffield looked up, saw me pointing, and smiled.

"Look at the way they all look to him," I said. "He's probably got them out there doing his bidding."

"Who? The whole football team?"

I started to say, *Absolutely*, but I really didn't have any evidence.

And then, on random unthinking impulse, I raised my camera. Looked through the lens.

"Shit," I whispered.

Because I could see it, in the air around them. Their guilt. Their damage. Sick wet clouds of it overhead. Slimy black spiders of it perched on their shoulders.

Tingles shivered up and down my spine.

Sheffield grinned, when I panned across to him, and then he started walking toward us. I felt a little like I'd aroused the attention of a lion on the grasslands. I wasn't afraid of him, but Jewel got social anxiety from harmless sitcoms, so I could only imagine how an interaction like this might mess her up.

"Ladies," he said.

Through the lens, he was framed with the blue hawk directly behind him, its jagged wings looking like they could be his. An angel with ugly wings. And a button nose, and an arrogant smile, and eerily rosy cheeks. I took the picture, more to flatter him than because I actually wanted it.

"Hey, Sheff," I said, when he sidled up to us. "Bummer about the parking lot."

"Such a *tragedy*," he said, although his smile said the exact opposite.

The other boys were watching us now.

"Who could have done such a thing?" I asked.

"Some very twisted, very angry soul," he said. "I hope he gets the help he needs."

"So you think it was a guy?"

"Forgive me," he said, "for my unconscious gender bias. It's wrong to have *male* be the default when dealing with someone of unknown identity. Blame my upbringing. That very twisted, very angry soul could very well belong to a girl." And he grinned.

"You coming to practice?" some random lunkhead called to him from across the hall.

"When I'm finished with my conversation, asshole." To Jewel, who had been pointedly ignoring him, he said, "God bless you, sister." She flinched.

"Hey, the lot," I asked. "Any connection to what happened with Marcy Brockelmeyer's house, do you think? Or Judy Saperstein's?"

He shrugged, his nonchalance exaggerated. "Hey—how's Solomon doing? Haven't seen him in school today."

His face gave nothing away, but still, my blood chilled

at the sound of my best friend's name in Sheffield's mouth. No good could come of this. "How is he? He's fucking fantastic," I said, anger getting the better of me. If this pink-faced little asshole was behind these random acts of cruelty, he needed to know to stay the hell away from Solomon. "I mean, you know how it is. Right? Such a gentle giant. When he gets angry, though? Guy could break your forearm like snapping a twig."

"Really," Sheffield said, nodding vigorously. "What a useful thing to know. See you around, Ash?"

"Not if I see you first," I said.

To Jewel, he doffed his blue baseball cap and bowed. She kept ignoring him. The tiniest of frowns flickered on Sheffield's face, and then he walked off.

Fuck.

Fuck fuck fuck.

I was a total idiot.

Everyone already thought Solomon was a lunatic. The last thing they needed was to think he was violent, too. And that was exactly the seed I'd just planted in Criminal-Supervillain-in-Training Sheffield's head.

All day long, I couldn't stop thinking about Solomon.

So, after school, I went to Cass's house. The door was unlocked, like it always was. She was on the couch, in her chaotic living room.

"Ash," she said, sitting up, and I could see at once that she'd been crying.

That's when I realized: I knew nothing about her life. Did she have kids? Were her parents alive? Did she have an intense long-distance letters-only love affair with someone? Had her heart just been broken? Was someone she loved very sick? More importantly, why hadn't I ever asked?

"Hey, Cass," I said, and stooped to hug her. She held on very tight.

"Excuse me," she said, making an elegant gesture in the direction of her face. "Moment of weakness. Never happens."

"Of course not," I said, and went to make us tea. By the time it was ready, and I brought it in on an ancient mirrored platter, she'd managed to pull herself together somewhat.

"So. What brings you here? To consult the Oracle?"

So many things I could have said. *I think that some guys in my school might be involved in hate crimes, and I'm worried someone will get hurt.*

Or, *I think I need to call Child Protective Services and tell them my best friend's location. Because if I don't, I'm afraid something worse will happen to him.*

"M-my project," I said instead. "There's things I want to talk about—stories I want to capture—but I don't know how to do it."

"You're so focused on this *project*," Cass said. "Forget the *project*. Focus on getting the truth. That's the photographer's job—and it's the hardest thing for her to do."

"What does that even mean?" I asked. "Everything a photograph captures is the truth."

"I'm not talking about truth as in, simple reality." She kicked the coffee table. "I don't mean this table was *here*, this person *smiled*. I'm talking about truth with a capital *T*. Something honest and real."

"Cass, are you okay?" I asked. "When I came in—"

"I don't know what you're talking about," she said, though she smiled when she said it. "That never happened."

"Right," I said. And I was glad. Because I didn't want to talk about it. Didn't want Cass to become any more human. Didn't want to know what might be making her miserable. Me, Solomon, Cass . . . Was everybody in the world this alone?

I could already feel it opening up: the hole inside me, the faulty plumbing that let the cold, dark water in. I had to do something about it.

I knew exactly what I needed. "Shit, Cass," I said. "I'm so sorry. But I really have to go."

"Of course," she said, waving her hand dismissively. "The Oracle dismisses you."

In her big black robe, with her oversize eyeglasses, she had never looked so small. And then she tried to smile, and it just made it worse.

"I could—"

"Go," she said, picking up a remote control on the table. "My dogs adore *Citizen Kane*. And they're way more fun to talk about cinema with anyway."

In the car, I called Connor. And twenty minutes later, I was at his house.

"Hi," he said, looking as pure and sad as a Roman sculpture of Apollo. Broad shoulders, inscrutable expression, classical nose. Though he could be melancholy, Connor never got upset about the things that bothered almost everyone else. He was a god, far above the petty hardships of mere mortals.

Yet he deigned to hang around with us anyway.

He hugged me hard. "Everything okay?"

"Yeah, sure," I said, and didn't ask, *Why?* Because I already knew the answer: *You only come by when you need something.*

"Come on," he said, and took me by the hand and led me upstairs.

It was exactly what I needed.

There was only now. Only us. He was good at it. And when we were together, I wasn't angry or sad or scared. I was just . . . alive.

This weird thing we have, it started when my depression was at its worst. When I felt so alone I could almost scream. When I felt like the weight pressing down on my chest would crack my rib cage and crush my heart. I loved him for it, for how he made me feel, for how much he cared about me, for continuing to do this even though it couldn't have been easy—because I suspected he wanted more.

Afterward, two squirrels fought and chattered in the tree below us.

"Dirty little things," I said, watching them through his bedroom window.

"I kind of like them," Connor said. We were spooned together. His bare skin was cool to the touch, but the heat of him warmed me up. This part was almost better than the sex itself.

"You would," I said.

"What does that mean?" he said, laughing.

"It means that you're a good person," I said. "We're not all like you. Some of us are monsters."

EIGHTEEN

SOLOMON

Two terra-octopi chattered and fought, in the tree above us. A perpetual problem, in the Underbridge. The side of Radha's hut was covered in dried ink.

"Dirty little things," Ash said.

"They really are," I said, marveling at the fact that she was almost using full sentences now.

"I'll be right back," Niv said, getting up from the floor where we sat. "I need to contact the Palace. See if I can connect with somebody there who trusts me."

"Okay," Ash said. "Tell my mom hello."

I laughed. Her sense of humor was returning too.

"Four slow knocks is me," Niv said, demonstrating on the door. "Anyone else, hide Ash in the back room. Okay?" He disappeared into the Underbridge.

Ash looked around the little house. Every inch of it was familiar and beloved to me, every cluttered shelf and worn-out appliance and sprig of dried herbs hanging from the walls, but I wondered how it would appear to someone used to living in a palace.

Her voice was barely a whisper, so low I didn't hear her at first when she said: "This is where you went."

"Not right away," I said. "I lived down at the docks for a while. Sleeping wherever I could find a safe, dark space to curl up."

"I'm sorry," she said, but her words were slurring and her eyes were getting a glazed look. Were the palace sorcerers working to strengthen their spell?

I took her hand, and pressed it to my face. Smelled the faint ginger scent of her.

"You're so warm," she said.

"You're so cold," I told her.

"I—"

But whatever else she had to say, she couldn't say it.

"It's okay," I said. "We're okay."

She smiled, squeezed my hand very faintly.

Four knocks at the door, and I let Niv back in.

"No luck," he said. "It's chaos over there. Stupid to even try. The princess is missing—of course it's madness. But—" And he handed me the *Clarion*. "There is some good news. You did it." My photo was on the front page: a line of broken othersiders; the Shield standing in front of them. "You exposed him. Showed the world his face."

My stomach clenched. "I did exactly what he wanted me to do."

"Maybe. But now that we know who he is, we can fight back. He released a statement, outlining his goals. He wants the queen to abdicate, he wants to break all othersiders, he wants to destroy all monsters in the city."

I took the paper, read it fast. I turned the page; tucked inside was a flyer. A propaganda-style image that showed a deep blue rendering of the Shield towering over a bloodred city skyline, with the words "The Truth Will Be Revealed" across the top. At the bottom it said:

**"What Queen Carmen doesn't want you to know
is what will be her undoing"**

Radha came in, her bright red sari instantly making me smile.

"How's Quang?" I asked.

"He's amazing," she said. "Still trying to run his restaurant like . . . nothing happened. He jokes like any other day, but when you look in his eyes you can see the pain. Connor will cheer him up, I hope."

"Solomon, outside with me," Niv said.

We went. A banner hung from a nearby tree, for the upcoming Unmasking Day celebration. Happy kids in dinosaur masks. I remembered being a happy kid. Even if I'd also been a miserable one.

"What's up?" I asked.

"This," Niv said, and kissed me on the mouth.

My body betrayed me, and I kissed him back. My lips were greedy, selfish bastards. I wanted to pull away, push him back, but when his arms wrapped around me, my own wrapped around him.

I kissed him for a long time. And then I said, without moving, "Stop."

"Why?" he said.

"Because I can't."

"So?"

"So I don't feel the same way about you," I said.

"With all due respect, Mr. Front Page Photographer, that's bullshit."

"I'm sorry," I said.

"You're telling me you don't feel anything right now?"

It took me so long to say *Nothing* that I knew he knew I was lying.

"Fine," he said. "I get it."

"You don't," I said.

"Then explain it to me."

"I can't."

Our arms were still around each other.

"Is it about me?" he asked. "Or about you?"

"Little bit of both."

I tried my best not to look him in the eye when I finally stepped away. But I couldn't help it. His eyes were wet and wide with surprise, with sadness. When he tried to smile, it just made it worse.

In that moment, I felt the thing they called me.

I felt like a monster.

NINETEEN

ASH

By the time I got there, all the excitement was over. The cop cars had driven off. The hauling company had brought the dumpster, and it was full of ruined carpets, curtains, books, furniture.

Jewel Gomez's house, flooded out. Someone broke in while they were away for the weekend, stopped up the sinks and tubs and both her toilets, started the water.

"No sign of forced entry," I overheard a neighbor say.

Jewel wasn't home, and she didn't answer when I called her. I sent a text—*Hope you're doing okay, let me know if you need anything*—complete with a GIF of a corgi puppy cuddle pile.

She sent me a thank you–themed GIF. We giffed back and forth for a while.

Next morning, the high school hallway was all grief and anger and betrayal. When I looked through the lens, everything was green and brown. Great slimy bubbles hung in the air around Jewel, splattering and popping. She stood beside her locker, pretending to look at something on her phone. I kept my camera aimed at her, but I did not take a picture. Her unhappiness was palpable, so much so that snapping the shutter would have felt exploitative. The stink of garbage filled the high school hallway.

"Hey," I said, stepping closer.

"Ash, hey," she said. She was dressed all in shades of blue, the better to blend in with the walls of Hudson High. The better to make herself invisible.

"I'm so sorry," I said.

"Thanks."

"You feeling okay? If you want to skip school, go up to Crossgates Mall or something, I got you."

She laughed.

It was a joke, after all. Super-religious Jewel never broke a rule.

"Well, let me know if there's anything I can do. I can't imagine how scary it must be, to have something like that happen."

"I'm fine," she said.

"I wouldn't be," I said. "It's okay to not be fine."

She nodded. "I feel . . ." And she took a long time but I didn't try to nudge her along. "I feel like I'll never feel safe in that house again."

I nodded. "Yeah. I get that."

Betrayal, I thought. That's what I was seeing in the air around her. How did I know? How could I tell the difference between guilt and betrayal? I wasn't sure. But since that day along the tracks with Solomon, when I'd held his trained penny in my hand, my understanding of the things I could see had gotten sharper. Stronger. Like I could read them now in a way I couldn't before.

"Do the cops have any theories about who did it?"

She rolled her eyes. "No," she said. "And they don't care."

Betrayal. Jewel feels betrayed by someone—maybe someone here. "And you? Do you have any theories?"

"My books all got ruined," she said, her eyes on fire. I knew how much her books mattered to her. She spent a *lot* of money on them. Bought new ones every week. Posted pictures of them online. Made memes out of her favorite quotes. She had a blog and everything.

"That sucks."

"No," she said. "You don't understand. They should have been fine. My house flooded, but the water didn't rise very high. Someone took all the books off my bookshelves, *and put them on the floor.*"

"Shit," I said, and then apologized for the profanity.

She nodded. "Whoever did this? They knew us. Knew *me*."

"Who?"

She shook her head. "I don't know. Yet. But when I find out? I'm going to punish them." She didn't curse, but the anger in her voice was just as frightening as a swear word would have been.

Shouts, from down the hall. Loud laughter. Which is when we all learned why the stink of garbage was so strong. Someone had taken all the trash bags out of the dumpsters behind the school, and ripped them open and dumped their contents in every classroom.

It pretty much scrapped first period, as everyone was busy cleaning up and wondering at what kind of vengeance the administration would rain down on us.

All day long, I looked for whoever wrecked Jewel's house. Watched faces, with and without my camera. I saw an awful lot of ultramarine tendrils. I knew without question what they symbolized. Guilt. But the thing is, guilt about what? Checking out those websites your parents told you were off-limits? Sneaking around behind your girlfriend's back? Or breaking and entering and destruction of property? One guilt looked like any other.

I even had some of my own. Because Jewel hadn't been on Sheffield's radar, before the two of us confronted him in the hallway together. Had I brought this on her?

That's when I noticed Bobby Eckels. Football player; second string, I thought. Even with the naked eye, you could see that he was twitchy. Through the lens the darkness I saw around him was fresher, rawer. When he caught me staring, his lips peeled back almost involuntarily into a snarl.

The football team. . . Sheffield.

That was when the idea popped into my head fully formed.

Maybe *that* was my photo project.

Maybe that was the Truth with a capital *T* that I could uncover.

The people doing these things. The monsters among us.

After school, I sidled up to Sheffield.

"Ash," he said, sliding his headphones down around his neck. They were oversize, ostentatious. Expensive.

"Word is, when it comes to the football team, you kinda run the show."

He smiled. His button nose wrinkled. "Those guys are my friends," he said. "They could have cut me out when I hurt my knee and couldn't play anymore, but they let me keep on tagging along."

"People say you do a lot more than tag along."

He shrugged. "Coach Barrett lets me help with strategy sometimes. Lets me come to games. He says we're a lot alike, him and me. Survivors. Why the interest?"

You and Connor's dad are not "survivors," I thought, but didn't say it. "I have this photo project. I'd like to take pictures of the team," I said.

Sheffield nodded, tilted his head to the side like it deserved careful consideration. Didn't answer right away.

Look at his face and you'd see an angel. I knew there was more behind his perfect facade.

"There's a party," he said. "Most of the guys will be there. Come hang out with us, and we can talk about it."

I frowned. "Can't I just come to the next practice? Or a game? When everyone's together?"

"You're asking for a lot," he said. "I'm happy to help you out, but I can't just make people trust you."

I thought of Bobby, flinching. Furious with me for daring to make eye contact.

"Fine," I said.

"I'll text you the information. Give me your number." He leaned closer when he said it, made his smile slimier.

The idea of him having my number made me instantly queasy.

"DM me," I said. "I follow you on—"

"Your *number*," he said. "That way I can call you, if I need to."

"Fine," I said, and gave it to him.

Later, I reached into my pocket to pull out my phone,

and almost burned myself on something.

Solomon's trained penny. It was hot, way hotter than it should have been just from sitting in my pocket.

I held it, and I could see him. Not like some blinding vision or waking dream— This was so clear it could have been a memory, except I was pretty sure I had never seen it before. A shabby little hut under a very big bridge. Solomon, staring into my eyes.

I headed for the classroom where he was supposed to be. Of course he wasn't there—but Mr. Taglia was, speaking to the teacher. I waited in the doorway.

"You're looking for him too," Taglia said to me, on his way out.

"Yeah. Is this about Child Protective Services?"

He frowned, and rubbed his beard. "They sent someone. She's in my office now. And that's the last step, before they send the police to do what they call a 'wellness check.' So if you see him, or talk to him, you have to get him to come in and meet with a caseworker. You know how cops are, in this town. And if Solomon gets an attitude with them . . ."

Mr. Taglia didn't finish the sentence, but he didn't need to. I could think up plenty of nightmare worst-case scenarios on my own.

I pinched Solomon's trained penny between my fingers, felt its sharp edges cut.

Calm down, Ash. You know how this goes. He is not your

responsibility. There's nothing you can do to help him.

Except, I didn't buy that.

I couldn't. He was broken, but I had to believe that he could be fixed. And I had to believe that there was something I could do to help him. Even if it was something that would make him hate me forever.

TWENTY

SOLOMON

I pinched Ash's penny between my fingers. Its sharp edges cut into my skin. I don't know why, but the pain made me feel the teeny-tiniest bit better.

"Make a fist," Radha said. "Make two fists."

She sat at the table beside Ash, her strong hands probing at the princess's arms and shoulders.

"Can you feel that?"

Ash nodded.

Radha didn't like to talk about her othersider ability, but I knew it had something to do with the body. Back in the day, she had been some kind of bad-ass warrior, a member of an elite othersider self-defense unit that used to patrol the city and protect our people, before the Darkside Police Department cracked down on them.

"Surprise is important," she said, when I was a kid and asked her what she could do. "Can't have word getting out about what you can do. When the time comes to use your ability on someone, you don't want them to know what's coming."

But Radha *was* well-known in the Underbridge for being able to track magic in the body, and help when there were blockages or defects. She'd agreed to take a look at Ash, see if there was something she could do. Secretly I hoped that maybe she could gain some insight into how the Palace sorcerers were continuing to control Ash, and whether there was any possibility of reversing it.

I sat down beside them. After fifteen minutes of tiny adjustments and questions, Radha sat back and shut her eyes.

"Anything?" I asked.

"It's powerful magic," she said. "Very complex. The combined spells of at least a dozen different sorcerers. She's strong, to be standing here despite it."

"Can you tell what her ability is?"

"It's not something that manipulates the elements, or any other class of object," Radha said. "Otherwise I'd see evidence of it in her muscles. Whatever it is, it's been buried too deep, and for too long."

"How do you feel, Ash?"

The Refugee Princess looked into my eyes, but did not seem to see anything. I took her hand.

She was broken, but I had to believe that she could be fixed. And I had to believe that there was something I could do to help her.

"The queen!" cried Connor, running into the room.

"What about her?" I asked, grabbing hold of him under the arms and hoisting him up into the air. He shrieked in delight.

"The queen is going to make a speech!"

"Wow," I said, because the queen never makes speeches. Barely comes out onto her balcony anymore. "What's the occasion?"

"People are scared," Niv said, following him in from the other room. The radio was still squawking away in there. "Attacks, home invasions. Vandalism. Just yesterday a library got flooded out. Half the city is angry at the other half, and each half blames the other."

Little Connor reached out his arms for Niv, and I handed him over. I'd avoided eye contact or alone time with Niv, ever since he kissed me, but it made me deeply happy to see how well he got along with Connor. Like, if Connor liked him, maybe he wasn't such a bad person after all. Maybe I was wrong not to trust him.

"The Palace says she wants to make a plea for peace," Niv said. "For calm. For understanding."

I thought of my front-page photograph. How we were starting to shine a light on the Shield—bring him out of the shadows.

I did that, I thought proudly. *Because of me, the queen has chosen to act.* But pride gave way to fear fast. There were so many people who hated us. Who would much rather we just *stay quiet.*

"When's the speech?" I asked.

"Sunday," Niv said. "Noon. All the radio stations are going to be broadcasting it."

"I want to go see Quang!" Connor cried.

"Well, you can't," Radha said. "I won't have you out there while things are so topsy-turvy."

"I can take him," Niv and I both said at the same time. I smiled, and let myself look at him. He looked back.

"No," Radha said, with harsher anger than I'd ever heard her use before. After that she paused for a couple of seconds, but she did not apologize. "Things are scary out there. If anything, the queen making a speech has me *more* frightened. She must know more than us—something bigger is going on than a few street fights and home invasions."

Connor looked like he was about to cry again, so Niv pitched him forward suddenly, stopping inches away from the floor, prompting a shriek of terrified happiness.

Niv laughed with him, and began to roller-coaster him around the room.

I hugged Radha. A train whistle sounded, crossing the bridge far above, and she flinched, and I held her tighter.

TWENTY-ONE

ASH

A train whistle sounded, far below. The strip mall on Wolf Road was at the top of a hill, looking down on all of Albany. Twilight. I could see the steam from the train as it headed toward Utica. I sat on the hood of my car with my latest triumphant purchase across my lap.

Albany was my last stop; I'd visited thrift stores in every decent-sized town within forty miles of Hudson, and found three guitars. All of them in shit condition, as far as I could tell, but none of them totally hopeless.

I would get them fixed up. I would leave one at my house, hidden behind the porch swing. One for the abandoned railroad shack by what Solomon called the Blighted Spaces. One for him to stash in another of his secret locations. That way, wherever he was, whatever he was going through, he'd be able to make music.

Albany was a shithole, but it had its moments. Like this one. An eerie calm; Friday night; the highway full of people heading home for the weekend. The full weight of Saturday and Sunday ahead of us. The sun was setting and the wind was picking up and the moon was already out. The place was magic. Across the parking lot, Albany's only Indian restaurant was making the night wind delicious.

The feeling came upon me out of nowhere: happiness. An overwhelming sensation, all through my body.

It wasn't the first time this had happened. It just didn't happen very often. The meds weren't exactly *causing* it; I knew that. But maybe they helped to quiet down the fear and the sadness and the rage that sometimes shattered this feeling before it could flower. The world around me was beautiful and I was wearing my favorite sweatshirt, and the hood of my car was still warm from driving and I had just bought a gift that I knew would make Solomon happy. I felt so full of love right then that I really could have cried.

Instead, I took out my camera. Snapped a picture, then another. Then five more.

But it was no use. I knew it without needing to go back to the darkroom and develop them. The images I caught contained none of what made me break out in goose bumps.

I could feel it in my arms, up and down my spine, like electricity—this bliss, this joy, this perfect contentment—but I couldn't capture it on film. All anybody would see, looking at these images, was a dirty, darkened parking lot where the lights were just coming on.

Love for the world, and hatred for the world. Somewhere between them, or in both simultaneously, lay the truth. About life, about Solomon . . . about me.

I got in the car. I drove back toward Hudson, but I did not go home. I went to Connor's.

And yeah, maybe part of me just wanted a hookup. But Connor was my friend too. He made me laugh. He thought I was way smarter than I actually was. He hated a lot of the same things I hated.

And I had questions.

The kind he was uniquely positioned to answer.

He was in the front hallway when I arrived, freshly showered and wearing a raglan-sleeve hoodie that did wonders for his profile. He smelled like clean clothes and Dial soap and cinnamon chewing gum.

"Ash, hey!" he said, and gave me a hug. His keys jingled in his hand.

"Where you off to?" I asked.

"Football stuff," he said.

"Not practice," I said. "This late?"

"Nah," he said. "It's a meeting."

"A meeting? Are you, like, selecting officers for your board?" I looked at him until he looked away, without answering.

I thought of Bobby, and all the other guilty-looking football boys.

"Have you guys heard anything about all that vandalism going on?" I asked.

He reddened. "No."

"You've always been a bad liar, Connor," I said. "It's one of the things I love about you."

At this, he chuckled. "But listen. For real. You need to let this go, Ash. Just so you know."

"I won't," I said. "Just so you know."

Connor reddened further. He looked at the floor for a while, and then he raised his eyes to meet mine. Still didn't say anything. We eye-wrestled like that for a little while, but he did not stand down. So I turned and left.

"Have a good *meeting*."

By the time I got to my house, I was so knotted up—with anger over the wave of vandalism, and with sadness over how Solomon was hurting—that I had looked up the number for Child Protective Services and was halfway through dialing it before I even realized what I was doing.

Here is a shortened, cleaned-up version of the

internal argument that went on in my head for several minutes:

What the hell, Ash?

I have to do this. Solomon needs help. He won't go get it willingly.

But is this the right way? And are you doing it for the right reason?

There is no right way. There are no simple answers. If I tell them about the brakeman's hut where he sleeps sometimes, maybe they'll send a social worker instead of calling the cops.

I finished dialing.

"Hi," I said, when a woman answered. "I wanted to provide information about the location of an at-risk minor who was recently flagged with you for a wellness check?"

I felt better, when I hung up the phone. But it didn't last long. The doubts came creeping in. And that stirred up that whole tangled nest of complicated emotions. Anger, that I had made the call—that I couldn't go back in time and take it back. Fury, that the laws of physics had to be so fucking rigid. In a few minutes I felt cactus-prickly and itching for a fight. So I went downstairs and found my mother watching television, and launched right in.

"What do you know about what happened between Solomon's mother and Connor's father?"

Mom frowned. She looked toward the shut door to

Dad's office. Which is what she does when what she has to say, she knows he won't like.

"She tried to burn the house down," Mom said softly.

I gaped at her. "What? Why would she do that?"

"You'd have to ask her," Mom said.

"I'm asking *you*. You were friends, weren't you?"

"Hadassah was not a well woman," Mom said.

"Who *is* well? Am I well? Are you?" I said. "Tell me what happened."

"It would be irresponsible of me to repeat it."

"But she's in prison."

"Yes."

Mom was watching a cop show. And here's something I learned from her cop shows: wherever there's a woman in jail for a violent crime against a spouse or partner, there's a man who did some especially heinous things to push her to that point.

What did you do, Mr. Barrett?

I headed for my room. A couple dozen gun shots echoed from the television.

TWENTY-TWO

SOLOMON

A couple dozen gun shots echoed from the canyon. The *Clarion* office's windows were all open and the smell of eucalyptus was strong. The front of the building faced out onto one of the most grimy, crowded streets in Darkside, but the back leaned over the beautiful wilderness of a Blighted Space. Brontosauruses munched happily on the tall trees.

"I need you to stop," Cass said.

"Stop?" I asked incredulously. I'd seen Cass scream at a reporter with a stab wound to the leg for not sticking around to interview the woman who stabbed her. More than once I'd heard her say that "self-preservation is not a helpful instinct for a reporter." "Are you . . . feeling okay?"

"Don't tell anyone," she said, "but it's getting too dangerous out there. And you're a great photographer, but you're also a kid. This is strictly me being selfish, by the way. I have enough to stress about without a dead teenager on my conscience."

I laughed. She laughed.

"Promise me," she said.

"I can make no such promise."

She frowned, and handed me a copy of the *Darkside Post*. "You saw this?" Darkside Police Commissioner Bahrr was on the front page, standing on the hood of his truck with a shotgun in his hands. Hunting chupacabras and rakshasas in the Northern Marsh.

"That asshole," I muttered.

"He's nervous," Cass said, "about the queen making a speech. He's threatened by her. Wants to get his own share of the press, so he poses for this." She threw the paper down. "One of my journalists is working a source. She found some paperwork, intentionally misfiled at police headquarters: a shipment of five thousand handcuffs reported missing last month."

"How do you misplace five *thousand* handcuffs?" I asked.

"You don't," she said. "This is no accident. The commissioner is supplying the Shield's soldiers with weapons and other tools. And with all those cuffs, they could kidnap literally thousands of othersiders—and the

Shield could break them. No one would be safe. *That is why I need you to stop.*"

"Okay," I said.

"I'm serious," she said. "I won't buy any more photographs from you. Not until all this blows over."

"I get it," I said. "Even if I see the perfect shot, I'll skip it." But I remembered what she'd said to me once: *Forget getting the shot. Focus on the truth. That's the hardest thing for a photographer to capture.*

She stood, and came toward me. And I flinched, because who had ever seen Cass express any emotion other than an angry one? She chuckled, at my fear, and then she hugged me.

"Take care of yourself out there, Solomon. Even when we're not looking for trouble, it has a way of finding us."

After that, I wandered. Away from the eucalyptus-smelling canyon, into the denser disorderly streets. Bright lights in some windows; dark patches where the Blight had struck and turned the land foul.

I loved Cass, trusted and respected her—but I couldn't stop. I was an addict, now. Hunting for the truth.

The world was full of monsters, and my camera wasn't much of a weapon against them, but it was the only one that I had.

Maraud was still paddocked, down at the Under-bridge. Which is why, when I heard the screams and followed them to the soccer field at the end of the alley in front of me, I couldn't do a damned thing to stop what I found.

The cry was distinctive. Nothing else sounds like a snake hissing and a lion roaring and goat bleating all at once. It was a chimera, but this one was in greater distress than I'd ever heard. Huge three-headed fire-breathing monsters are usually the things that inspire fear, but this chimera was itself very much afraid.

Sure enough, I found it roaring; swinging its terrifying tail; belching fire in chaotic jets. Only when I got up close could I see what it was fighting.

Destroyers, soldiers of the Shield. A horde of them. They came in pairs, swinging chains, and alone, with torches and long, sharp weapons.

Trees burned all around the field. Two people were already sprawled motionless on the ground, but there were an awful lot more where they had come from.

An unarmed Destroyer walked out, waving his arms. Taunting it. The chimera charged—and another Destroyer swung a chain, which wrapped around the monster's hind legs. Thrown off-balance, it came down in a heavy crash. The taunting Destroyer was firmly in its jaws, and it bit down hard.

That triumph did not amount to much. More came, closing in on it now that it was down, sharp weapons aimed for soft parts.

"Stop!" I screamed, but I might as well have been speaking to people in another reality. They were laughing. Cheering. Hooting, hollering.

Abruptly, the animal's cries went from angry roars to heart-hurting whimpers.

A crowd of people stood and stared. A couple of them were crying. I looked to a woman who I felt certain was an othersider—but if she was, she was too afraid to use her ability to intervene.

"Hey!" said one of the Destroyers, seeing the camera around my neck.

"Take a picture," another one said, holding up the chimera's forepaw. The thing was bigger than his torso, and he could only hold it aloft for a couple of seconds.

"Go fuck yourself," I said, which was when I noticed how hard it was to breathe.

I sat down on the dead grass. A white stripe of chalk ran past my feet. In summer, kids played here. I looked up, trying to focus on the stars, something faraway and safe that could help me calm down. But I couldn't see the stars.

Smoke billowed up from the burning trees set ablaze by the chimera's breath. The cylinders of flames burned like bonfires on a chilly beach. They hooted and bellowed, these monstrous murderer savages, and I clenched my eyes to shut out the feral sight of them, but I could still hear them.

TWENTY-THREE

ASH

Smoke billowed up from the bonfire, a cylinder of flame, warm and safe on that chilly beach. The fire lit up the faces of my fellow partygoers, almost all of them boys, and made them look feral and wild and exaggerated. Very *Lord of the Flies*. It occurred to me to be afraid. Maybe Sheffield had lured me here to be murdered.

"Put more wood on it!" someone yelled.

"There's too much wood on it already," someone else yelled. A buoy clanged, out on the Hudson River. Someone splashed kerosene, from a massive red metal jug.

"They're animals," Sheffield said, sitting down in the sand beside me. "Cavemen, at best."

"That's not a very nice thing to say about your friends."

He shrugged, sipped from a bottle of root beer. "Not sure about that."

All the other boys were drinking actual beer. I wondered why he wasn't. Maybe what Sheffield liked more than being drunk, was being in control.

"You're not sure whether it's not a nice thing to say, or you're not sure whether they're your friends?"

"The second one," he said, and turned to look at them.

Most but not all of the football team was there.

It wouldn't do, for photography—not with lighting like this, the dark of the night and the creepy shifting illumination of the bonfire. The sand was cold. I planted my hands in it, and shivered.

"So why are you hanging out with them?"

"*Some of them* are my friends," he told me. He looked like he had more to say, but left it at that.

"What about Bobby Eckels?" I asked, pointing to him. He stood at the edge of the firelight, sharing a bottle of something stronger than beer with a friend. Watching me.

Sheffield laughed. "A bit of an idiot, isn't he?"

"I have no idea."

"He's a bit of an idiot."

"This is a great conversation."

Sheffield laughed again. He laughed a lot, seemed like, but rarely because things were funny. More like because it bought him time—time to think of something to say. "Why the football team, Ash?"

"School spirit," I said, because I had anticipated the question, and practiced my response. Nothing further; no expression on my face.

"Some of the guys were suspicious. You're not the school spirit type. When was the last football game you went to?"

Answering his questions would only lead me further onto his turf. "I appreciate that other people appreciate it."

He nodded his head, like a chess player whose opponent has made a particularly skilled move. I stood up, and raised my camera, and aimed it at Bobby. Sickly green flames swirled around him. He saw me, and his face broke into a snarl.

"You don't like to get your picture taken," I called to him, across the fire.

"I don't," he said, and even on just those two words I could hear how drunk he was.

"Why not?"

"Who the hell are you, anyway?"

"A fan of the team," I said. "And a friend of Jewel's."

He lost his cool completely. His mouth went slack. His eyes widened. He took a step back.

"You used to be friends with Jewel," I said. "Didn't you?"

A couple other guys around the campfire had stopped talking, to better pay attention to us. I kept on.

"You ever go to her house?"

"Calm down," Sheffield said to me, standing up. "Obviously Bobby is still very upset about what happened. Poor Jewel."

"Where were you?" I asked. "When it happened?"

Sheffield put a patronizing hand on my shoulder and said, "Shhhh."

Bobby breathed a little easier, with Sheffield coming to his rescue. So I raised my camera, and took a picture.

"And what happened, exactly?"

He made a choking noise in his throat, and I took another picture.

"Someone broke in," I said. "Someone who knew her."

"I . . . ," he said, but didn't finish the sentence. I took two more pictures.

"Screw you," he hollered, and he sounded like a little kid—but like a guilty little kid, one who'd gotten caught when they didn't think they would. He took a step toward me, and stumbled, and fell to his knees. Everyone laughed.

This was where I went too far. I knew it; I just couldn't help myself. The tingle in my spine was back. I could see him through my lens, his face angry and embarrassed, and his body . . . His body was covered in shadow-spiders—fat, oily, gruesome creatures. Their spiky bodies and pincer jaws dripping with poison. They swarmed his face, poured into and out of his mouth.

Irrational hatred, uncontrollable anger. That's what I read.

I took his picture.

He took another step forward, and stumbled again. Everyone laughed, and that made him holler into the darkness.

"You think you're so fucking smart," he said, and picked up a big red jug of kerosene. "So much better than any of us. But you're no different. You'll burn just like anything else." He uncapped the kerosene. A couple people gasped. Someone else laughed.

"Chill, bro," said a voice from the far side of the fire, and Bobby told them to shut the fuck up. Which they did.

You think people are decent. You think, *Okay, maybe they're idiots or macho jerks or they've got a chip on their shoulders because of whatever they've been through, but at the core, underneath it all, they're decent. They'll come through in a crisis.*

But they aren't. Not all of them.

Bobby splashed kerosene into the fire and onto the sand in front of me. It sizzled and burned there. I opened my mouth to say something smart, but of course I couldn't. All my words were gone. No one had my back.

He could set me on fire and none of them would lift a finger to stop him.

Fear paralyzed me.

But fear also made me remember. Opened something inside me. A bridge, to the last time I felt so afraid.

Twelve years old. Going to see Solomon. Summer twilight; the air smelled like someone cooking pork chops. Ringing his doorbell—Connor's doorbell. Getting no answer. Going around back, calling his name up to the treehouse. Still no answer.

Climbing up.

Seeing Solomon.

Little twelve-year-old Solomon turned around, startled by my arrival. Caught. Horrified. Frightened. His mouth a wide dark circle of terror. And then . . . I fell.

I don't know how long we stood there, Bobby and me and the jug of kerosene. It couldn't have been too long. The flames of the bonfire were frozen in time. Sheffield's eyes had never been so big. His face was wide open, taking this all in. What Bobby did, what I did. I couldn't be sure what I saw there on Sheffield's face, but it was pretty damn close to pride. Like he'd engineered this moment, and it was turning out better than anything he could have imagined.

That was Sheffield's thing. Controlling people.

Manipulating them. He liked to be the boss. I saw it, and I shivered.

And then time sped up, again. And Bobby roared, an ugly inarticulate garble-sound of idiot rage, and he swung the jug.

Two people screamed.

And the jug—stopped. In midair. Midswing.

No one saw Solomon coming, or knew how long he'd been standing there. In the dark. Watching. Waiting.

Or had he just arrived, his timing perfect to reach out one strong arm and grab hold of Bobby and stop it? To take the kerosene jug out of his hand, and hurl it into the Hudson River? The splash sounded super–far away. A bell tolled, out on the river. Solomon stomped out where the sand was still burning in front of me.

"Come on," he said, holding out his hand for mine. "Let's get out of here."

TWENTY-FOUR

SOLOMON

A bell tolled, from a buoy out on the riversea. I had no idea how long I'd been wandering like that, through the crowded streets, deaf and dumb to the world around me, trying to pretend like I hadn't just watched a monster get murdered.

Shouts jolted me back to reality. A bunch of kids, taunting a green dragon. Screaming at it; running up and poking it and running away.

Most monsters in Darkside are pretty chill about random antagonism. But this one was pissed. All the monsters were on edge that morning. What had happened to the chimera—they could smell it in the air. And people were messing with monsters everywhere.

I called out, "Dumb move, kids. They're vegetarians,

but you still don't want to piss them off."

"Shut up, monster!" one of them hollered.

"Yeah!"

"Your funeral," I said, and kept walking.

But then I stopped. Turned around.

It wouldn't kill them. But it might slap them with its tail, give them a gentle kick, and the last thing this powder-keg city needed was a couple crying kids talking about how a monster attacked them.

I looked at the coffee cup in my hand. It had gone cold. I did not even remember buying it. Any other day, kids harassing a dragon would have amused me. Like ants annoying an elephant.

But now, I wasn't amused. I was afraid.

The dragon let loose an angry roar. Fear spiked, made me dizzy, unstable. But fear also made me remember. Opened something inside me. A bridge, to the last time I felt so disoriented.

Twelve years old. Wandering through the Palace halls. Going to see Ash. Summer twilight; walking the ramparts high above the city. Black clouds piled high like a cliff in the distance. Air smelling like someone roasting a pig. I knocked on the door of Ash's room. Got no answer. Remembered it was time for her daily combat session with her nine soldiers.

I headed for the Magic Rooms. I climbed up to the High Tower.

I saw Ash.

Little twelve-year-old Ash turned around, startled by my arrival. Standing, with her nine bodyguards seated in a circle around her.

Their faces: horrified. Frightened.

And then, as one, their nine faces went from horror to anger. Fury. They stood up all at once.

Thunder boomed outside. The night had suddenly gone from clear to stormy. Rain fell in heavy battering sheets.

That storm. The Night of Red Diamonds.

Just two days before my abrupt eviction from the Palace.

The memory went no further. It faded out, like the smoke dispersed by the wind as soon as I breathed it out. What did it mean? And why was I remembering it now?

I looked at my cigarette. Sucked air in, watched the little fire blaze up.

And saw . . . something else. Some other place.

Smoke billowing up from a bonfire on a chilly beach. The fire lighting up the faces of strange men— overgrown boys, really—making them look feral and wild and exaggerated. A bell tolling, from one of the buoys out on the river. Lights glimmering on the far side of it—but how was that possible? No one could see to the other side of the riversea. What was I looking at?

Was this a memory, or a vision?

Whatever it was, Ash was there. I saw her standing in the wind. Unafraid. Unsedated.

My other side. That's what I was seeing.

I didn't even try, this time. Didn't try to fight it, didn't try to force it. It just happened. That's the only explanation I can offer, for why I might have been able to access my ability in that moment, without going into a full-body freak-out. The fear I'd already been feeling, over what I'd seen the night before, was amplified by the fear I felt at seeing Ash in peril.

My spine shivered. I let it. I let the tingles roll all through me. A long low moan escaped my lips.

And then, a second moan sounded, this one from above me.

The dragon wasn't angry anymore. It was afraid. And animals who are afraid are the most dangerous of all. It reared up onto its hind legs, kicking at nothing with its forefeet. It lowered its neck to bellow at the kids, who as far as I could tell hadn't done anything new to annoy it. In fact, nothing had happened that could have turned its anger into fear.

Nothing except . . . my own fear.

It roared again, and swung its tail, shattering the plate-glass window of a shiny luxury shopping center. The sound of breaking glass was so loud.

"Calm down," I whispered, as much to myself as to

the dragon. I took one deep breath in, and then let it out slow. Did that nine more times.

The dragon blinked, and lowered a foot that had been set to kick out at the kids. Went back to calmly munching eucalyptus leaves.

Had I . . . changed its mood? Its mind?

Holy.

Shit.

TWENTY-FIVE

ASH

"Tell me more," I said, stroking Solomon's hair. He lay on his back with his head in my lap, looking up at the stars.

"I don't know where to start," he said.

After we left the party, we'd gotten into my car and I'd driven us south. Parked by the river; walked out along the Germantown waterfront. A group was there cooking fish they'd caught that day, over a fire in a barrel. And drinking, apparently, and breaking beer bottles. After what I'd just been through, dumb drunk kids should have scared me, but I wasn't afraid of them. With Solomon at my side, I wasn't afraid of anything.

"But I'm a *princess*," I said. "I want to be superclear about that part."

He laughed. "You are."

"And I have superpowerful magical abilities."

"Probably. But no one knows what they are. Because you've been under an evil spell."

I clapped my hands. "I always wanted to be under an evil spell."

He turned over onto his side, so that the back of his head was against my stomach. Looked out across the river.

"How did you know?" I asked. "Where I was? That I was in danger?"

Solomon shrugged. "I don't know how it works. I was . . . elsewhere. Over there, the Darkside. Wandering the streets. Drinking coffee. And then I was back, and standing by the bonfire."

Of course, I wasn't really a princess, and there were no brontosauruses blocking traffic anywhere that I knew of. But the spiders I'd seen, crawling into Bobby's open, angry mouth; the guilt that had helped me connect him to the break-in at Jewel's? The fact that Solomon found me, at precisely the right moment?

Something strange was happening.

I kept telling myself it was impossible, but it was harder and harder to deny. Something was changing in the very air around us, and I had to follow it to the end—whatever that was.

"Some lady with a clipboard was sniffing around

the brakeman's hut when I came back this afternoon. Luckily I saw her before she saw me. I could run away. And then the next thing you know, I was on that beach. . . ."

October wind made me shiver, which made him shiver. "Tell me more," I said again. I could have listened to him for hours. Because it was fascinating, and because I could tell it made him happy to talk about it. And because when he stopped, I'd have to tell him that I was the one who called Child Protective Services.

"Darkside is the only place where monsters and humans can coexist. The queen's great-great-great-grandmother brokered a magical truce among all the sentient species to create a safe place for everyone."

And then there's this—and I think once again that we're just going crazy in tandem.

"Do you ever write this stuff down?"

"No," he said.

"You should."

"It scares me," he said. "I don't mind talking about it with you, because you're part of it, but the more I think about it, the more confused I get. Like, right now, while we're talking, I'm fine. Magical truce, whatever. But when I stop talking? When I look off into the distance? And I can hear the wind, and the cold, and the dark? It gets blurrier. Especially if I shut my eyes. Like I come unanchored."

"So keep them open," I said. "Look at me. I'll be your anchor."

Or we'll come unanchored together.

He nodded, rolled onto his back again. Our eyes locked. He smiled; so did I.

"Thank you, Ash."

"I think . . . I'm seeing things too. Only when I look through my camera lens."

"I told you," he said. "Everything is changing. The balance is being upset. Something terrible is coming, and if we're gonna stand any chance of stopping it, we need to see it clearly."

"What's that?" I asked, pointing to the book he held, only partly because I wanted to change the subject.

He handed it to me: *Out of the Dark,* by Helen Keller.

"Did you know she was a socialist?" he said.

"I didn't know anything about her, except that she was deaf and blind and mute and I cried like a baby at that movie about her."

"Back then, lots and lots of disabled people got that way because of accidents and diseases that only happened to them because they were poor. Children who'd lost hands in the factories where they were forced to work. Children who went blind from syphilis they had contracted at birth from mothers forced into prostitution. Helen saw that poverty was the real evil, and believed that the only solution was to overthrow all the powerful men who exploited people."

This was the old Solomon. The kid so smart it was scary. Crazy, that he could coexist with the one who believed in sky whales.

"She was a revolutionary," he continued. "Like you."

"Would that be Princess Me, or Boring Me?"

"Both. There's really only one. I saw what you were doing, down by the river."

"What was I doing?"

"You were gunning for them. The bad guys. They were afraid of you."

I ran my fingers through his close-cropped hair. I shut my eyes, but I could still feel Solomon's on me.

"Solomon," I said, "I remembered something."

I told him what I remembered: seeing him up in the treehouse, caught in the middle of something. Me, falling. As I heard the words come out of my mouth I suspected it was a mistake, but I respected him too much to keep a secret from him.

Solomon's eyes widened. He sat up.

"What?" I said. "Did you—remember—something—too?"

He stood up. He was breathing heavily. Already, sweat stood out on his forehead.

"No," he said. "Oh no. No no no."

"Solomon," I said. "What do you remember?"

He turned, from staring across the river at a single

flickering green light, and looked at me.

I'll never forget that look, as long as I live.

It was utter pain.

He turned and ran off into the night. Along the river, where I couldn't follow in my car.

"Solomon!" I called, even after I knew it was no use.

My belly gurgled at the peppery smell of grilled fish. A girl laughed. A buoy clanged.

TWENTY-SIX

SOLOMON

The street vendor had used too much pepper on my grilled-fish kebab, but it had been a long time since I ate and I scarfed it down in a couple of massive bites.

"Hey, girl," I said, arriving at Maraud's stall in the Underbridge paddock.

When I stepped into the enclosure, she pushed her head against mine. Too hard, but that's pretty standard for my big mauve allosaurus. It's not her fault she's too affectionate, and humans are so much smaller and more fragile than she is.

"I know, girl."

I had gotten all the fear out of my system, and most of the desperation, but a low-level sadness was still throbbing inside me. She nuzzled me, hard enough to push me back a step.

"Come here," I said, and put my arms around her snout. Rubbed her cheek. She shut her eyes and let her breath out in a long slow snort-sigh. Her head was as big as my whole torso.

I shut my eyes too. Tried to think about anything other than what was happening to my city. To monsters everywhere. Tried to tame my fear, so it wouldn't touch Maraud.

"You okay?" asked a voice from the darkness.

"Niv," I said, when he stepped into the light. "How long have you been in here?"

"Couple of hours. Waiting for you."

"And she didn't eat you," I said, impressed.

"We've been having a great time, actually."

"You left Ash alone? Unguarded?"

He laughed. "Unguarded? She's with Radha, and I'd wager a lot of money that woman's a way scarier fighter than I'll ever be."

I nodded in agreement.

"So," I said, dreading it. "Why were you waiting for me?"

He smiled. Hopefully.

I wanted to step back, but I didn't. I kept one hand on Maraud's forearm, feeling the tiny feathers across her skin.

"Can we try this again?" he asked.

I didn't speak.

"I know how hard it's been for you—out here. I know I can't imagine what you've been through. But I've been through stuff too. And I care about you. I think we could be good for each other."

I shrugged, feeling a lump in my throat grow bigger and bigger.

He kissed me. I let him. Put my hands on his chest, as if to push him away, and then just let them rest there. And then I kissed him back. Hungrily, until he pulled away.

"Are you okay?" I asked.

"We need to get out of here," he said, sliding down to sit in the straw. "Me and Ash. It's not safe for her, and it's not safe for your family."

I sat too. "Yeah." And then I remembered the burlap sack I'd dragged in with me, and handed it to him.

"What's this?"

"A present," I said. "For Maraud. Give it to her."

He opened it up, and then winced at the smell, and then laughed. "Here, girl," he said, and hoisted up the coelacanth steak I'd purchased. She ate it greedily, exactly like I'd eaten my fish kebab.

"Ash's personal guard," I said, because this one detail had been bugging me ever since I regained my memory of Ash in the High Tower. "The nine soldiers."

Niv frowned. "Yeah?"

"What happened to them? They were trained to be by her side until the end of her life or theirs."

"Well, then—it sounds like you already know what happened to them," he said.

"They died?"

"I assume so. The truth is, nobody knows. But they vanished. One rumor is, they were executed by the Palace, because one or more was going to betray Ash—but I don't believe that. I know those women. They adored her. Another rumor is, Ash killed them herself. By accident—she attempted to access her power, and it overwhelmed her. Went haywire."

"She had a freak-out," I said, thinking of my own blackout moments. "When they disappeared—was it around the Night of Red Diamonds?"

Niv nodded. "It was that same night."

Neither of us said anything for a long, long while. We had spent our whole lives protecting Ash from the outside world. It never occurred to us that the world would need protection from her.

At our feet, on the cover of the *Clarion*, Darkside Police Commissioner Bahrr had his hands on his hips. He wore a polo shirt and seersucker shorts.

"That asshole," I said. "What'd he do now?"

"Eyewitnesses described a secret meeting that took

place between Commissioner Bahrr and the Shield."

"Are you serious?" I said, eyes widening. "That's huge! That proves—"

"Not really. He played it off, said they were just meeting 'to coordinate efforts for the annual Unmasking Day celebration.' And also he 'denied all involvement in the growing Destroyer movement.'"

"Of course he did."

I couldn't stop thinking about Ash's eyes, in that vision of the other side that I'd seen. How they held pain and anger I knew nothing about. How she was my whole world, and I didn't know what to do to help her. How helpless that made me feel.

Maraud stepped forward, lowered her head to lick my hair. And then she licked Niv's. And I felt safe, even though I knew we were not.

TWENTY-SEVEN

ASH

"Ash!" said Mr. Barrett, when he opened the front door. He wore an olive green polo shirt and blue seersucker shorts. They fit him way too well.

"Connor around?"

"Football practice," his father said, putting his hands on his hips in a way that showed off the muscles in his biceps. This was probably not intentional. He just had a lot of biceps. Everything he did showed them off.

"Shoot," I said, even though I'd known damn well that Connor wouldn't be there. I'd jogged over, so I'd arrive out of breath and get invited in for a drink of water.

He smiled, the kind, generous smile he'd always favored me with. "You look exhausted. Do you want to come in for a glass of water?"

"Sure," I said.

I was there for information. Whatever had happened between Mr. Barrett and Solomon's mother, maybe it could help me figure out the roots of Solomon's current crisis. We are our damage, at the end of the day. And if I knew the truth, I could help Solomon confront it. Learn from it. Move on from it.

I couldn't stop thinking about Solomon's eyes, when he remembered something, in the instant before he ran off into the darkness along the river.

I followed Mr. Barrett into the house. He smelled like cedar and eucalyptus.

"Here," he said, handing me a bottle of water from the fridge. "Do you want some electrolytes?" He opened a cabinet, full of canisters of whey protein and bags of pills and PowerBars and who knew what else. He and Connor are both super-health-obsessed.

"Sure," I said.

"Good answer," he said, and squeezed something from a tiny plastic bottle into my glass. Dark red swirled in the water like blood. "This stuff is really good for you." In seconds, the whole thing was crimson. I took a sip: fruit punch.

"Glad to see you're exercising," he said, and I wondered if the sentence carried an unspoken follow-up— *because you're so chunky*—or whatever. Mr. Barrett could be rough like that. It was something I felt sorry for Connor about.

"How are your mom and dad?" he asked, continuing the sandwich assembly I had evidently interrupted. A whole stack of ham and cheese on whole grain bread, cut diagonally.

"Fine," I said, draining most of my punch and deciding to dive right in. "I saw Solomon yesterday."

Mr. Barrett shook his head. "Such a sad case, that kid. I tried, you know. To help him. I would gladly have let him stay here, after she got locked up. But he wanted nothing to do with me."

"What happened, exactly?" I said, all innocence. "My mom said something about a fire?"

Mr. Barrett put his knife down, and looked at me. Was he wondering how honest he could be? Why I wanted to know all of a sudden? "She torched my car," he said. "Doused it in gasoline, flicked a lit cigarette at it. It was inside the garage at the time."

"Oh my god," I said. "Why did she do that?"

He rubbed his beard. "She thought I was cheating on her."

I laughed, but there wasn't a lot of humor in it. "Were you?"

"No," he said, laughing too. Then he stopped abruptly. "Hadassah was not a well woman." *The exact same words my mom used.* "Whatever sickness Solomon has, I wouldn't be surprised if he inherited it, you know? And she was raised in a very strict Orthodox Jewish community. Turned her back on all that, but it really messed her up."

Sounded a lot like gaslighting to me, but I just said, "Wow."

"I try to keep tabs on him, you know. Even though he pushed us away, I still care about the poor guy. I hear he's not doing so well in school. How did he seem, the last time you saw him?"

"Tough to say," I said, and I stopped myself, without really knowing why.

Mr. Barrett did care about Solomon, as far as I could tell. Wanted the best for him. So why did it feel wrong to share Solomon's stories with him? The dinosaur city and the Refugee Princess? Even to say he was experiencing hallucinations, losing track of what's real and what isn't, felt like a betrayal. So all I said was "He's pretty unhappy."

"He's lucky to have you," he said. "Solomon needs something stable in his life. Something he can trust. You know how he's prone to persecution fantasies."

"Yeah," I said, but the words made something click in my mind.

Persecution fantasies—my father had used the exact same phrase. Except how would Mr. Barrett know that? Solomon hadn't developed those until pretty recently.

"Did you want a ham sandwich?"

"No, thanks," I said. "Seems like you've got a system here. Everything in its proper place. Just enough. I should get going."

"Did you want me to give a message to Connor?"

"Right," I said. "Yes. Tell him I stopped by."

"That's all?" He grinned. I wondered if he knew that Connor and I were sleeping together. Or if he thought we were boyfriend and girlfriend. Or if he'd think less of me, if he knew we were just Friends with Benefits. There was something old-fashioned about Mr. Barrett, under all that scruffy, hip *GQ* silver-foxness, and I didn't imagine he'd be super-open-minded about our arrangement.

So I stopped myself from saying, *Tell him I can't wait to feel his hot body pressed up against mine.*

"No, that's all," I told him.

As I was walking down the driveway, Sheffield came up it.

"What are you doing here?" I asked, not bothering to hide my anger at him.

"Me and the coach have to meet to coordinate efforts for the annual Halloween dance. How are you doing, Ash? After the dramatic events of last night? I was going to call you, but—"

"You mean after your little asshole friend tried and failed to murder me? And you and the rest of your little asshole friends didn't do a damn thing to stop him?"

"Relax, sister," Sheffield said. "Everything turned out fine, didn't it?"

"No thanks to you. And I'm not your sister."

"We would have stopped him."

"You're a liar," I said.

Sheffield laughed. "Jeez, okay, Ash, I'm super sorry about what happened. Really. I don't know what came over Bobby. Except that you *were* kind of fucking with him. It doesn't excuse how he acted, but still . . . You're not completely blameless here."

"Don't you both-sides me," I said. "Calling someone out on their bad behavior is not the same thing as the bad behavior itself. And you can go ahead and scratch *Call Ash to apologize* off of your to-do list."

"I wasn't going to call to *apologize*," he said, button nose wrinkling up in an ingratiating little smile. "I was going to call to say that if you still wanted to photograph all my *little asshole friends*, we're cool with it. The whole team."

I blinked. "Why? I pass some kind of test? Is that what last night was?"

"People were impressed, that's all. Everybody knows Bobby's a psycho. The way you stood up to him was pretty impressive. You know, we're not as diabolical as you seem to think we are."

This, I did not believe.

"Maybe I don't want to photograph you anymore."

"Well, whatever," he said. "That sucks. But I get it."

Silence. Long enough for the artist in me to start whispering.

Because, actually, last night made me *more* convinced there was something the team was hiding. Something solid. If I shot them, it would give me *more* to say about them. About who they were, and what lurked behind their handsome smiles and rugged cheekbones. The terrible things that they did. The terrifying unphotographable darkness behind their eyes.

As Cass would say, the Truth.

"I get to pick the place," I said, after thirty solid seconds of silence. "And the time. And I get to bring people with me."

"Well, shit, Ash, this isn't a damn peace talk. I mean, yes, of course, all those things, but you make it sound like you're a mobster agreeing to venture into hostile territory to negotiate a ceasefire."

"Bye, Sheffield."

I left him and walked back to my car. I called Connor. He didn't answer.

Sex was best, for feelings of frustration and fear and depression, but when it wasn't available I'd settle for food. I drove to McDonald's and went to the drivethrough and the man who handed over my burger and french fries had his arms densely tattooed, a giant squid on one forearm and a sperm whale on the other, forever locked in battle, and I wanted him so bad I had to roll up my window fast before I said something stupid.

And then, miracle of miracles: Connor called me.

"Hey!" I said, shivering with anticipation, but as soon as he spoke I knew this would not be an intimate encounter.

"Come over," he said, his voice small and frail-sounding. "I'll tell you everything."

Five minutes later I was back at his house. My head spun.

"I won't even bother to ask you to keep this a secret," he said, when I found him in his backyard. "I know you couldn't."

I sat down in the dirt next to him. Handed him my french fries without thinking about it. He didn't look up at me. "I should start at the beginning," he said. "He calls it the Induction Ceremony."

"Sheffield?" I asked.

Connor nodded. "He gives you a task. You have to do it."

It was dark out. I could barely see Connor's face. The treehouse was a black shape in the sky above us, blotting out the stars.

"A task like flooding Jewel Gomez's house," I said. "Or spray-painting *fucking swastikas* on a Jewish girl's house."

Connor nodded.

Of course. It was that simple. Sheffield was a manipulative little fucker who liked to be in control. For some reason, he had the entire football team wrapped around his finger. They danced like his puppets, and he got off on every second of it.

"Once it's done, his task—once he's confirmed that it was acceptable—he certifies you as Inducted. And then you get to choose the next person to Induct."

"Shit," I said.

Thunder boomed in the distance. "Storm coming," Connor said. "Saw it on the news just now."

"Why are you're telling me all this?" I said.

He looked up at me, and even in the dim light from his kitchen windows I could see the pain in his face. "Because I just got my assignment today."

I grabbed his arm, squeezed it. "Can't you refuse?" I asked.

"I thought I could," he said. "My dad is the coach, for Christ's sake. But they chose me, and Sheffield made the assignment."

"He tells you what to do?"

"Not what. *Who.* Who to target. The task you do, it's up to you—although Sheffield can veto it if he thinks you're letting someone off easy. It just has to be directed at someone specific."

"Like Jewel Gomez," I said. "So? Who is your assignment?"

It's me, I thought. Sheffield knew how close Connor and I were. And he had plenty of reason to hate me, since I was apparently the only one who objected to or even cared about his little Ponzi Scheme of Infinite Cruelty. He wanted to mess me up badly by having my Friend with Benefits hurt me somehow. What an absolute—

"It's Solomon," Connor said.

Thunder, again. I gaped at him. Well, that made even *more* sense. And made me even madder.

"Of course," I said. "That sadistic little shit. Well, you're going to refuse. Right? Obviously."

"That's the thing," Connor said. "If you refuse, it's worse. Because Sheffield will assign that target to someone else. And he'll devise the task himself. And it will be way more vicious than I would ever be."

"This is all completely crazy," I said. "I can't believe you all go along with this. Have you told your dad?"

Connor shook his head.

"Why the hell not?"

"Sheffield told us not to."

I groaned, in exasperation. "I can't believe everyone on the team knows about all this, and won't, I don't know, call the police or tell the principal or *something.*"

"I'm doing something," he said. "I'm telling you."

"And what the hell am *I* supposed to do about it?" I kind of yelled.

"I don't know. But I know you'll do *something.* You're

the strongest person I know."

Thunder. Lightning. Far away, but getting closer. I had a lot of questions. But I was too angry to ask them.

"I gotta go," I said. Clouds were moving in overhead, looking like massive sea monsters getting ready to fight. I thought of the squid and the whale on the arm of the McDonald's employee.

"I'm sorry," he said. "You have to understand—it all started out really chill. Goofy pranks, things like that. I didn't realize how out of control it was until—"

"Save it, Connor," I said sharply. "You all have a lot of people to apologize to, but I'm not one of them."

TWENTY-EIGHT

SOLOMON

The night of the queen's speech, a sky whale and an air kraken were fighting in the air around the bridge. A bad omen—certainly for the kraken, who put up a good fight but was clearly doomed from the start. The squid spewed black-ink clouds in a spiral from one end of the bridge to the other, as the whale chased it relentlessly around and around. The whale was black against the deep blue twilight sky.

A battle like that was a rare enough sight that a big crowd gathered, and the oddsmakers were trying their hardest to get people to place bets. Radha and I were out there with them, with Connor holding both our hands, until the fight entered its final stages and Radha hurried us inside so the little boy would not be too badly scarred by the carnage.

"Is the squid going to win?" he asked.

"Maybe," I said. "But we have to hurry to listen to the queen's speech."

I hoisted Connor up onto my shoulders and roared around the living room until he got distracted from the high-pitched noises coming from the sky.

"March forward, tyrannosaur," he said, drumming on my scalp with his little fists.

"I'm not a T. rex," I said, making my hands into three-clawed paws. "Are you blind? I'm clearly an allosaurus."

"March, allosaurus," he said, his voice high with delight.

Ash smiled at the sound of it. Niv was frowning over something in the newspaper.

I marched in slow circles of the kitchen, roaring occasionally. On the radio, commentators were filling the dead air until the Palace broadcast began. *Virtually unprecedented*, they said, and *The impossible task of saying something that will make both sides happy, or at the very least not make either side any angrier.*

"She doesn't make many speeches. How come?" Connor asked.

"She's a very busy woman," Radha said, and her eyes flitted to the little shrine in the corner. Small paintings of the gods, Radha's personal pantheon of chosen protectors: the bone-white royal tyrannosaur, and the queen herself at the center of it. "She's busy working to keep us all safe."

"Is that true?" he asked me, sounding skeptical. Niv and Ash avoided eye contact.

"Of course," I said.

You have to kind of lie to kids. The truth is too messy, too ugly, too confusing. You have to give them this little bubble, this all-too-short time when they believe the world is okay. And my lie made Radha smile. She knew about my time in the Palace, but I'd never told her anything about the queen herself and she was too in awe of the woman to even ask.

The talking heads on the radio cut out, and a blare of trumpets announced a Palace priority message. Usually that meant some kind of emergency—a wildfire, or kraken lord attack. Sometimes it meant that on-street parking would be free for a remembrance or royal birthday. But this time, instead of the mellow spokeswoman who normally made those announcements, a clipped and proper male voice simply said:

Ladies and gentlemen, Her Majesty, Queen Carmen.

None of the lengthy honorifics of her full title, the one we all learned by osmosis from street signs and radio clips—*by the grace of the gods Queen-Empress of the Middle Valley, Regent-Mayor of Darkside and Governor of the Lower Riversea, Grand Duchess of the Carnivores* . . . and so on.

None of that. Just a short pause, a hiss of static, and then—her voice.

My subjects, I speak to you tonight from a place of great love, and great concern.

The last time I heard her voice it was literally saying, *Get the hell out of my house.* But now she was precise and formal and strangely accented, a mask she put on when it was time to be The Queen.

These are difficult times for many of us. We are angry. We are frightened. We think that our neighbors are our enemies.

I looked to Radha. Her face was so beautiful. Her lips came together in a tiny, strange smile.

Like Connor, she was better off believing that the woman was perfect, all-powerful. The pride she took in her queen was worth more than anything I could offer.

I implore you all to look past our differences. We are all of us brothers and sisters.

I hadn't told any of them about what I saw. The chimera, murdered. The crowd of people—half of them terrified by the sight, the other half excited.

I am announcing the formation of a new royal commission, said the queen, through the tinny speakers of Radha's ancient wireless. Ash smiled, at the sound of her mother's voice, and then she frowned. *It will be tasked with investigating the deep divisions that are splintering our city, and recommending the best way forward. If actions are required—if new laws must be passed, if ancient injustices must be remedied—I am not afraid to do so.*

Shouts, from outside. Faraway explosions.

Niv's fists went up, tendrils of lightning sparking in the air around him. Instinctively, he stepped between Ash and the front door. I envied him, his training, his skill. His ability.

Then the screaming started, in the distance.

"Stay here," Niv told us, but I followed him outside. Ash and Connor stayed with Radha.

Flames raged atop the far tower of the bridge.

"Explosions," a fellow gawker told us. "People are saying it's all over the city. Synchronized."

I asked Niv: "Is this the Shield?"

He nodded. "If I had to guess. He wants to show how powerful his movement is. How the Palace can't protect the people. We should go back inside. Could get crazy out here."

We got back in time to hear the queen say, *May the gods bless you, and may the gods bless Darkside.* The trumpets sounded. The radio people began to squawk again. The smell of smoke drifted in through the open window.

TWENTY-NINE

ASH

Someone set Walmart on fire. Kind of a sophisticated operation, evidently. Walked through, dribbled gasoline from concealed containers up and down every aisle, trailed it out the door, dropped a lit cigarette onto it. *Fwoosh. Attention, Walmart associates, code orange in aisles one through fifty.*

We live close enough that the smell of burning drifted in through the open windows. Lots of smoke, but not so much damage once it was all under control. No one injured.

Still, it was serious, now. The police were all over it.

Walmart, they cared about. Jewel Gomez, not so much.

Another one of Sheffield's Induction Ceremonies; it

had to be. The whole football team knew about this. Knew who did it. Was protecting them. And things were escalating. Getting scarier.

The day after Walmart, I phoned Connor from his driveway. I was still angry at him, but I hoped maybe I could talk some sense into him. Get him to help stop all this before someone got seriously hurt.

"Hey," he said, just like that, with no exclamation mark. Normally, he's superhappy to answer a call from me.

"Hey," I said. "I'm outside. We need to talk."

He didn't answer right away. "Door's open," he finally said. "I'm in the basement."

I went inside and walked down the hall, and I had a moment, opening the basement door, when the mildew-and-cinnamon smell of it transported me briefly back in time, to childhood, to Solomon and me standing at the top of the stairs and daring each other to descend to the darkness.

But I was a grown-up now, and I was alone. And the broken bulb at the bottom of the stairs had been replaced. So I didn't think about Solomon, didn't spend even a second getting sad over where he might be, because I was on a mission, I had to stay focused, and I didn't let myself feel the slightest bit of fear following the sound of clanking metal to where I knew I'd find Connor.

His basement had a better weight room than most actual gyms. Connor didn't like lifting, but he wanted to please his dad, spot for him, be bros.

And there he was, shirtless and sweaty, on the rowing machine. Resistance set so high I probably couldn't have pulled it a single inch.

"Hey," he grunted, when he got to the end of his set.

"I know you don't want to talk about this," I said. "But someone just tried to burn down Walmart. Was that you guys?"

He frowned, looked at his hands. They were patterned with the checkerboard imprint of the machine's metal handles.

"Jesus Christ, Connor. People could have been hurt. You could have—"

"Look. I want to talk. But it has nothing to do with any of that."

I sat down on the floor. There was real pain on his face.

Crazy fears filled my head. But then Connor opened his mouth, and it was so much worse than anything I'd been imagining.

"I don't want to be your pick-me-up anymore. The person you hook up with when you're feeling down," he said, avoiding looking at me. "I'm sorry. I don't want to be insensitive. I know it helps you. But it's been messing with me, and I can't handle it anymore."

I put my hand on his leg. He pulled it away. "Are you okay?" I asked.

The words looked superhard for him to say. "I care about you, Ash. A lot. And I can't just do this and pretend it doesn't mean anything to me."

"Oh, honey," I said, and reached for him, and then stopped. Because I didn't want to touch him if touching him made him upset. Like even that would be leading him on. "I'm so sorry. I didn't know."

He looked at me, for what felt like the first time. His eyes were round, hazel, electric. "Didn't you?"

And I had. On some level, I must have. I didn't want to see it, because seeing it would mean I was an awful person, playing with his emotions, hurting him, ignoring his pain for my own momentary sense of well-being.

Humans are so strange like that. When we don't want to see something, we just don't see it. Or we tell ourselves it's something else. That's pretty much an essential part of how we survive in this world.

The smell of his sweat was strong in the air. Normally the scent was sexy to me, exciting. Now I could see it more clearly. All this "manliness" . . . it didn't match up with the soul behind his eyes. He was something softer, kinder, more sensitive than the world wanted him to be.

An image flashed in my head: irrational, absurd. Connor as a six-year-old, being carried piggyback by a fully grown Solomon . . . in a weird little hut. Laughing like the happiest kid on the planet.

"If you want to go out on a date sometime, call me," he said. "Roller-skating. Bowling, over in Catskill. But without that? I'm sorry. I thought I was mature enough to handle it, but I'm not."

I didn't answer, not right away. The easy thing to do was say, "Yes, let's go roller-skating."

But the thing was, I couldn't. And he deserved better than that. So all I said was *okay*.

For a second he looked surprised, and then he nodded. "See you around, Ash."

I wanted to say more. It felt wrong, after everything we'd done together, to have so little in the way of goodbye. But I didn't want to make things worse. So I just went out the door.

Me, and all my unanswered questions.

THIRTY

SOLOMON

Niv scoured the airwaves for a while, but all the news was awful. Only an hour had passed, since the synchronized explosions all over the city. Dozens of people were injured; each side was blaming the other; spontaneous street demonstrations turning into brawls. Fires were burning out of control. All the mammoth-drawn trolley lines were out of commission for the foreseeable future.

The city was in a state of raw panic. The Shield himself phoned in to speak with one radio station, his voice sounding eerily young and cheerful.

These terrorist atrocities are not our doing, he said. *This is just another example of criminal elements in the othersider community attempting to discredit us.*

Police Commissioner Bahrr was on the radio as

well. Demanding the queen take action immediately, to make magic illegal, to mandate that all othersiders wear an identifying mark on their clothing, to establish a curfew.

"He's been demanding she do all that for years now," I said. "He knows she won't. So why keep asking?"

"Because every time she refuses, the press hammers her over it," Niv said. "Says she won't keep her people safe. Some even call for her to abdicate. Very smart of him, actually. He knows he can't attack her directly—she'd fire him. But he can play the press against her. The constant media attacks have diminished her popularity, the past couple years, and made him more popular."

He switched the radio off. We sat on the floor with our backs against the bed, side by side, knees touching. Connor snored from the top bunk; Ash slept silently on the lower bunk, right behind us. Only a couple of hours had passed, since the queen's speech.

I pulled two tatamis out from under the bed, and unrolled them.

"You sleep," he said. "I should stay awake and . . . stand guard."

Sirens sounded, from outside. He turned and looked at Ash, her noble sleeping profile, and then he reached out to touch her arm. As though he was convincing himself she was real, she was alive, she was safe. For the moment.

"Don't be an idiot," I said. "You're exhausted. I can see it in your face."

He started to protest, but I put a hand over his mouth. I felt him smile. When I took my hand away, he yawned.

"See? Get some rest. We're safe here."

I blew out the lantern. Niv lay on his back, and I lay down beside him on my side. Facing away. Six slim inches separated our mats. I could still feel the heat of him. People said firesiders and lightningsiders had abnormally warm bodies, but I was pretty sure that was faulty folklore masquerading as science.

"They'll kill me for this," he said. "For running away with her. Kidnapping her, essentially."

I opened my mouth to say, *Of course they won't*, but of course they would.

"Ash will fix it," I told him. "We'll bring her back to herself, and she'll explain what happened, and we'll be forgiven."

"Not just us," he said. "Ash is the secret to saving the whole city. Queen Carmen can't stop the Shield, and won't challenge his movement. Or the police, for that matter. But Ash has an awesome power inside her. She could stop them. Save us, save this city. But it seems so . . ."

Unlikely. Impossible. Overwhelmingly difficult. Likely to end in at least one of us ceasing to breathe. Neither one of us finished the sentence, because there was no good way to end it.

We lay in silence. I didn't shut my eyes. Someone was hollering through a megaphone from far away. Cops, conducting random sweeps of anyone out on the streets, likely. A bad night not to have a place to sleep.

Of course I couldn't sleep myself. My head was too full of the things happening all over the city at that very moment. One part of me wanted to grab my camera and go find them. Another was frozen in place. Eventually I opened my eyes and turned around. In the dark I could make out the shape of Niv's body, his bare shoulders, his sturdy chest. I could see that his eyes were open as well.

"Can you . . . come over here?" he asked. "Lay with me?"

I wasn't sure if that was such a good idea. My feelings about him were messed up enough already. I didn't know what it would be like, pressed against him on the floor. If I'd be able to keep from kissing him. If there was any reason not to. "Sorry," he said, when I hesitated just a second too long. "That was silly of me. I'm not a little kid."

"Don't be an idiot," I said, feeling bad for my indecision, knowing what it was like to be lonely. To feel frightened. I shifted my body back and forth, inched my mat over until it was up against his. He rolled over onto his side and I spooned in behind him.

"This used to be my favorite time of year," he said. "The week before Unmasking Day. As a kid, it was always the best holiday."

"The food alone," I agreed with him. "The fried dough. We'll feel better after a good night's sleep."

"Thanks, Solomon," he said, and kissed my forearm.

I kissed the back of his head. It felt so easy, the way we fit together. I didn't want any more than this. The moment was magnificent the way it was.

And then he spoke.

"You were right," he said, turning around so we were face-to-face. "Not to trust me."

THIRTY-ONE

ASH

I didn't trust them, so I made the arrangements myself. I chose a public place, the strip mall on Fairview Avenue, against the white-painted wall of what used to be the back of the Fairview Cinema. I picked a date and time, and called Sheffield to tell him to have the whole team there, then.

"We just got the invites for the Halloween dance," Sheffield said. "Can I give you a bunch, when we see you? We could really use help handing them out."

"Fine," I said, fully intending to deposit them in the trash as soon as I was out of his eyesight.

The Halloween dance is a weird tradition in Hudson. It's held at the high school, but it's open to the whole town. Hosted by the football team, to thank their neighbors for their support. Two dollars a ticket, and the proceeds go to fund their end-of-season party.

"You're the best, Ash," he said, before I could hang up on him. The saccharine sound of his voice started my eye twitching. Ever since my accident, this has been a sure sign of a headache on its way.

I put the shoot into my calendar. I prayed it wouldn't rain, and then I bought three giant umbrellas to cover my camera and tripod. And then I thought to myself that it might make the shots better, all of them standing in the pouring rain; it would wear down their resistance and help me get to the core of who they were—the Truth—so I prayed it *would* rain.

Walmart was packed. Parts of the store were shut down due to fire damage, but the rest of the place was full of people. The stink of burning plastic was almost completely gone from the air. I picked my way through the crowd, sneaking glances at every passing face. Connor's revelation about Sheffield's Induction Ceremony scheme had me all shaken up. Suddenly everyone was a potential arsonist or criminal.

How many of these people had done terrible things—and how many more of them had simply gone along with it when others did, or turned a blind eye?

To practice, I took pictures of my mother. Put her up against a plain beige wall.

"Don't smile," I said, but she kept smiling.

"Stop," I said, maybe a little too harshly.

"Sorry, honey," she said, laughing. "I can't help it. It's like a reflex at this point. Aim a camera at me and I break into an idiotic grin."

It was a strength, really. The ability to smile through every calamity. To be calm when other people—usually my dad—were trying their best to lose their minds. Through the lens she looked like some kind of queen or diplomat. Short hair, tiny earrings, just enough makeup. Her darkness was distant, an orbiting swirl of little black stars blooming and bursting.

Distant—but I could sense it. It existed.

There was some of it in everyone.

THIRTY-TWO

SOLOMON

Niv's darkness was there. Had always been there. Distant—but I could sense it.

"Tell me what you mean," I whispered to him, there on the safe, warm floor of Radha's home, with the whole world falling down around us.

He did not answer me right away. When he did, I could hear that he was crying. "They've got me, Solomon. Going back years."

"Who's they?"

"The police," he said, and his breath smelled like cinnamon and chocolate, like the little boy he had been. "When I was ten, when I first started working as a stableboy at the Palace, they came to me. My mom was in prison, and they told me that if I didn't work for them, they would make life hard for her. Kill her, even, if I disobeyed, or if I told anyone at the Palace about what was going on. My handler would come check in with me once a month. Ask me what had been happening. What I'd seen, heard. It made me sick to work for them, but in the beginning, it wasn't such a big deal. I didn't have any power or responsibility back then, and certainly nobody ever told me anything valuable—but pretty soon I started getting promoted. They made sure I moved closer and closer to the center of the inner circle. Until pretty soon I was the Refugee Princess's number one aide."

"I knew it," I said, and I wondered if that's why I didn't feel angrier.

"I pretty much hated myself, for what I did. But you have to believe me, Solomon. I love Ash more than anything, and I've never *ever* given them any information that could help them to hurt her. And I never would."

He was crying harder, now. I held him tighter. Told him *shhhhhhh*. Told him we would figure it all out. Told him everything would be okay.

"They have her," he said, through sobs. "My mom. What're they going to do to her, now that I've run off?"

"I don't know," I said.

"My handler liked me," he said, rolling over, onto his back, away from me. "She came by the safe house, told me that the cops had learned about the Shield's plan for the attacks, during the queen's speech. Told me the Destroyers would be coming for Ash at the same time, and they'd kill her guards if they had to. Told me I should go out for a kebab when the speech started, if I knew what was good for me. As soon as she was gone, I took Ash and headed straight for the Underbridge."

I touched his face. It was the only thing I could think to do. Pressed my hand against his cheek.

"I'm so sorry," he said.

"I'm sorry too." Like clouds after a storm, all my complicated hostility toward him had been whisked away. I could see him now for what and who he truly was. "I'm sorry this is the situation you're in. I'm sorry for the situation Ash is in. All of us, really. It sucks. But it's who we are. So let's try to get some sleep."

"You have to take her," he said. "In the morning. Take Ash and run. They have spies everywhere. I tried to keep a low profile, but it's not safe to stay in one spot. They'll come for me—and for her."

"Okay," I said.

"You promise?"

"Of course."

"I'll go too. Somewhere. I don't want to bring the heat to Radha and Connor."

"Okay."

I lay there until Niv fell into a fitful sleep, and then I scooted up into a seated position. I watched Ash, the way her chest rose and fell. I didn't know what horrors lay ahead of us, or how much longer we'd have, or whether I'd be able to save her. But I knew that I would be there for her, all night long, and I would be there for her in the morning.

THIRTY-THREE

ASH

I drove as fast as I could. I was exhausted—I'd barely slept, I was so excited. It was the morning of my football team photo shoot and I wanted to get to the location well ahead of the rest of them. The streets were still coming awake, the whole town dressing itself up in blue and gold, the Hudson High colors, for the Halloween dance.

"If anything creepy goes down, just call my name," said Solomon, fiddling with the car radio. He'd been asleep on my front porch when I woke up, and I hadn't known until I saw him how badly I needed him to be there with me. *I'm here for you,* he'd said, rubbing the sleep from his eyes. *All night long, and into the morning.*

"Where are you going to be?" I asked.

"In the movie theater, probably."

"The movie theater is closed. Has been for years."

He flexed his fingers. "No problem for a skilled criminal such as myself."

I rolled my eyes. "Let's not get arrested. Mmkay?"

"They'll never take me alive," he said, but not like it was a joke.

We pulled into the movie theater parking lot. Today was the day.

I would get to the Truth, complete with a capital *T*. I would capture these brutal boys on film. How they were flawed. How they were human. I would penetrate to the core of who they were. I would put all of Cass's lessons and insights into action. I would find the secret unphotographable essence of each boy, and I would photograph it.

And the day was perfect. A gray blanket of cloud completely obscured the sun. There would be no harsh shadows, no tricks of the light to get in the way. The air was cold. The wind had a smoky edge to it. Each boy would stand before me in his team T-shirt, as I'd specified in my instructions, bare arms exposed and goose bumped, shivering. My sense of triumph as I came to a stop was complete.

And then I saw him. Sheffield. Standing beside his car, waving at me.

"Shit," I said.

"Shit," Solomon said.

"What the hell is he doing here so early?"

"Same thing as you," Solomon muttered. "The first to arrive controls the space."

"I'll let him think that," I said, and remembered that Sheffield had assigned Solomon as Connor's target. "Don't talk to him, okay? Like, at all. He's a manipulative little shit and he'll get inside of your head."

"He's a punk," Solomon said, getting out of the car, smiling, waving at Sheffield. "And he's smaller than me. He won't do shit, not without his army behind him. He's weak. That's why he's a bully."

I nodded. Sometimes Solomon lived in a fantasy world full of horrors, and other times I could see that he understood our world way better than I ever would.

I got out, and took a picture of Sheffield, grinning, leaning on the hood of his car. His proud smile shrank, the slightest bit. Weird shapes swung through the air around him.

Past the theater, there were only woods. Walk through them far enough and eventually you'd come to the freight train tracks.

Sheffield shook hands with both of us. "Good to see you, Solomon. What's shaking?"

Solomon glared down at the shorter boy, then made a low snickering sound. "Have fun, Ash," he said, without breaking eye contact, then stalked off.

"Strange dude," Sheffield said to me.

"Everybody's strange, if you really get to know them," I said, and busied myself with setting up my equipment. He tried chatting me up a couple more times in the hour until the rest of the team started arriving, but I deflected each attempt.

Where had Solomon gone? Into the theater, like he said? And what would Sheffield do about his being there—since he'd already hung a target around his neck? Would he tell the others? Would he tell Connor? Would he call off the shoot? Or—the more likely scenario—would he do something worse than anything I could think to anticipate?

But then I couldn't think about it anymore, because the shoot was underway. I had light tests to do, sample shots to make. Finding the right balance of ISO and shutter speed and aperture. I decided to err on the side of a longer exposure, to allow a smaller aperture, which would give me greater depth of focus.

Because I wanted focus. Clarity. Perfect precision. Whatever was written on their faces, I wanted to capture it.

With sadness—and with relief—I noticed that only one of the thirty team members was missing. Connor.

For the best, really. He wouldn't want to see me after the way we left things. After he told me he didn't want to be my Friend with Benefits anymore. And after he spilled the truth about the whole football team's conspiracy of vandalism and hate crimes.

I took shots of the whole group of them, chatting nervously, standing awkwardly.

Watching Sheffield interact with his teammates, the way they deferred to him, the Induction Ceremonies made perfect sense. And while now wasn't the moment to bring any of it up, confront any of them about what they'd done, my eyes would be open for it when I looked through the lens.

"All right, assholes," Sheffield called. "Ash is ready to get started."

"Thank you, Winthrop," I said, pleased to see him wince at the sound of the first name he hated so much. Other boys giggled. "You first, Justin."

For the portraits, I had picked out a stretch of wall where the paint was perfectly clear and even. No graffiti, no cracking or chipping or bullet holes. A plain white background for each boy.

Justin stood there, and gave me the grin you give to the photographer for school pictures. Broad and dumb and childish. I took a picture, just to set him at ease.

"No smile," I said.

"Yeah, Justin," somebody yelled. Six different conversations were going on behind me. They were uncomfortable, bored. Getting rowdy.

"Tell them to be quiet," I told Sheffield. And, after

a second, he did. And the feeling of power I got from ordering him around—ordering all of them around—was like electricity all through me.

"You're still smiling," I told Justin. "Give me nothing."

He gave it. The swirling ink blots behind him were calm, modest.

I felt the tiniest beginning of a tingle up my spine, and then I reached for it. Grabbed hold. Focused on it. Felt it swell. Watched the shapes change, clarify.

"Good," I said, after taking twenty different shots of Justin. "You can go, now."

I was on my third football player when I heard a car pull into the parking lot.

"Connor!" someone called.

"Hey," he said, and I shivered at the sound of his voice. Connor got into line and if he looked in my direction, I didn't see, didn't look back.

"You're up, Will," I said.

The shiver in my spine was getting stronger all the time. I could feel it, an energy pulsing through my eyes and into my fingertips.

And this time, when I looked through the lens, I really looked. Focused on the swirling black ink in the air around him. Blocked out everything else, until the shiver of my spine was all I felt. Watched the ink expand, take on concrete shapes. His damage, his demons. His darkest moments. I could use what I saw.

Night. Ski mask on his head, gloves on his hands. Spray-painting a line of dark blue swastikas along the back of Judy Saperstein's house.

"Hey, have you seen Judy lately?" I asked.

His jaw dropped. Panic filled his eyes, and then was replaced by anger.

I pressed the shutter. *Click.*

"No," he said.

"Got the shot," I said, and waved my hand dismissively. "Your turn, Hector."

And so on, down the line. By the eighth player we had hit a groove. Their awkwardness was gone, replaced by a kind of impatient boredom. Which was good. A place of frustration to start from, when they stepped in front of me.

I could see so much more, now. Which ones were monsters, and which were just scared little boys trying their hardest to be men. The shiver in my spine—the visions through my lens—they were under my control.

They all left, when I was done with them. The crowd shrank fast. Connor was the very last in line. It was only me and him and Sheffield—and Solomon, somewhere. Watching us, I felt certain.

"Hey," Connor said, taking his place before me. The first word he'd said to me, since I left his house that night. I had been angry before that, at his complicity in the Induction Ceremony scheme, and then ashamed of how I might have hurt him. Now I felt only sadness for him. Because he was such a sweet and kind person—now. But Sheffield was already at work on him, and so was the whole horrible world. Sweetness and kindness were so easily broken. Crushed into oblivion.

"Hey," I said.

His smile was weak, thin. Forced. Proud. Sad. I took a single shot of him. Trying my hardest not to tap into my ability. It switched off easily, and I saw only Connor. "That's perfect," I said, and smiled back. My smile broadened his, made it real—wide and happy.

"Goodbye, Sheffield," I said, turning to him.

He blinked, startled at being dismissed, and then recovered. Sheepish, calculated grin. "Later, Ash. Seems like it was a success, yeah?"

"You did good. Thanks for your help."

We eyed each other, for a second or six, before he saluted and turned to go to his car.

"Why *are* you helping me?" I called.

"Why wouldn't I?" he said, his voice sounding different—lower, sadder—and for a very short second I felt like I was getting the real Sheffield, a boy with no schemes or plans or power plays. A boy who wasn't good at sports, who wasn't strong or creative or funny, who developed the art of manipulation out on the elementary school recess field from sheer, sad loneliness.

"You don't strike me as the kind of guy who does anything that won't benefit him in some way."

He frowned, and then nodded. "I guess I get that. Maybe I wanted to help you out. Maybe you asked me for something and I could help you, so I did. Or maybe I just one day, maybe, want to call in a favor."

They all felt partially true.

I watched him drive off. Neither Connor nor I said anything right away.

"I'm sorry," he said. "I should never have gone along with them."

"I know," I said, and I smiled, because I really did understand, but I also didn't have anything else to say to him. I got into the car and after a few seconds he walked back to his own.

"I want Indian food," Solomon said, startling me. He was laying down in the back seat.

"How long have you been back there?"

He shrugged.

"Indian food sounds really good, actually," I said.

I watched Connor's car pull out of the parking lot. Midafternoon, and already the shadows had swallowed us up. Soon the sun would set. We'd be alone in the dark. Winter was halfway there.

"It was me," I said. "I called Child Protective Services, told them where you've been sleeping."

"I know," he said. "Of course I know that."

"How did you—"

"Ash," he said, and *Don't be stupid* was implied in his tone of voice. "There's no one else who cares enough about me to snitch."

He chuckled. I couldn't tell if he'd had to make himself do that.

"You're not mad?"

Solomon shrugged. "I was for a little while. When I found you on that beach, I was fully intending to curse you out. But when I saw that asshole about to hurt you, I realized my anger wasn't meant for you. I love you."

I breathed in, out. Relief flooded me, and shame. "I'm so worried about you, Solomon. That's why I did it."

"I know."

"I'll go with you," I said. "To CPS. So you won't be alone."

"Maybe," he said, his voice shrinking, and I could almost hear the fear pressing down on his chest. "I'll think about it."

"We'll have to drive down to Red Hook," I said. "For Indian food."

"That's cool?" he asked. His hands were behind his head and he was smiling.

"That's cool," I said, excited already at the thought of the strong, sweet milky tea that would provide badly needed caffeine at the same time as it soothed my frazzled nerves.

THIRTY-FOUR

SOLOMON

We drank sweet milk tea, and ate soft fluffy *idli*. Radha had packed us two little breakfasts, when we woke up at dawn and told her that Ash and I had to go. Niv had given us the last of his money. Enough to paddock Maraud in a safe place, and get a hotel room if we absolutely had to.

He'd hugged us. And I kissed him, in front of Radha and Ash. His smile was like the last gulp of air you take before diving under water, when you don't know how soon you'll be able to breathe again.

Logistics were worked out. Ways to get in touch. Worried looks were hidden away. We all kissed sleeping Connor on his forehead. And then we headed out, and went our separate ways, and Ash and I were alone.

And now we sat along the riversea, miles away from

home, with no clear idea of where we were going. Drinking tea and pretending like we weren't scared shitless.

"How do you feel, Ash?" I asked. All morning long she'd been present, saying little but responding in ways that made it clear she was aware of what was happening around her.

She nodded, then reached out her hand for mine. "I'm okay."

"Better today than yesterday?"

"I can see and hear things . . . better."

"Excellent."

"What happened?" she asked. "Last night. The attacks, during my mother's speech?"

That was the old Ash, all right. Concerned for everyone else's safety. Worried more about her city and her people than about herself. I told her the little that we knew, from the news reports on the radio. Thirteen people were confirmed dead. Fifty-seven known instances of sabotage and terrorism. Monsters slaughtered, all over the city. DPD had made no arrests.

I took both of her hands in one of mine, and pressed them together. "There's something I need you to remember. Something that I think will help. Will you let me try something?"

Ash nodded.

I shut my eyes. Breathed in, straightened my spine,

focused on the sensations there. Tried not to try. Tried to just let it happen, like it had with the brontosaurus. Tried to feel happy, stable, strong. Things that would help her out, lend her the power she needed to break through the spell she was under, access her own ability. But where do emotions like that live? Wherever happiness and stability and strength were, I couldn't snap my fingers and summon them up.

A breeze came in from down the shore, bringing with it the smell of the riverfront laundry vats, and I had my answer.

Because I thought of Connor. The day we met. When he was two and I was twelve. The clean-clothes smell of him. The happiness, coming off of him in waves, so strong that my sadness about being cast out of the Palace blew away like raptor feathers in the wind.

Memory can make you feel things.

"Shut your eyes," I told Ash.

She did.

"Do you remember the time you found out your mother was going to let you attend a meeting of her governing council?"

"Yeah," she said, and my eyes were shut but I could feel the smile in her voice.

I let myself drift back into the body of the boy I'd been. Only a month or so before my banishment. I could smell the familiar interior: stuffy like a bank, safe like a church. Summertime; thick stone walls kept the inside of the place a solid ten degrees cooler than the rest of the city.

I saw us, in front of a long line of mirrors. Because of course the queen had an entire room just for getting dressed. Ash stood there, holding a dress in each hand. One gray and one mauve. I was sprawled on a massive round blue velvet couch.

"They're both awful," I said.

Ash threw them both on the ground. "They *are*."

We wore the simple tunics used by Palace guards and soldiers for their training. Ash had just come from there—the nine guards stood outside in the hallway, dressed identically—they'd spent hours drilling martial arts, but she still only had the one move, where she grabbed an attacker by the wrist and by the elbow and bent the arm the wrong way.

"You should wear that," I said, sticking out my leg to touch the tunic with my toe.

"You're ridiculous," she said. "This is a very big day for me. I don't want to meet them dressed like a soldier-in-training."

"Why not? Is it better to meet them looking like a duchess whose mother is trying to marry her off? Go in there as the princess that you *are*, not the one your mother wants you to be."

She nodded. Of course I was right. I was only repeating stuff I'd heard her say before. Ash understood things in a way I never would.

She tried on several more gowns, but I knew the argument was over. I'd won.

I let it swell and grow inside of me, the same pride I'd felt back then. In that moment I'd believed that I belonged in the Palace, that I was part of that world, that I had something to offer. That Ash and I would change our city, fix everything that was wrong with it.

My spine tingled. It got stronger and stronger—my hands turned cold and started to shiver, like a freak-out might be moments away, but I breathed deep and calm and soon the shivering subsided.

Ash gasped.

"What?" I said, opening my eyes, startled to see that we were still sitting beside the riversea.

"I feel something," she said. "Like . . . a smell that's not a smell. Or a sound that's not a sound."

"Another sense," I said. "Right?"

She nodded. "I can see things. Almost. They're there, in my peripheral vision, but they move when I turn to look at them. Like I can't ever quite catch up."

"You'll get there," I said. "You're still coming out from under the spell."

I had done it. I conjured up an emotion, and I used it to help Ash. I'd made her stronger. And the weird thing was, I felt stronger too. More confident in my ability. Strengthening her had strengthened me.

Thunder boomed in the distance.

"Storm coming," said a woman with a shopping cart, picking up cans from the trash, accompanied and assisted by a small flock of gremlins. "Heard about it on the radio just now."

"Thanks," Ash said, with a smile.

"Here," the woman said, shuffling over, and handed us a battered old radio, the size of a book. "Found this in the garbage. Looks like hell but works fine. Full battery. Got one of my own already."

"Thank you," I said. She could have sold it, gotten a moon cake or two. My people were the kindest and most generous in the city. It was baffling to me, how anyone could hate or fear us.

"Solomon," Ash said, when the woman was gone.

"Yeah?"

"Thanks. For . . . everything."

"Psssh," I said.

She took my hand and held it. "I've got you. I may not have anything else, but I've got you."

"Likewise."

Lightning lit up the sky.

THIRTY-FIVE

ASH

Thunder sounded. I'd counted the time since the lightning: six seconds.

Rain began to pelt my windshield. I was parked in my driveway, savoring the silence. After our trip to Red Hook I'd dropped Solomon off under the Rip Van Winkle Bridge, at his—characteristically bizarre—request. That had been hours ago. I'd driven all the way to Albany to get more photo paper, developer, stop bath, fixer.

I sat there and watched the rain get stronger. I didn't want to go inside. Didn't want to talk to anyone. I wondered if in Solomon's magical world there was a way to teleport directly into one's bed and sleep forever. Or if somebody could put me in a coma so I'd never have to deal with humans ever again.

My phone vibrated in my hand. *Unknown Number* flashed on the screen.

I almost didn't answer it. Everything would have happened so differently, if I hadn't. But I did.

"Hello?" I said.

Static. Someone yelling in the background. Finally: "Ash?"

"Solomon!" I said. "Where are you? What number is this?"

"I wasn't sure if I had your number right."

Metal clanged, wherever he was. A loud buzzer sounded. I started to get a bad feeling. "Solomon. Tell me where you are."

"I'm in jail," he said, and laughed, not like it was funny, but like he could hear how ridiculous the situation was. "I'm breaking the rules right now. I already used my one phone call. But these people are pretty bad at their jobs. They just left me in the hallway where the phone is. I could make all kinds of calls. What's the number for the Psychic Hotline, do you know?"

"In *jail?*" I said, too loudly, before my rational mind kicked in and I dialed back the panic. If I got upset, so would he. Emotions were contagious like that. "What happened?"

"I ran into Bobby," he said. "At Fairview Plaza."

"Oh, honey, no," I said. The little psychopath who

almost set me on fire—there was no way that interaction went well.

"He started it."

"It doesn't matter!" I said.

"Anyway I beat the shit out of him."

"Solomon, you—"

"They're coming," he said. "I gotta go. I called my aunt but she didn't answer. So I don't know what they're going to do with me."

"Don't tell them anything until you have a lawyer," I said, finally thankful for all the awful cop shows my mother watched, which I'd absorbed by osmosis. "They have to provide one for you, even if you can't pay for it. Better yet, just don't speak. To anyone. I'm coming. Okay?"

"Okay," he said.

"Breathe, Solomon. Don't get stressed."

"I'm not stressed," he said. "And I'm not sorry."

I had to chuckle at that. At his strength, his bravery—his ignorance, his naïveté. And then there was a harsh boom, as someone slammed the receiver down. It rang in my ears like thunder.

THIRTY-SIX

SOLOMON

For most of the day it was almost like everything was normal. We walked; we ate; we talked to strangers. Only a few charred tree skeletons gave any indication that anything unusual had happened in Darkside the night before.

The thunder endlessly booming in the distance should have been enough to set us on edge. Keep us from getting too comfortable. Like the storm was toying with us, biding its time, waiting to rush in and flood us out.

One minute we were in the central market, trying to decide which noodle vendor to go to, and the next minute we were running for our lives.

I noticed the first watcher when we stopped at a citrus

cart. Ash was picking through bright pink oranges, and I caught a woman staring at her. She wasn't wearing ultramarine, so I didn't think she was a threat. Which just goes to show what a shitty bodyguard I make. But Ash was hooded, and she'd hardly ever been photographed, so I didn't think we needed to be so on our guard.

The second one wasn't wearing ultramarine either. She owned the salamander cart we stopped at, looking for the shed skin of a rainbow hellbender, which supposedly helped calm the mind and strengthen othersider abilities. The woman whispered something in the ear of her domesticated baboon, and it hurried off.

And I got very, very scared.

"Ash. We should go," I said.

She looked around carefully. "Are we in danger?"

"I think we might be."

Smiling like happy idiots, we turned and started walking.

"Place is packed," she said. "We can't run."

"Neither can they, at least."

Everything went great, for a solid eleven seconds. And then someone yelled, "Hey, Princess! There! It's the princess!"

And everything went to hell.

Ash just kept walking. But people stopped, pointed, stared. And out of nowhere stepped three men in ultramarine.

"Your mother's a monster lover!" someone shouted. Someone else shouted at them to shut up.

Fear. Hate. I felt it all around us. And I felt it inside me as well.

I would have loved to have summoned up a bunch of peaceful, happy vibes to calm them all down, but calm seemed impossible right then. All I had at hand was hate. Anger. But maybe I could use that to throw them off-balance. So, trying my hardest not to try—I focused on it. Felt the tingling up my spine. Let it take hold of me.

And then . . . I pushed it out. Let it fill the air. Aimed it for the faces that frightened me.

Shouting swelled, all around us. Faces reddened. Weapons were drawn. Rage confused people, muddied the waters of who they were mad at.

"On three," Ash said, slowing down alongside a spice cart.

"Mm-hmm."

"One," she said.

"Two," I said.

"Three," she said, and seized two huge brass bowls of powdered lightning bugs, slammed them together, tossed them high.

A cloud of bright blue dust filled the air, and we vanished into it.

THIRTY-SEVEN

ASH

Lightning turned the night bright blue, lit up the long, flat, plain-looking building that was the county jail.

I hadn't even known where it was; that's what a sheltered life I'd led. But I'd mapped it on my phone and found it, behind where the match factory had been, beside the giant domes where the county kept its mountains of rock salt for snowy winter roads. I'd driven by it a hundred times in my life at least. Ignorant, every time.

I sat in my car and tried my best to think clearly. Why had I come? What was I going to do? They wouldn't just hand Solomon to me. According to the cop shows, if he was charged with a crime, they'd keep him overnight and in the morning he'd go before a judge who would either set bail or keep him in county until his trial came. And even if he wasn't, Child Protective Services practically had an all-points bulletin out on him—they'd probably hold him until a social worker could inspect him in the morning.

I had come because I couldn't *not* come. Because Solomon was in trouble, and I had to help him. Even if I didn't know how.

The rain got harder. Louder. I didn't have an umbrella.

I turned off the car, silencing the punk rock singer of Destroy All Monsters! midshriek. I looked around for something that could shield me from the rain, and found a giant sweatshirt across the back seat.

Solomon's. I could tell by the smell. A man's smell, but there was more to it than that. He was there, somehow—Little Boy Solomon, a shred of the child he had been. Before his brain broke, before the world began to betray him. I breathed it in. The smell opened up something—a doorway to memory—but I didn't have time to go through that doorway, not just then.

I opened the car door. Wind made it difficult, drove rain in stinging slaps against me. I stepped out, slammed the door shut again, held the sweatshirt over my head. It didn't do much good with the wind so strong, pushing the rain so it seemed to come at me sideways. I walked toward the front door to the jail. A single bare bulb was lit, above the entrance.

When I was halfway there, the door opened. And I stopped. Because Mr. Barrett came out the door, with his arm around someone.

Around Solomon.

Mr. Barrett was smiling, saying something to someone back in the jail, but Solomon's face was twisted up with agony.

I took off my hood. I let the rain punish me.

In nightmares, for the rest of my life, I'll see that face. So much pain, so much fear. Little Boy Solomon was back. The Solomon with the big muscles and broad shoulders was gone. Forgotten.

Oh god, Solomon, I thought. *What has you so afraid?*

And the really awful thing? The proof of how being an artist and being a bad person are all bound up together? My first reaction, my gut instinct, the only thought that popped into my head: more than anything, I wanted my camera. What I saw on Solomon's face, in that instant, it would have been the most perfect photograph I'd ever take. Pure emotion, captured on film. The truth I'd been hunting for.

I thought about calling out to him. Yelling his name. But fear paralyzed me. Fear and a little voice that said, *Stay hidden. Don't let them capture you.*

Thunder burst overhead, like God knocking at my door.

THIRTY-EIGHT

SOLOMON

Thunder burst. Rain began to fall. We did not stop running. Through crowded, noisy streets, down narrow, lonely alleys. Long after we knew we lost them. I'd never run so far before in my life, and although Ash had gotten a ton of bad-ass warrior training once upon a time, she'd also spent four years sitting still. So I don't know where all that stamina came from. Fear, partly, but more than that. From our clasped hands, I think.

Ash and me, we made each other better.

Finally, we arrived at the stable where we'd left Maraud. The place had the sweet coffee stink of dragon droppings, and under that the smell of bleach.

"Cops stood by and watched," the attendant said, talking to her coworker, when she handed me the reins.

"Watched what?" I asked, wishing immediately that I hadn't.

"Attack on the Underbridge," the woman said. "Biggest one in ten years, they're saying."

Radha. Connor.

"Hundreds of Destroyers," the stranger continued.

She looked at me. I looked back. Both our faces were rigid masks.

We didn't know each other. Maybe she was an othersider; maybe I was a Destroyer or a sympathizer. Maybe we would have been friends; maybe we hated each other. But we were both scared.

"Thank you," I said, and smiled, and she smiled back.

Ash switched on the little radio the woman had given us. Steered the dial through a sea of static until we arrived at a polished voice saying—

Multiple eyewitnesses report hearing the attackers call out for the Refugee Princess, who they believe was in hiding at the shantytown, and who may have been the target of the raid. . . .

All the air went out of me.

"We abandoned them," I croaked.

I tried to say something, and couldn't. Tried to take a breath, and couldn't. Collapsed into coughing.

"Let's go," Ash said. "*Solomon,* let's go."

THIRTY-NINE

ASH

Solomon stopped and began to cough, and somehow that helped me regain control. Shook me out of my paralysis. I took a step forward through the rain, and then another. I still didn't know what I was going to do, but I had to do something.

Mr. Barrett came down the steps, into the rain, and Solomon followed. Looking for all the world like a pig going to slaughter, one who knew exactly what was waiting for him. His hands were shoved deep in his pockets, his shoulders hunched. He wasn't cuffed. That had to mean something. He was free. Neither one of them seemed to notice the rain. Neither of them had noticed me, in the darkened parking lot.

It's true that Solomon was unstable. But why was he so afraid of Mr. Barrett? And why had Mr. Barrett come to get him out of jail? There was no way Solomon called *him*. Why was he here?

There was something about *this*, I told myself. This moment. The truth I'd been after was inside it somehow. I knew it. I could feel it.

"Solomon!" I called, stopping.

They stopped too.

By now I was close enough to see that Solomon was crying. I hadn't noticed with the heavy rain streaming down his face. And he was shivering.

"Ashley," said Mr. Barrett, his voice firm, bossy, used to being obeyed. "What are you doing here?"

"Ash," Solomon said, or anyway his mouth made the shape of the word. I couldn't hear him.

"It's all under control, Ashley," Mr. Barrett said. People only ever used my full name when they were trying to make me feel small. "Go home. We'll call you tomorrow."

Movie heroes always know what to say. I didn't.

With a strangled cry, Solomon ran. He pushed past Mr. Barrett, ran past his car—which I hadn't noticed when I pulled in—and ran to mine. Pulled the handle. It was locked, but he pulled it again and again.

"Ash, please," he called.

"Don't do something stupid, Ashley," said Mr. Barrett. "Solomon is very sick. We got lucky—one of the guys at the station knew Solomon, gave me a call, and I was able to get the charges against him dropped, but only on the condition that he—"

"Ash!!" Solomon wailed.

I was not interested in anything Mr. Barrett had to say. Maybe he was right, and I was doing something stupid. But I couldn't not do it. I couldn't let Solomon go home with him. I fumbled in my pocket for the key fob, and unlocked the door. Solomon scrambled inside. Very calmly, very slowly, I turned away from Mr. Barrett and walked to my car.

"Ashley," he called. "If you leave with Solomon, there will be consequences."

I opened the car door, and I heard a new sound in Mr. Barrett's voice. Fear.

"For god's sake, Ashley! You can't—"

I slammed the door. Locked it. I didn't care what he thought Solomon needed. I started up the car.

"Drive," Solomon hissed. "Fast." Mr. Barrett was walking toward us, and he had completely lost his Good Guy Composure. I put the car in reverse and the lights lit up his face a bright, angry red. I slammed my foot on the gas, turning the wheel in a wide arc, and then put it into drive without braking. I fishtailed away.

When we were out on Route 66 and the miles

between Solomon and Mr. Barrett piled up, he finally spoke. "Oh my gods, Ash," Solomon said, "thank you."

"Any time," I told him.

Wind howled.

"What the hell do we do now?" I asked, but it was a rhetorical question. Neither of us knew the right answer. Probably there wasn't one.

FORTY

SOLOMON

I howled. So did the wind.

Nothing made sense. I knelt in the mud and looked at my hands, watched them shiver. Black stars bloomed and burst in my peripheral vision. The world felt like it was about to crack down the middle. Shatter into a thousand pieces.

The last hour, the last day, the last several weeks— all a blur. Maraud had run at full gallop through the pouring rain, all the way to the Underbridge. I'd climbed off, told Ash to take her to a safe place nearby. Couldn't have the Refugee Princess showing up. Cops might take her into custody, or Destroyers still lurking in the crowd might snatch her up.

And then I entered the crowd, weaved my way through the chaos of ambulances and police cars and weeping and rage. I recognized people, thought about stopping to ask what had happened, but the only thing that really mattered was confirming Connor and Radha were okay.

"Solomon!" someone said, and clapped a hand on my back, and I whirled around with my fist cocked back until I saw who it was.

"Quang!" I said, and hugged him as hard as I could. "How are you?"

"I'm alive," he said. "I thank the gods for that."

He looked hungry, weak. Like he hadn't been sleeping. Or eating. I said, "I'm so, so sorry for what happened to you."

"Forget about me," he said. "You have to come. Now."

He grabbed my hand, pulled me with him. Toward Radha's house.

She was standing in front of it. Surrounded by friends. I had never seen her face like that. Transfigured by grief, but not only grief. Rage was there too.

She wasn't weeping. But something about her stony face was more disturbing than any amount of tears would have been.

"No," I whispered, to myself, as the pieces came together in my mind.

"You!" she said, when she saw me.

Grief fled from her face. Only rage remained. And I knew.

Connor.

"Radha, please," I said.

"You did this. You brought her here. They came looking for her in our home—because of you."

Shortness of breath dropped me to my knees again. I had to cough, but couldn't. All I could do was look up at Radha as she closed the few feet between us, this woman I loved with all my heart, who loved me more than probably anyone—who I had hurt so, so badly.

"I'm sorry," I said, maybe out loud, maybe not.

And then I was up, off the ground. Hovering in the air. Radha held me there without moving at all, using only her mind.

Every muscle was on fire. Ankles, knees, wrists, elbows—every joint was aching, bent at an unnatural angle. I felt her power, felt how easy it would have been for her to jerk her head to the side and split me into a thousand pieces. How hard it was for her not to.

No wonder you wanna keep that a secret, I thought. *Pretty nasty surprise for anyone unlucky enough to piss you off.*

And then I thought: *I totally deserve this.*

Our eyes locked. I saw hers widen.

"Oh my gods, Solomon," she said, and the fog of

rage lifted, and I fell to the ground. She knelt down in the mud next to me. "I'm so, so sorry."

Looking at me, the way my limbs were bent, the way my face was still twisted up in agony—that finally started her crying. And when she did, so did I.

I felt her inside my muscles again, soothing this time, finding every little stab of pain and snuffing it out.

All the pain except the one in my heart. That one just kept getting bigger and bigger, as the truth set in. She gathered me up in her arms.

"I'm sorry," she whispered. "He's gone. No one knows what happened to him."

Connor. Gone.

Was he kidnapped? Broken? Dead?

Radha held me, and I held her.

Three charred corpses lay in the mud around us. "Your friend fought like hell," a neighbor said. "Took out a whole bunch of them. But there were just so many. They got him too. Took them both away."

Niv. Ready to sacrifice himself, for the people he loved. Just like when he ran away with Ash, knowing he'd be risking execution, because he put her safety above his own.

Pretty soon I'd have to get up from the ground, go meet Ash. Figure out how the hell we were going to save our friends.

I was so, so tired.

I howled. Wind echoed it. Rain fell down on us like we had done something horribly wrong, like we hadn't suffered enough.

FORTY-ONE

ASH

It rained like we had all done something terribly wrong. Like God was punishing us. My windshield wipers could hardly keep up. Nobody was out. The roads were ours.

"Stop the car," Solomon said, after fifteen wordless minutes. I'd tried talking to him—asking him questions, about what went on back at the precinct—but he hadn't answered. Just cried, as quietly as he could.

I couldn't take him to my house. That's the first place Mr. Barrett would have gone to. And I'd turned my phone off, so my parents couldn't reach me when he told them about the idiotic thing I'd done. And I didn't know where else to go. Where it was safe. So we kept driving.

"Please, Ash," he whimpered. "Please stop."

"Solomon, we're in the middle of nowhere," I said.

We'd somehow ended up along the river, on the narrow rarely used roadway between the railroad tracks and the Hudson River, south of the Rip Van Winkle Bridge.

"Stop the car," he said again, and reached for the handle.

Too late, I thought to lock the door. He'd already opened it, and the wind howled through the opening like a savage monster that had been waiting for its chance to get in. Only the seat belt he'd forgotten to unbuckle stopped him from leaping out.

"Okay, okay, Jesus," I said, slowing down. "You'd fucking break a leg if you tried to get out at that speed."

He sat back in his seat. Unbuckled his seat belt. He did not shut the door. As soon as I'd slowed to a stop, he was out of the car and off again.

"Shit," I said, turning off the car, following him into the rain. I screamed: "Where the hell are you going?"

FORTY-TWO

SOLOMON

"Where the hell are you going?" I screamed.

Ash didn't answer. She kept walking, along the rails, into the dark.

"What the hell, girl?" I asked Maraud, but Maraud was just as confused by her behavior as she was by all human behavior.

"Ash!!" I called. I could see her in the darkness ahead of me.

I'd returned from the Underbridge to find her sitting on the rails in a kind of trance, with Maraud standing guard over her. When I squatted down and touched her hand and said her name she'd opened her eyes, looked startled, then gotten up and walked into the darkness.

Was there something here she was looking for?

Something she needed? Or was she broken beyond repair by the Palace's powerful magic? Was this part of her healing, or part of her damage?

I ran after her. Already the storm had soaked me so thoroughly that I didn't feel it anymore, couldn't tell the difference between air and rain, water and wind.

And then she stopped. Stood still. Tilted her head back. Lifted her face to the downpour. Turned toward me. Her eyes were shut, but I could see her smile.

"I feel it," she said, when I reached her side. "I can feel it breaking. The spell I'm under. The rain helps. It's real. It's here, now, in this moment. I'm here."

"Okay," I said. I had to say it loud, to be heard above the wind. "So . . . we just stand here?"

She opened her mouth, let rain collect there. Laughed, spat it at me. In her face, in her eyes, the old Ash was coming back.

We were standing on the railroad tracks. Riversea waves crashed at our feet. I knew what she was talking about. I felt it myself. The elements were strong, here. Everything else was stripped away. We were rooted firmly on the Earth, on the stone and metal of the train tracks. Breathing in air, surrounded by water. Fire burned inside of us, and twinkled in the distance—lights on the riverboats; cooking fires along the quay.

"It's not safe here," I said to her.

"It's happening," Ash said. "I remember."

FORTY-THREE

ASH

.

"What do you remember?" I asked.

"That night," Solomon said. "The night you fell."

He grabbed me by the arms, pulled me into a hug. His whole body was shaking. Not from the cold.

"It's okay," I said. "We're going to be okay."

A bell clanged on a buoy out in the river. Thunder thudded, distant now.

"I'm slipping," he said. "It's like the rain is washing me away. Washing all of this away, this Solomon-shaped person I've constructed. The walls are coming down. And I can't tell if that's a good thing or a bad thing."

FORTY-FOUR

SOLOMON

So we didn't talk for a long time. Just stood there in the rain, holding each other tightly, eyes shut, tuning out the whole world around us. Until I wasn't sure what world we were in anymore. Or who I was. Until I thought we were somewhere else—a place like ours but twisted, different, incomplete. I could see its outline, the shape of it, so close to ours, but not.

We held tight to each other. Like nothing else mattered. Like literally nothing else was real.

Lightning snaked along the edge of the sky. I braced myself for the thunder, prayed it would never come, wished I could stop time, keep this moment from ending.

But I knew I couldn't.

I felt her, now. Coming back. Felt the way her posture and her face took on a new strength, a new confidence. Something they'd been lacking. And then that confidence, that fearlessness, began to bleed into me. My fear began to shrink. Not by magic. Just because we were together, we were united, we were strong. "Tell me," I said.

"I can't tell you," she said, her eyes wide with excitement. "But I can show you. That's what I can do. *That's* my ability."

Vision magic: a rare and valuable power. To be able to see with perfect clarity what would happen in the future, or had happened in the past, or was happening far away in that very moment—people had built huge and powerful empires on the strength of a gift like that.

"Show me," I said.

She pressed her index and middle fingers to my forehead. Shut her eyes. The sound of the rain faded out. So did the darkness.

I was dry. There was no rain. No thunder. The smell of cold stone and chrysanthemums was in the air.

The Palace. The High Tower. Four years ago. Ash knelt on the floor of the central training area, twelve years old.

Ash's voice was in my ear, back in the here and now.

"My nine guards had spent that whole day, walking me through a seventy-two-movement martial arts routine, to focus the flow of energy through the body and awaken my ability."

Twelve-year-old Ash stood up. Shut her eyes.

"I felt so powerful. Like I could finally save my city. Show everyone what was really happening."

Twelve-year-old Ash stood in front of her guards.

"I looked, and saw this."

She showed them. And she showed me. Screaming in the streets. Fires burning in storefronts. Fists flying. Daggers pulled. Bodies. Bloody puddles. Broken glass.

"The Night of Red Diamonds," I said.

"I saw it all. The army of goons gathering at that very moment to go out and bash some heads. Me and my guards, we were going to stop it. I wanted to go with them, but they said it was too dangerous."

The guards held hands. One of them teleported the whole group of them away. Ash's vision shifted again, showed me the scene in Raptor Heights. No cops in sight. The goons arriving, brandishing sticks. A lot of them: thirty, maybe forty. Led by a woman in ultramarine. When Ash's soldiers showed up, the hooligans laughed at first. They had them so outnumbered.

Then the mayhem started. Fire arced through the air. Lightning descended from the sky. Windows shattered. People screamed.

Both sides were angry. Both sides were afraid. Everyone was out for blood.

In the morning, the crowds came. I saw the Shield standing on the sidewalk. Indistinguishable from all the other gawkers. Looking young; looking scared. One of the corpses was the woman in ultramarine; his mother.

The dark returned, and the rain. Ash and I were both crying by then.

The night that split our city wide open. The moment everything went wrong.

"It was me," Ash said. "I'm responsible for the Night of Red Diamonds."

"You weren't," I said. "Those jerks came to start trouble, and they got it."

"No," she said. "You don't understand. I thought I could stop it from happening, but I *caused* it to happen."

Thunder made her jump. I opened my mouth, but there was nothing I could say.

FORTY-FIVE

ASH

Thunder made him jump. He stiffened, stood up straighter.

"Shhhh," I said. "It's okay."

"It's not okay," he whispered.

He was right, of course. But I couldn't let him know it. "It's going to be okay," I said. "You'll be okay. Whatever he did to your mother—"

Solomon pulled back from me. Looked at me. His eyes were wild, haunted. "Did . . . to my mother?"

"Yeah," I said, afraid, then, that I'd made a bad mistake, prompted him to remember something he wasn't ready to remember. He'd said he recalled everything, but how would he know whether his memories were incomplete? "Mr. Barrett. He hurt her, didn't he? And you were so small and helpless compared to him, you couldn't help her. That's what started all of this. You—"

Solomon laughed. I was expecting a lot of responses, but not that one. "Is that what you think?"

I opened my mouth, but then I shut it. Because why *did* I think that? Why *had* I jumped to that conclusion? What evidence did I have?

Only the fact that Mr. Barrett was lying, and Solomon was afraid of him. And Solomon's mom was in jail.

Rain coursed down his face, flattening his hair to his forehead. He looked like a little kid who had just climbed out of a swimming pool. But when he spoke, he sounded less like a child than he ever had before.

"That night," Solomon said, and pain settled into my heart as he spoke, as his words unlocked memory.

That night. No one answers the door when I knock. Solomon's mother's car is gone from the driveway, but his stepfather's is there. A big bright red pickup truck, like something from a cartoon, except the smell inside is bad, like wet, dirty clothes. I hate when Mr. Barrett takes us anywhere in it.

So. Fifty-fifty chance. Either Solomon is home with his stepfather, or out with his mother.

Bingo, I remember. Wednesday nights his mother

plays bingo at the American Legion. Solomon loves the game, but hates the smoky room where they played it. So he's probably home.

I go around to the back. It's so dark there. I raise my camera to try to take a picture, but there is not enough light.

I open my mouth to call his name, and then decide not to. Solomon's imagination is very vivid, and when he plays his weird little game—Darkside City, he calls it—he hates to be jolted out of it. So I shut my mouth and begin to explore the yard. All the places he could be hiding: the shed, behind the trees, under the patio furniture. Even though I'm pretty sure I know where he is. Where he always is.

I climb the rungs nailed into the side of the really big sugar maple at the far end of the backyard. It is easy, now. I remember how hard it had been, back when Solomon first moved into the house four years ago. How much smaller we'd been. How we always had to stretch to reach the next rung. My camera swings slightly, around my neck, as I climb.

When I get to the top, I hear them on the other side of the tattered old red flannel blanket that hung in the doorway. Mr. Barrett, talking. His voice low, harsh, scary. Like how he talked to little Connor when Connor wasn't doing well at soccer practice.

Solomon, crying.

I decide to turn around. If Solomon is in trouble, if he is crying, he wouldn't want me to know. Walking in would only humiliate him.

I decide not to pull the blanket-door back.

I pull the blanket back.

I don't know why, or even how. I don't think about it. My mind makes one decision, and my arm makes another. Looking back on it so many years later— standing in the rain, between the river and the rails, there but not there—I realize why. Mr. Barrett had made my best friend cry. That was all I knew. My anger at him outweighed everything else. I grabbed hold of the curtain and I yanked it open, prepared to do . . . what exactly?

The film breaks down, at this point. The celluloid strip has snapped. Only freeze-frames remain. Photographs. A whole series of horrible images imprinted indelibly on my brain, stacked neatly in a folder. Hidden away for so long, but found now, and unforgettable.

Solomon, on his knees. Mouth open, fear and shock on his face. He is a child. Anyone can see it. He is saying my name, yelling it, but I can't hear him. All the sound is gone.

Mr. Barrett, on the far side of Solomon. Sitting on the bench. A cigarette in one hand. The other makes a fist. His face is clenched too, with so many emotions. You could spend a long time looking at the photograph, sorting them out. Frustration. Embarrassment. The struggle to come up with a Good Explanation for This. His eyes, however, hold only anger. They look like lightning might shoot out of them.

Close-up: Mr. Barrett's gray sweatpants, down around his ankles.

In my brain: raw confusion. The pieces do not add up. The images do not compute.

The confusion fades. I understand exactly what I am seeing.

Rage.

My little fists.

I take a single step back. I want to go back in time, unsee what I'd just seen, unhappen what was happening, undo what had been done to Solomon.

None of these things are possible.

My fingers go to my camera. Even at twelve, this is my instinct.

I take a small step backward, into space.

I fall.

FORTY-SIX

SOLOMON

The rain had mostly stopped, by the time we finished piecing the rest of the puzzle together. We assembled it from what I remembered, and rumors I'd heard and newspaper reports I'd read, and Ash's memories, and the scraps of images she could summon up. She wasn't back completely, not yet. Her ability was still chaotic, uncontrollable. We sat on the rails, facing the riversea, watching waves lap at the shore.

"My mother," Ash said. "She convened an emergency session of her governing council, told them about what I had done. Police Commissioner Bahrr used it against her—threatened to tell the press that it was my fault, reveal that I was an othersider and that I had instigated the attack."

She picked up rocks, threw them into the water.

"It was a way to gain control. He told my mother I was dangerous, my power couldn't be contained, and talked her into having the palace sorcerers sedate me. They agreed to cover up the alleged proof of my guilt, but forever after it was a threat hanging over her head. She knew if she pissed them off too much, they could reveal to the public the intel they had on me, and the public outcry could destroy the monarchy."

"Did your mom even care what your side of the story was?"

"It didn't matter. She thought that I wasn't in control, that my gift involved some kind of dark magic."

I stood up. "And now Commissioner Bahrr and the Shield are working together. And he has Connor, and Niv. How are we going to stop him?"

Ash shut her eyes. I saw them twitching; saw them move back and forth beneath her eyelids. Trying to control what she saw; trying to track down information that could help us.

Finally she opened her eyes. Shook her head no.

"You'll get it," I said.

Queen Carmen had kept her a secret. She was afraid her daughter wouldn't be safe if everyone knew she was an othersider. But what if the opposite was true? What if the secrecy made us vulnerable? Darkside had so few proud, visible othersiders. We stayed in the shadows.

Hate and fear kept us quiet.

Ash could change all that. If she stepped into the spotlight, if everyone knew what she was, maybe we could stop being scary stories that people like the Shield told to make people afraid, and to make themselves more powerful.

"We need to get out of this rain," she said.

"There's a brakeman's hut over there," I said. We headed that way.

A sound like thunder echoed through the sky, but unlike thunder it just kept growing.

"Ash," I said, pointing to something very high up, bright lights flickering on the wing of something impossibly far away.

"That's an airplane," she said.

"What the fuck is an airplane?"

"A machine," Ash said. "Like a really big trolley that flies. It can go very vast distances very quickly. Over sea, over land."

"How do you know that?"

She shrugged. "Ever since I woke up, I know lots of weird things that don't make a lot of sense. Stuff from . . . the other side?"

"So why can I see it now?"

She shrugged again. The airplane's howl echoed across the sky. "Maybe we broke the universe."

FORTY-SEVEN

ASH

There is no other word for it: I howled.

I knew there was nothing to say. No words that would fix this. But I couldn't be silent. Couldn't shut my mouth. I wept, and I wailed, and I screamed, and I howled. I dropped to my knees, because it was getting hard to breathe. Probably I was hyperventilating. Hopefully I was dying. It would be so much easier to never have to stand up again.

The universe was broken.

I howled until my eye twitched uncontrollably, until a headache wrapped all the way around my cranium.

"Ash," Solomon said, high above me in the rain.

"Oh god, Solomon," I said. "Oh god, I am so, so sorry."

"Ash, no," he said, and got down on his knees beside me. "It's not your fault."

I remembered everything. Lying on my back, on the ground. Moving in and out of consciousness. Seeing him in the doorway up above me, holding on to the tattered red blanket. Seeing Mr. Barrett behind him. His pants hastily, sloppily pulled up.

The hospital, after. My arm, broken. My skull cracked, around my eye.

More importantly, I remembered the not remembering. The days of darkness. The way nothing was clear. The dream I'd had, that city of rain and fire and monsters, giant squids and manta rays that swam through the skies, spiders as big as people who infested vacant buildings.

I lay back, into the mud. Solomon lay back too. I grabbed his hand. Our fingers interlaced.

"I'm so sorry," I said. "I should have done something. Said something. But I didn't remember. Not enough . . ." Since that day all that had remained was a suspicion. A fear. A knowledge that Solomon had been hurt in some irrevocable way. And that I couldn't do anything about it. And sometimes there wasn't even that.

"You blocked it out by accident," he said. "I did it on purpose. I was so scared, all the time. I used to have nightmares. They started bleeding into when I was awake. I tried my hardest not to think about it. To lock it up tight. And eventually, I guess it worked. I knew I hated him—I knew I was afraid of him—but I never knew why. The other night, after the bonfire, things started to come back to me. But now . . ."

Thunder boomed twice in the time I spent waiting for Solomon to finish his sentence.

I pressed the heels of my hands into my eyes, trying to calm the headache that originated there. The pressure helped only a very tiny bit.

I said, "We have to make him pay."

"We can't," he said. "Football coach, All-American dad. Who do you think they'll believe?"

"It won't be your word against his," I said. "I saw it. I remember it, now."

"He's buddies with lawyers," Solomon said. "And they'll say 'How convenient that you remember everything, all these years later.' Poor kid, she fell out of a treehouse, went weeks in the hospital. Her best friend is a fucking mental case and he's in trouble. She's desperate to help him. She'd say anything. She may even believe what she's saying. Poor kid."

He was right, of course. Apparently he watched the same shitty cop shows as my mom.

"Some other way," I said. "We *can* make him pay. I don't know how, but . . ."

"Like what?" Solomon said. "Cut his brake lines? That man already did enough damage to me, Ash. I refuse to let him hurt me anymore. Or you."

A train whistle split the night.

"We should move," I said. "We're pretty close to the tracks."

"We'll be fine where we are," he said. "I come here all the time."

We could hear the metal rails whine. These weren't the freight tracks, where the trains came through slow and solemn. These were the passenger lines, that stretched north to Montreal and south to New York City, and from there to every city in the country. Follow them long enough, and we could get anywhere.

I took my hands off my eyes. The world looked different, now. Brighter. Weirder. I couldn't see the other side of the river anymore.

The ground shook, as the train came nearer. I propped myself up on my elbows, to see it better.

The headlight cut the night in two, swinging around the bend, catching us in its wide, bright sweep. The conductor, who must have seen us, blew his horn. Three short toots, a friendly sort of hello. Probably train conductors saw a lot of weird shit out their windows.

And then it was screeching past us, and the light from the windows turned us a deep shade of amber. Solomon wasn't looking. His eyes were on the sky. The rain. The spot where the moon was showing a rip in the clouds, in the distance, to the west, where they were ragged and torn, like maybe this storm would finally be coming to an end.

I looked. I saw the people inside, asleep or reading or watching things on phones or tablets. Some were looking out the window, but they were all peering into the distance, the Catskill Mountains, the lights of the Rip Van Winkle Bridge up ahead. Dreaming of their destinations.

Only a little girl saw me. Just for a split second, but I saw her eyes widen. I wondered what she thought of the filthy wet woman in the mud, in the night, in the pouring-down rain. At first I hoped she wasn't too scared, and then I decided it was okay if she was. The sooner you learned there were monsters in the world, the better.

I watched the train until it was long gone, leaving us alone with the river and the rails and the sky.

The sky, where something moved. Too solid to be a cloud. Moving too fast. Black as the night. Swimming through the air with broad slow strokes of a massive tail.

"Do you see that?" I asked, pointing.

"The sky whale? Of course."

"Of course," I said, and watched a massive sea creature as it descended from the sky and dove into the river.

Of course the world would never be the same again. We had passed through something, Solomon and I.

Fighting it wouldn't do me any good. Whatever weird shit came along, I would roll with it.

"I know what to do with you," I said.

"Do with me," he said, and laughed. "Is this the part where you take me out in the back, tell me about the rabbits, and shoot me in the head?"

"Shut up," I said. "I never liked *Of Mice and Men*, anyway. I'll sneak you into my basement; you can sleep there tonight."

He sat up. "I'll be fine out here. There's an old duck hunter's shed, in the swamp not far from here."

I sighed. "It's late October and you've been out in the rain and it's going to get cold as hell tonight. You're not sleeping alone in a dark shed in a goddamn swamp."

"Well, when you put it like *that*," he said. "It does sound kind of terrible."

We went back to my car, and got inside. I turned the key, cranked up the heater, but didn't put the car in drive right away. Instead, we sat there, listening to rain hitting the roof.

FORTY-EIGHT

SOLOMON

Rain tapped away at the tin roof over our head. The brakeman's hut smelled of oil and stale tobacco, but it was dry. Ash lay with her head in my lap. We held hands. Our teeth chattered.

I thought, *I could really go for a cup of Radha's hot milk tea right now.*

And then I thought, *My gods. Radha.*

Connor.

"What?" Ash asked, when I sat up with a start.

I leaned forward, pressed my hands to my temples.

Thirty whole minutes had gone by, and I hadn't thought about him once.

They took him. This beautiful kid, this boy with an incredible gift. They were going to take it away from him. If they didn't do something way, way worse.

"What's the matter?" Ash asked, sitting up, rubbing my back.

"It's Connor," I whispered, hating how much it hurt to say his name. "And Niv."

I told her everything. The rhythm of the rain slowed down, in the time it took me to tell her. And then we just sat there. Something huge and heavy moved through the night outside our little hut—maybe a titanosaur, maybe a land dragon. Then it stopped, and let loose the most heart-rending wail. Like a foghorn on the edge of forever, crying out for ships that never come.

Ash stood.

"This is my fault," she said. "Those Destroyers came looking for me."

I took her hand, started to say, *No, don't say that, you couldn't have known, it wasn't even your choice to come to the Underbridge.*

"We'll get them," she said, before I could get out a single word. "I promise you that."

I believed her. I had no reason to, but I did. Something in her voice was unshakeable. I should have known right then and there what she was planning. What she was willing to do.

I wasn't scared. I should have been, but I wasn't. Ash and I were together, and together we were unstoppable.

FORTY-NINE

ASH

Long after midnight. The streets were dark and wet. No one was out. The world belonged to us and us alone. I should have been scared, but I wasn't. Solomon and I were together, and together we were unstoppable.

The whole drive home, I practiced my lying. Said things out loud over and over again. Practiced my responses to every conceivable thing my parents would say. Kept my face blank, empty. Rooted out all my tells, every little tic and jerk and eye movement that might let on to them when I wasn't being 100 percent honest. Until I felt . . . ready.

Two blocks from my house, I pulled over. "Get in the back and lie down on the floor," I told Solomon. "Stay there for the next thirty minutes. Do you have a watch?"

He shook his head no.

"Phone?"

"No."

"Well, shit. Try counting to sixty thirty times. Then get out—don't slam the door—and go around back. I'll have unlocked the door to the basement by then. I'll leave you some sheets and blankets and stuff."

"You still have that big Totoro beanbag chair?"

"Yeah."

"I want to sleep on that."

"Of course," I said, touching his wet arm. "Although it might not be as big as you remember it. We've both grown a lot, since we were ten."

He frowned, got out, went around to the back seat. When he was in the car again I pointed to the side of the road, where a trio of rabbits as big as dogs, with antlers like deer, were chewing on a bush. "Should I be concerned about those?"

"No," Solomon said. "They're jackalopes. Harmless scavengers." He got down on the floor, curled up into the smallest ball he could.

As soon as I pulled into the driveway, I knew at once that all my preparations were insufficient. Woefully inadequate. Because Mr. Barrett's car was parked in our driveway.

Which, of course it was. Because he'd known that sooner or later I'd have to come home. Because finding

Solomon was his number one priority. Because he was afraid of Solomon. What Solomon could say, what he could do.

But, as far as he knew, only Solomon knew the truth of his crimes. I hadn't said a word in all that time. He believed I had completely forgotten. I needed to make him think I still had.

So I sat in my car in the driveway and took ten deep breaths, and then went inside.

"Ash!" my parents exclaimed, when I slammed the door shut, intentionally too loudly, so they'd come running. Which they did.

"Hey, guys," I said, making my face expressionless, making my voice sad.

They saw I was okay. They hugged me. And then they got mad. Assaulted me with questions, one on top of the other.

"Where the hell have you been—"

"We called a hundred times—"

"Left you a million messages—"

"This bad weather—"

"Anything could have happened—"

"All kinds of awful car accidents—"

"Super sorry," I said, and took out my phone. "It got soaking wet, out in the rain. I had to turn it off. Take the battery out. Wait for it to dry."

This mollified them slightly. An explanation was all

they needed. Even a kinda stupid one.

"Hello, Ash," Mr. Barrett said, stepping out of the living room. Looking concerned . . . but also looking intimidating. The smell of beer was in the air; baseball gabbed from the television. They'd been sitting around, probably for hours.

"George was telling us what happened," Mom said.

"What you did was very irresponsible," Dad said.

"What?" I said, eyes wide, all innocence. "What did I do?"

"Solomon was signed over into my custody," Mr. Barrett said. "You were wrong to take him."

"I am so sorry," I said, eyes sad, truly penitent. "But maybe I misunderstood. I thought you said no charges were filed. So he couldn't even have been technically under arrest. So . . . why would he need to be in anyone's custody?"

He frowned. And my father tilted his head slightly. Only I, and maybe my mother, knew that's what Dad did when something didn't quite add up. "Not *formal* custody," Mr. Barrett said. "But they released him into my care. I felt a sense of responsibility. I was very worried."

"He wanted french fries," I said. "He said you hated McDonald's"—this was true—"and would never ever take him or Connor there." Also true. "He asked me to take him. Nothing wrong with that, right?"

Mr. Barrett opened his mouth, but in the split second

of hesitation that followed I saw exactly how to proceed.

"I took him to your house right after," I said. "Why weren't you there?"

"I was here," he said, and something was gone from his voice, a small degree of his normal cool and control.

"Why?" I asked.

"I was waiting for you. The way you two ran off—"

I laughed, but just a little. "Yeah, I mean, I get that. Solomon *was* pretty spooked. The county jail will do that to you."

"It's been hours, Ash," Mom said. "Where have you been all this time?"

"Me and Solomon went for fries, and a long drive, then went back to Mr. Barrett's. Like I said, he wasn't there. If only someone had been home . . ."

Both my parents looked at Mr. Barrett. Waited for an explanation. Even a stupid one. While he fumbled for it, I proceeded to line up the last few straws that would be needed to break the camel's back.

"He was worried," I said. "Thought you'd be mad at him. Asked me to leave him there. Sitting on your front stoop in the rain."

My mom made a small *awww* noise. Mr. Barrett doesn't have a porch. No shelter from the storm.

"You should find him there. That is, if he stayed," I said. "He might have run off. Gone anywhere, really. You know how Solomon is."

No one spoke, not right away.

Boom. My work here was done. Mr. Barrett was the irresponsible one here. The one who they believed had acted irrationally.

"Damn," he said, and chuckled. "You're right. I guess I wasn't thinking straight. Figured this would be the first place the two of you would go, so I came over, and then me and your mom and dad got to talking, and before you know it, here we are." He smiled, and my parents smiled back. An explanation; even a stupid one. "Better get home, then."

Goodbyes were said, embraces and handshakes exchanged. When Mr. Barrett looked at me, I could see the frustration in his face. He had underestimated me. He didn't know my intention, but he *did* know that this conversation had not gone the way he'd fully expected it to.

And even though I knew it was stupid, dangerous, ran the risk of exposing how much I knew, I couldn't stop myself from saying, "He seemed pretty shaken up to see you. Scared, almost. What's that about?"

"Who knows," Mr. Barrett said, rubbing his chin. Looking dead at me. Eyes ablaze. "You know how Solomon is."

"Yeah," I said. "I do."

A rusty hinge screeched as Mr. Barrett shut the door behind him. Me and Mom and Dad hugged. Talked for a little while, and then they returned their attention to the television. A regrettable incident, as far as they knew, but small, and settled now. The smell of our living room had never been so comforting.

And I needed to go get some blankets.

FIFTY

SOLOMON

"She should be fine until the morning," said Anchal, our neighbor from two doors down. She emerged from Radha's bedroom, holding a blanket. Anchal was a sleepsider, able to make anyone doze off no matter how stressed out or addled they were. Anchal spent an awful lot of time helping people rest in difficult moments.

"You're amazing," I said, and hugged her.

"He's going to be okay, yeah?" Anchal asked. "Our little boy?"

"We're going to find Connor," I said. "Nothing will happen to him."

"Give these to Radha when she wakes up," she said, and handed me a plate of cheesy biscuits. I set them down on the table, beside dozens of other delicious foods brought by neighbors.

Anchal nodded at Ash on her way out, but clearly did not recognize her. Between an oversize hood and some of Radha's makeup, expertly applied, the Refugee Princess had rendered herself invisible before we returned to the Underbridge. We'd gone back to be with Radha, hold her hand through the agony of this moment, but apparently she'd been so stressed—and so hell-bent on storming out to slaughter every Destroyer in sight—that her friends had intervened and talked her into accepting Anchal's help first.

I sat on a floor cushion, beside Ash. The smell of Radha's hut had never been so comforting. What did it smell like, wherever Connor was? Was someone being nice to him?

Images flooded me, against my will. Ugly dark rooms. Harsh words. Disgusting food, or none at all.

My spine shivered. My bones throbbed. Ash looked up at me sharply. My own anger had risen fast, and spread to her. I smiled and focused on breathing. Ten breaths later, I asked her, "Can you find him? See him? Wherever Connor is right now? And show me him?"

Ash looked into her hands. They were empty. It was a long time before she said, "I can try."

"I can help," I said, hoping it was true. Strong emotions had helped her remember the Night of Red

Diamonds. *Emotion is the key to memory.* Maybe it could unlock vision as well. "What kind of feeling would be most helpful?"

"Let's start with calm," she said.

But calm did not work. Five minutes of slow peaceful breathing produced nothing but images of the riversea rushing by, herbivorous dragons munching chestnut tree leaves.

Ash asked, "How about anger?"

I let myself drift back into the nightmare images. Connor in chains. Connor screaming. People laughing at his pain.

That worked better. Ash blinked, and we were gone from the little hut.

A massive movie theater. Abandoned now—the place smelled of mold and dust—but packed with people. Ultramarine armbands; posters that said "Destroy All Monsters."

Ash's voice echoed in my ear, in the real world. *"This is his headquarters."*

"Where is it?" I asked.

More scenes of hustle and bustle. Thick red carpet had been torn up in spots, and was worn thin in others.

"I can't place it. And I don't know if Connor and Niv are here. The things I see—I can't control what I see, or when, or why."

Giant crates were stacked along the wall. The seal of the Darkside Police Department was emblazoned on the side of each.

Ash said, *"Gifts, courtesy of Commissioner Bahrr."*

Of course. "The Shield is nothing without Bahrr," I said. "But it doesn't go both ways. If the Shield falls, Bahrr will be just fine. To take *Bahrr* out—we need your mom. We need to go to the Palace as soon as possible. You need to speak with her. Convince her. Make her—"

"Yeah," she said. *"Sure."*

The images kept coming. Me and Ash, in weird clothes, sitting inside of a giant metal box that smelled of leather and gasoline. Eating weird food: fried brown ovals. Both exhausted, both looking bleary-eyed and rough. Was it the other side?

"I *am* kind of hungry," she said, pulling us out of the vision.

"We should go get breakfast," I said. I grabbed the little radio, and we walked out into a weirdly warm day.

FIFTY-ONE

ASH

"Welcome to this weird, beautiful day," Ms. Jackson said, through my car radio, her gravelly smoker's voice soothing as ever. "Seventy degrees out, sun shining like summertime. They're saying it might get up to seventy-five. Doesn't seem right, for the end of October. Global warming, beloveds. We'll enjoy our nice days for as long as we can, I guess, until the rising seas swallow us up."

Solomon and I sipped our McDonald's coffee and picked at a pile of hash browns. Seven thirty in the morning and we were both exhausted, both looking bleary-eyed and rough. We'd driven around until McDonald's opened, and then we'd found a quiet place with no people.

"We have to tell Connor," I said. "We have to get him the hell out of there."

Solomon's eyes widened. "Oh my god," he whispered. "Oh my god, Ash. You don't think—"

"Hey," I said, reaching for him.

"Oh my god," he said again, and lowered his face into his hands. When he spoke again, I could hear how hard he was working to keep from crying. "All this time, I—"

"Mr. Barrett is a monster," I said. "Okay? His behavior is not on you."

"He always made me feel like I was less than Connor. Back then I kept thinking I was being punished for something. So I assumed Connor was safe. . . . What an idiot I—"

"Stop," I said. It was so hard to think and speak rationally about something so irrational, something that made me feel so full of rage and nausea.

I took out my phone, dialed Connor's number. No answer.

"It's a school day," I said, and laughed. "I forgot all about school." I must have been way more exhausted than I'd initially thought, because I laughed a lot longer and louder than the joke deserved.

"Almost eight," Solomon said. "So he's probably at the high school already."

"We'll get him," I said. "When school lets out,

we'll be waiting for him. Okay?"

"Yeah," he said, and looked out the window, to where the movie theater used to be. Everybody in town had a ton of happy memories of that place. I felt something die inside when it closed two years ago. "Can we go over to the old Greenport School?"

"Sure," I said. "You're missing your purple dinosaur?"

"Yeah."

I let him eat the last hash brown, then started up the car. Outside the McDonald's, three mummies stood around looking bored.

"What are those?" I asked Solomon.

"Mummies," he said, like that was totally normal.

I watched them. Waited for the sun to come out from behind a cloud and reveal them as nothing more than our own harmless local meth heads.

Was I losing my mind? Was the trauma of learning what had happened to Solomon so extreme that my hold on reality had been broken? Was I falling under the spell of his world?

When we got to the Greenport School, four girls our age were sitting on skateboards and smoking cigarettes in the parking lot. I didn't know them, though they looked familiar in that way everyone does in a small town.

"Hey, Solomon," one of them said. "You got your

guitar today? Gonna play us something?"

"Nah, sorry," he said.

I waved awkwardly. So did they.

His allosaurus awaited us, looking rough. Paint mostly peeled off, rusted over everywhere. But he hugged her like she was the prettiest sight he'd ever seen.

I lay on my back on the gravel beside him. I tried to explain Sheffield's Induction Ceremony. I wasn't sure why. Exhaustion, mostly. My brain wasn't working right. Made me talk a mile a minute. But then Solomon said, "He's a very good student."

"Who's a student?"

"Sheffield. He's like Mr. Barrett's, what do you call it? Protégé. His power comes from him. Sheffield is nothing without Mr. Barrett, but it doesn't go both ways. Why the hell is he still on the team if he doesn't play anymore? Mr. Barrett probably sees something of himself in him."

I sat up suddenly. He was right, of course.

Maybe there was nothing I could do about Mr. Barrett. Maybe he was too big and too well-respected for me and Solomon to hold him accountable.

But Sheffield . . .

I wasn't sure how, yet, but Sheffield was the weak link we could use to break the chain.

"I need to get that film developed," I said. "From the football team shoot. Want to come?"

Solomon stared off into the woods. Sound came, from a little transistor radio he had been carrying in his back pocket.

"What a beautiful day for Halloween," Ms. Jackson said. "My favorite holiday of the year."

"Solomon?" I asked, but if he heard me at all, he did not respond. I looked off to where he was staring, as if there might be something there to explain where he'd gone.

The woods had closed in on the school in the years since it shut down, tall grasses and shrubs and vines inching forward to encircle it. That ramshackle forest cut like a river through the whole town, or rather the town had been carved into the woods. Trailer parks and rows of identical duplexes and gorgeous old mansions all nestled in it.

"I used to be so scared of the woods," I said. "Anything at all could come out of them."

"Only animals," Solomon whispered, and it was like he wasn't really there. "The real monsters—they're all human."

FIFTY-TWO

SOLOMON

"Girl?"

Something had happened to Maraud. I squatted down and touched her cheek, and felt cold steel instead of warm pebbly skin.

"Who did this to you, girl?"

She was a sad, broken, rusty piece of metal, with most of her face flaked off. Smaller than me.

I staggered back, clamped a hand over my mouth to keep from crying out.

Maraud was not a monster at all, but some ancient toy that no one loved.

"This isn't real," I whispered—and looked around— and saw that we were gone from the Underbridge—that we stood outside some miserable broken-down building, covered in graffiti, where a couple of kids did drugs in the shadows.

There were no whales in the sky. No brontosaurus necks arcing high overhead.

"Solomon?"

It was Ash—but not. This person was stronger, in some ways. No wicked spell held her back. No faraway look glazed over her eyes.

But she was weaker, too. Not a princess. Not an othersider. Just a person. Like anyone else.

And the woods were empty. No monsters lived there.

I held out my hands, and felt how empty they were. Nothing lived in them. No magic.

As far back as I could remember I could feel it inside me, even if it took me years to figure out what it was and how to use it. Now there was nothing.

Once, when I was a hungry little kid—before the Palace, before Radha—sleeping wherever I could find a safe place, eating only what I could scavenge—I'd had the most wonderful dream.

A table was spread before me. Covered in candles; so long it disappeared into the distance. Piled high with food; a thousand plates of weird and wonderful dishes. Some were real, like the sweet-spicy–smelling wyvern kebabs I'd never been able to afford, or the cheap roasted chestnuts that kind fellow citizens would buy for me from time to time—but some were not, like a strange giant circle of dough that had red sauce and melted cheese on top of it, or tiny, little pale pink sausages crammed into strange little loaves of bread, or pink oranges that were actually orange.

At first I'd been afraid to eat it. Clearly it was meant for someone way more fancy and wealthy than me. But I took a handful of pomegranate seeds, and no one stopped me, so I went to town. Spent hours, it felt like, eating all that food.

I ate it until I woke up.

And I lay there, in the dark warm basement where I'd been lucky enough to fall asleep, and felt how I had nothing. No food in front of me. Nothing in my stomach. Nothing but pain and hunger.

Never in my life had it been so painful, to wake up into cold, drab miserable reality. And it never was again—until that moment, when I looked around and saw that I stood in a world with no magic, no dinosaurs, no monsters. How could humans survive in a world so ugly?

"This isn't real," I whispered again, and shut my eyes and focused on the red light of the sun that filtered through my eyelids, praying that when I opened them I was home and safe again.

FIFTY-THREE

ASH

Red light turned Solomon to stone, a statue carved from a massive ruby.

"I thought light would ruin the picture," Solomon said, looking up at the bare amber bulb. "Overexpose it."

"It's a safelight," I said. "Its light comes only from parts of the visible spectrum that photographic chemicals—especially those on the paper—are almost completely insensitive to."

"Almost," he said, dipping a finger into the stop bath. "So *something* is lost."

I swatted his finger away. "Shhh," I said. "Let me concentrate."

I still didn't know why we were there. What I hoped to achieve, looking at these photos. Why we were hiding in my basement instead of finding a way to punish Mr. Barrett. The only thing I knew was that I had to expose Sheffield somehow, and for the moment these images were the only tricks up my sleeve. To fight Sheffield, I had a plan. I had hope. To fight Mr. Barrett I had neither.

My parents were at work, but Mom had called me. Apparently, Mr. Barrett had phoned in the morning, to let them know Solomon had not been at home. And to imply that I hadn't been completely truthful with them. My father had said, *You really should have been there, George.*

Connor hadn't responded to any of my texts or calls. It was still only ten in the morning, and school let out at quarter to three.

The darkroom was my sanctuary. The only place I felt connected to something bigger than myself. Something all-powerful. I'd get a little sliver of the same sensation sometimes, taking pictures, when everything was right and I was connected to that essential *thing*—a shiver up the spine, a tingle all through my skeleton—but it was fragile and could come and go as it pleased. Only here could I really revel in it, tune everything else out. Dip my fingertips into warm water, move the squares of white paper back and forth, watch the world emerge. Taking pictures felt like capturing reality; printing them felt like creating it.

"Who's that?" Solomon asked, watching a boy slowly take shape in the tub of developer.

"Just watch," I said.

The darkest spots came in first. His black hair; the shadow he cast on the wall. And then the warmer grays, the shape of his smile and the arc of his shoulders and his jug-handled ears.

"Tom," Solomon said, when he saw what football player he was, sounding peaceful and calm in a way I could not imagine.

"How are you so chill right now?"

"Because I know my brother is going to be okay."

I didn't think I'd ever heard him call Connor his brother before. I didn't ask him how he knew he was okay. I tried to focus on feeling what he felt. Believing what he believed.

He sat down on the floor, and began to strum the guitar.

And, somehow, it helped. Calmed me down.

I plunged Tom into the stop bath, and then the tub of fixer. And then I moved on to the next negative.

I placed a piece of photographic paper under the enlarger. Focused the bulb and switched it on. Justin's face frowned up at me. I switched the bulb off, and the paper was blank once more. I shut my eyes again, and slid the paper into the bath of developer. The steps were familiar, mechanical. I ran my fingers across the smooth, glossy wet square, felt its potential, all the images it could come to carry.

Photography was magic.

Keeping my eyes closed, I remembered what I had seen when I looked through the lens. How different my visions had been, lately. The scenes I could summon up. Specific things, not the abstract senses of guilt or shame or anger I'd been seeing before.

If it worked when I took the pictures, could it work when I developed them?

"Hey, Solomon," I said, and the strumming stopped. "Did we ever figure out what my ability was? On the other side?"

"Seeing things you shouldn't be able to see," he said. "Visions. Secrets. The past, and the present."

I turned around to look at him, sprawled on the Totoro beanbag chair he had once been swallowed up in, and now dwarfed. But the look on his face, in the dim red light, was the same. Excitement over things I couldn't get my head around.

Maybe he lived in a different world. A crazy one. It didn't mean he couldn't be happy there.

"How do I do that?" I asked.

"You think of an image you want to know more about," he said. "Concentrate on it. Let it grow. Show you its connections to other things."

I shut my eyes. Imagined the photo of Justin. The pouty look on his face when I told him what to do.

A tremor went through my chest. Like a second

heart, beating beneath my breastbone. Like something was flowing through me, from some other place (*the other side*), some other me.

I smelled old popcorn, spilled soda. Body odor. Burning.

Eyes still shut, I focused on the dark clouds around Justin. They bubbled and swelled in my mind's eye, and I began to try to . . . push them. Show me what I wanted to see.

His worst moment, I thought. *His Induction Ceremony.*

I opened my eyes and watched it take shape on the paper. First, the dark spots. Shelves stuffed with giant sacks of dog food. Distant people. And then the lighter pieces: Justin standing with his arm out, dropping a match. Bright flames blooming.

Justin setting the fire in Walmart.

"Solomon," I whispered. "Come here?"

He stood, and came to my side.

"What do you see?" I asked.

"Just stupid Justin," he said. "It's a good picture, though. You captured how stupid he is."

"Thanks," I said, stepping back from the developer, mind racing, wondering what this meant, what I could do with this.

Solomon couldn't see it. But—I thought, with sudden, electric certainty—what if Justin could? It was an unbelievable idea, an impossible one. Yet somehow it felt like another puzzle piece falling into place.

"Go upstairs and make us some tea?" I asked Solomon. "I have work to do."

He went.

My phone rang. *Connor.* I answered it immediately, smearing the phone with wet chemicals.

"What the hell, Ash? What's the emergency that has you blowing up my phone?"

"Connor, thank god." I looked at my phone—it was almost eleven. Plenty of time before school let out. "Wait for us after school, okay? Me and Solomon are going to pick you up."

Silence. "Solomon? Is everything okay?"

"Basically," I said. I didn't have the heart to lie. "We just want to talk to you, that's all."

A sound from upstairs. Solomon fumbling around in the cabinets. "Solomon hates me," Connor said.

"Solomon has never hated you," I said. "And . . . I can't explain it now. We'll pick you up by the side cafeteria door right when the last bell rings, okay? Don't get a ride with anyone else. Anyone."

Especially your father.

"Fine," he said, sounding small, sounding young. "I was gonna call you anyway. Got a few discussion topics of my own."

I'll add them to the meeting agenda, I started to say, but he had already hung up.

A whole lot of work was ahead of me. Two hundred and fifty exposures, five to ten of each player, with one frame of each circled in black Sharpie.

I poured out fresh chemicals, savoring the sharp stink of them, and got to work. Solomon came down, with two cups of tea and his transistor radio.

"Weird weather today, children," Ms. Jackson said. She always called her listeners *children*, like she was older than absolutely everyone in earshot. "All that glorious warm sunshine seems to be fading fast, and the mercury is dropping along with it."

I told Solomon about the call from Connor. We each took a long sip of tea.

FIFTY-FOUR

SOLOMON

"Weird weather today, children," Ms. Jackson said, on the radio perched on the table between us. "Might want to bundle up after all, wear a sweater or two under your Unmasking Day disguise."

I opened my eyes. Maraud's face was inches from my own, staring at me with great concern. Her real face, not that pathetic rusty thing she had been in—wherever that horrible place was.

"Hey, girl!" I said, with a laugh, and hugged her huge snout. "I went away for a second. But I'm really happy to be back."

Pterodactyls squawked in the dockside air overhead. The smell of the riversea was strong. I breathed it in deep. I'd never have imagined I could be so happy to smell kraken ink.

Ash asked, "What happened to you?"

"I went somewhere," I said. "Somewhere horrible. What about you?"

"I just saw a lot of weird shit."

"Nothing that could help us find Niv and Connor?"

"A couple things might be clues. I have to go back under."

Ms. Jackson continued: "News now on the story that has the whole city talking—the abduction of the Refugee Princess."

"Shit," Ash and I said at the same time.

"With no word yet on her whereabouts—and in light of recent violent incidents all over the city—the Darkside Police Department has been conducting raids on known othersider gathering places." Ms. Jackson sounded as unhappy as we were, about this abuse of authority. "Queen Carmen has so far not responded to Commissioner Bahrr's call for a sunset curfew on all othersiders, and while the police department has no power to take a step like that without royal approval, the commissioner maintains that the city charter does grant him full authority to ask all uniformed officers to conduct random stops of Darkside citizens, and detain any othersiders for further questioning—"

Ash switched the radio off.

"He can't do that," I whispered.

"He's doing it," she said. "He's been waiting for this moment for a long time, and the Shield finally handed it to him. If I hadn't—"

"Stop saying that this is your fault," I said. "This city was full of hate and fear long before the Night of Red Diamonds."

She did not look convinced.

"We have to get in touch with your mother," I said.

FIFTY-FIVE

ASH

After the fifth time I nodded off, standing there in the darkroom with my fingers in the tray of stop bath, I decided I needed a nap. Solomon said that sounded like a great idea. We went up to my room, spooned together on the bed. I set my alarm for two hours.

What I needed was some good deep empty dreamless sleep, but as soon as I shut my eyes I was . . . somewhere else.

I was not in my bedroom. Not in Hudson.

Solomon and I still lay together. His forehead was still pressed into the back of my neck. But we were in a weird little hut that smelled like sweet milk tea. And there were birds calling outside that sounded like no birds I'd ever heard.

I got up and went to the window. Thinking I was ready for what I would see.

I was not ready.

Not for the massive bridge that arced overhead, a hundred times bigger than any bridge in the real world. Not for the old woman pushing a shopping cart, accompanied by a velociraptor. And not for the little kids practicing magic, summoning up images of monsters.

The other side. Where I was the Refugee Princess.

And it wasn't just the world around me that was different. I was different too. I felt it inside. Some of it felt like weird fuzziness, as if I was drugged or half asleep.

Some of it felt . . . amazing. My arms tingled.

And I could see things. Whatever I wanted to see.

The Truth, even.

I lay back down beside Solomon. Still asleep, he wrapped his arms around me again. I shut my eyes to breathe in the smell of him. Of this moment.

I cannot keep you safe, I thought.

FIFTY-SIX

SOLOMON

Ash opened her eyes. She'd had them shut for fifteen minutes, fingers twitching like she was shuffling through a deck of cards.

"I know where they are," she said.

"Connor and Niv?"

"Yeah. Darkside Cinema Palace. I saw it. And I can control it, now—what I see."

We lay there in Radha's hut, listening to children laugh outside. I wanted to ask her to show me Connor, see how they were treating him. But if it was bad, I didn't want to know.

Ash stood up. Went to the window, and smiled at whatever she saw out there. I wondered if she had gone away as well. To whatever awful, magicless world I'd been to.

She tilted her head to one side, and then the other. Flexed her hands together in front of her.

The spell was gone. I could see that now. Nothing was holding her back.

She did not need me.

"We should go," I said. I debated waking Radha. Her powers would certainly come in handy. But the Shield's headquarters would be packed with angry, powerful soldiers and I felt weirdly certain that we would be walking into our own doom. I couldn't get Radha hurt too.

"First, I need to try to reach my mother," Ash said.

"Okay," I said, but neither one of us moved. The smell of the river was strong. Birds squawked in the air overhead.

I didn't want the moment to end. Soon this would all be over, one way or another. One or both of us would go down in the attempt to rescue our friends—but even if we emerged victorious, she was still the princess. In the unlikely best-case scenario where we brought down the Shield and saved the city and she reclaimed her rightful place running it, she'd have a whole crowded life with very little room for me. She would leave me behind forever.

Either way, I felt like she was already half gone.

FIFTY-SEVEN

ASH

"It happened more than once," Solomon said.

The smell of the river was strong. Seagulls squawked in the air overhead. Connor was crying. We sat on the rocks at the river's edge and shivered. Looking across to Athens, to the abandoned quarry's loading dock and the empty silo that used to hold— I didn't know what it held. The lights of the Rip Van Winkle Bridge were just coming on.

"This is real? This really happened?" Connor asked me, but I could see in his eyes that he already knew, already believed.

"Yeah," I said. "I saw it. I blocked it out for a long time, but I remember it now. I remember everything."

"Why didn't you say anything?" Connor asked

Solomon, and I gasped, because of course I'd wanted to ask the same question, but I'd had too much sense.

"This isn't on Solomon," I said. "He was a kid."

"I know!" Connor said. "I'm not an idiot. I just mean— I wish I could have . . ."

He didn't finish the sentence. He wanted to think he could have done something about it, protected his brother, helped him, stopped the bad man from hurting him, even if the bad man was his father.

"It's okay, Ash," Solomon said. Then he turned to Connor. "Honestly, for the longest time, I didn't remember any of this. I had blocked it out, too. I was ashamed. I felt like it was my fault, at least a little bit. Ash and I used to joke about having crushes on your dad. For a long time I thought I'd said or done something to make him think I—I wanted it."

"Don't say that," I snapped.

"Don't tell him what to say!" Connor snapped back.

A bell clanged, out on a buoy. Seagulls screaked by overhead in the ultramarine sky. The world was very beautiful, and very ugly.

I could see things differently, ever since I'd returned from (the other side) that weird dream under the giant bridge. Like the Truth was closer now. Just out of reach.

"It had been happening for about a year," Solomon said. "The night Ash saw us—that was the last time. He got spooked, I think. He wasn't sure what you had

seen—what you'd remember. Whether you'd say anything. And then I ran away. . . ."

"Oh, Solomon," I whispered, and my hand went
to my mouth. It was stained and stinking from photo
chemicals. It felt like a whole other reality, the darkroom and the photos I'd developed.

But I'd done it. Somehow. Channeled the feeling; fed
it, stoked it, pushed it out through my fingertips. And I'd
captured images of each member of the team taking part
in his Induction Ceremony. Graffiti, arson, all of it. They
were blurry, sometimes, or awkwardly cropped, but real,
and convincing. When I switched on the full, bright flu-
orescent overhead light, the pictures hadn't gone away.
Solomon saw only portraits, but I saw. I knew.

And the photos were good, too. Some of them were
great, even. They captured something real and vital and
complex about each player.

*Maybe—somehow—someday—when all of this is over—I
could go back to Cass. I could have a future in this.*

"You really didn't remember anything?" Connor
asked me, and then hastened to add, "Not that it was
on you either."

"Those days, in the hospital and afterward . . . ," I
said. "They're still fuzzy. I remember being scared. And
confused. I knew something awful had happened, but
I didn't know what. I had these nightmares, so vivid I
couldn't tell them apart from reality. Monsters running

through the streets. Bloody broken glass."

"Me too," Solomon said.

"Did your mom know?" Connor asked, looking at his feet, at the rocks, at anything but his brother.

Solomon shook his head. "I never told her. I was scared of what he might do. To both of us."

"She burned his car—"

"Easy, Ash," Solomon said, and chuckled. "I know my mom. If she had any idea what really happened, she'd be in jail for murder right now. I don't know what he did to her, but he deserved whatever she did in response. And worse."

"I wish she *had* killed him," Connor said, and slid off his rock and buried his head in the crook of his elbow, the way you do when you sneeze, but he screamed instead. I rubbed one shoulder. Solomon rubbed the other.

I grabbed Solomon's hand.

"I'm going to be sick," Connor said, doubling over, pressing his forehead into his knees in a very Solomon kind of gesture. I felt bad, to have split his world down the middle like that. What would it do to me, to know my father was a monster?

But I'd rather know, than not know.

"No wonder you wanted nothing to do with me," Connor groaned.

"You look like him," Solomon whispered, but the

wind was strong and I wondered if maybe Connor didn't hear him. I hoped he hadn't, because I had, and that four-word explanation had gutted me.

Solomon looked out across the river. His eyes widened. I turned, and gasped at what I saw. Flying through the air, two animals: as big and long as trains, glinting in the sunset.

"A water dragon and a fire dragon," Solomon whispered. "Dragons wander—they never nest or build a home. And when two meet, they have a dance they do. A different one for every two elements. It's a super-rare sight."

Connor looked, but then looked down at his feet again. The way you do, when someone describes something that must be a figment of their imagination. Or their madness.

But I could see them. Serpentine creatures, Eastern-style dragons instead of the winged long-neck lizards of Western folklore. They coiled and looped together in an intricate, gorgeous dance. So complex I worried they'd get knotted together. The weird world Solomon lived in was so much better than this one. I almost envied him, that he got to live there all the time.

My meds were working, mostly, but I wasn't cured. I'd live, but I would never be cured. Not of this.

Solomon said, "I just . . . I had to get as far as possible

from everything that reminded me of him."

"I can't believe I never knew," Connor said. And then he opened his mouth and said, "I'm—" But then he stopped, because what could you say? *I'm sorry* was insufficient, almost insulting. He shut his mouth.

"Words are bullshit," Solomon said understandingly.

Impulsively, with the urgency of a frightened child, Connor leaped forward and hugged his brother.

I wanted to join in, but I checked myself. There was so much pain between them, so many obstacles, so many walls they'd built up around the little boys they'd been. The brothers who loved each other. They needed to get there together.

A barge moved past us on the river, its deck crowded with crates. I shut my eyes, breathed in and out, memorized every sense impression. The raw, wet muck smell of the river. The cold wind. The sniffling of the boys beside me. It was one of those moments I'd want to be able to remember, years and years later. The little instants that turn us into who we are.

"You had something you wanted to talk about," I said, twenty minutes later, when we picked ourselves up and brushed off our behinds and headed for the car.

"It's nothing," Connor said, wiping one eye. "Stupid bullshit, compared to this."

"Is it about Sheffield?"

"Yeah."

"Tell us," Solomon said. "Even if we can't punish Police Commissioner Bahrr for what he did, we can still stop the Shield if we know what he's got planned."

Connor and I made quick, furtive eye contact, but both of us promptly decided to leave it alone.

"I told him all about the Induction Ceremonies," I said.

"There's gonna be one last one," Connor said. "The final prank, to close it all out. Sheffield's own."

"I thought you still had to go," I said.

"I've been stringing him along, putting it off over and over. So much so that he's mad at me now. Sheffield's prank is the biggest and it's got to be during the Halloween dance, which is why he can't wait on me anymore. He's going to burn down the old Greenport School."

"What?" I said. "Why?"

"Because that's where all the weirdos hang out," Solomon said. "Right? That's who he's been targeting with all this. The people who are different."

Connor nodded. I hadn't connected those dots. But Solomon had.

Jewel was religious; didn't smoke, didn't drink. Didn't curse. So she made the people who did do these things extra uncomfortable.

Judy was Jewish. That was reason enough for lots of people to hate her.

The nerds and geeks, the suck-ups, targeted in the parking lot minefield.

Solomon, the crazy kid.

It tracked.

"Except that if it burns, so do the woods," I said. "And so does half of Hudson."

"He doesn't care about that," Connor said. "And he won't even be getting his hands dirty. He's got everybody on the team taking on a little piece of it. He says it's to divide the guilt up, but really it's because then *everyone's* implicated."

I thought for a moment.

The team. They could stop this. But I'd have to convince them to. The photos I'd developed, using my gift—once I confronted the players with them, I might be able to scare them into doing the right thing.

The sun was hidden behind the clouds, and the sky was getting darker and darker even though sunset was a long way away. On the radio, Ms. Jackson had said the weather was strange, and now out of nowhere we were looking at a thunder and lightning storm, and maybe even snow, if the temperature kept dropping.

I had a lot of driving ahead of me. A whole bunch of football players to visit, and confront.

But before any of that, I had to talk to my mother and father. I didn't know if they'd know what to do about Mr. Barrett—or if they'd even believe me when I told them—but I had to try.

Movies make a lot about the hero setting off alone to vanquish the monster. But those are movies. In real life, I needed all the help I could get.

FIFTY-EIGHT

SOLOMON

The sun was hidden behind the clouds. The sky was getting darker and darker even though sunset was a long way away. Out of nowhere we were looking at a thunder and lightning storm, and maybe even snow, if the temperature kept dropping.

"Nothing," Ash said, stepping out of the phone booth. "Couldn't reach anyone I trust."

She couldn't very well call and say, *I'm the princess, I need to talk to my mom*, not if the Palace was as full of spies as Niv had said. If they were cops, they might be able to trace the call.

"The place is on such high alert that even my asking for someone specific got them all suspicious."

"You sure you know where the Shield's holed up?" I asked.

Ash nodded.

"Should we start to head that way?"

She frowned. Doing so was almost certainly suicide, but if we had other options, I didn't know what they were.

"Wait," she said. "I want to try to reach my mother one more time. Not in person or on the telephone—with my ability. But for it to work, we need to get as close to the Palace as we can."

Maraud carried us through the busy late-afternoon streets. Posters with our faces on them had been put up in bus shelters and store windows. Ash wrapped a scarf around her face, and I had acquired a ridiculous hat from one of Radha's neighbors.

On every street corner, people argued. We caught snatches of conversation as we ran. Tensions were so much higher. Everyone seemed to be on edge. Afraid, and angry. Arguments started easily, over the smallest things. People said horrible things about the Crown and the Palace that they'd never have dared to say before.

But this was still our city. We could still smell roasting chestnuts, and garlicky noodles, and mammoth-milk ice cream. Stalls sold Unmasking Day tools and supplies, for a city full of people building masks for themselves.

The city belonged to the good people who just wanted to live their lives, not the wicked ones who wanted to divide us.

Two blocks from the Palace, Ash tugged at my sleeve. We stopped, and she whispered in my ear. "Go get us something to eat, okay? I want to be alone for this."

I climbed off Maraud, and went into a nearby bakery. Pretended to browse through breads and cookies, when what I was really doing was watching Ash. How her face darkened. How her lips moved, ever so slightly, like she was whispering in the ear of the queen.

And then I had to wait, until she was done crying.

"I don't think it worked," she said, when I came back out. "I don't even know if she could hear me. Or if she heard me, and was trying really hard not to."

I handed her a cinnamon roll, and climbed back onto Maraud.

Ash turned around to watch the Palace as we left it behind. Shimmering gray stone. The home she had never felt completely at home in, but loved all the same. I switched the little radio on, eager for some news, some distraction, but Ash turned it right back off.

FIFTY-NINE

ASH

Solomon turned the car radio on, but I switched it right
back off.

I looked up at my house. Pristine gray paint. The
home I had never felt completely at home in, but loved
all the same.

"What do you want to do?" I asked Solomon. "Wait
out here? Down in the basement?"

He looked off into the distance, and I was afraid he'd
want to leave. Go off on another one of his weird, wild
journeys. The time we'd spent together was making me
feel strong, stable . . . and I hoped it wasn't just pride
that made me think it was helping him too.

"I'll take a nap in the back," he said, opening his
door. "I'm so tired."

I hadn't told him, that I meant to tell my parents. Half of me thought maybe he wouldn't want me to. Wanted to keep this secret. Because telling my parents meant something might happen. And maybe that would get Mr. Barrett punished, but it also might make headlines, become gossip, cause a backlash . . . make Solomon's life even more hellish than it already was.

But staying silent couldn't be the right call. Could it?

"That sounds great," I said, watching him curl up across both back seats. "I love you, Solomon."

"I love you too," he said.

I headed inside. "Hey, honey," my mother said, when I got to the kitchen. Dad was there too, and I said a prayer of thanks that I'd only have to have this conversation once.

"Hey," I said. "I need to talk to you two."

I looked at my hands while I tried to figure out how to do this. Where to start. What to ask. They were ruined, my hands. All those photo chemicals. They looked like they belonged to an eighty-year-old. I'd need to moisturize, soon, and often.

"I saw something terrible," I said, without really putting any thought into how to say it. "I saw Mr. Barrett molesting Solomon."

"What?" my mother yelped.

My father spoke too. "Ashley, what are you—"

"It was up in the treehouse," I blurted. "When we

were twelve. The day I fell out of the tree."

"No," my mother whispered, but it wasn't the *no* of "I don't believe you." It was the *no* of "Please, God, no."

They stared into each other's eyes. Grasped each other's hands. Their faces searching.

I knew they were trying to make sense of a world that seemed to crack open. A world they didn't recognize.

"Ash," my father said, but it wasn't the *Ash* of "Come on, Ash, don't be ridiculous." It was the *Ash* of "Oh my god."

"Fuck," my father said, and clamped both his hands over his mouth. "Fuck." Stumbled backward, leaned against the wall.

I felt the tears threaten to spill over my cheeks. "I'm sorry, Daddy. I—"

My father shook his head. Held up his hand to silence my apology.

"All these years," he said, his voice so low it was hard to hear. "George, he—he always said that Solomon was crazy. Said he had *persecution fantasies*—told me that, over and over. Said he tried to hurt Connor. Implied that he had something to do with your falling out of the tree. And I believed him. I treated Solomon like a criminal."

I remembered what Mr. Barrett had said to me, about Solomon's mother coming from an Orthodox Jewish background. The casual, quiet anti-Semitism of it,

implying: *You know how those people are.* How many times
had he repeated that line, to the people around town?
How many people had he convinced she was crazy?

"Abusers they—they discredit their victims," Mom
said, her voice barely bigger than a whisper. "Make
everyone think they're liars or—or crazy. So if they ever
do ask for help, they . . ."

They won't get any. My mother couldn't finish.

And then my father started to cry.

I hadn't expected this from him. I'd expected denial,
him trying to tell me how his Good, Good Buddy Mr.
Barrett wasn't capable of anything so awful.

My mother took me by the arm, pulled me into a
hug. Eventually my father joined in.

An hour later I returned to the car, with two mugs full
of black coffee.

"Hey," Solomon said. He was lying there, eyes open,
looking past the ceiling. Holding his guitar, picking out
haphazard strings of notes.

"Hey," I said, handing him back his coffee. "Did you
nap?"

"Yeah," he said. "It was nice. You've been crying."

"Yeah," I said, and left a little silence, in case he
wanted to talk about it, but he just kept strumming. I
felt weird, light-headed. Powerful.

I need to do some research, my father had said. *Talk to some people. See what we can do about this.*

I'll call Jocelyn, Mom had said. *She's a lawyer. I'll give her the general info—nothing specific—and see what our options are.*

Promise me, I'd said. *You won't do anything without telling Solomon first. Making sure he's okay with it. We can't hurt him any worse than he's already been hurt.* And they'd promised. My parents hadn't fixed anything, but Solomon and I weren't in this alone. That made a difference.

"I'm going to Justin's house now," I said. "I'm confronting them all. The whole team, one at a time, for what they've done."

"Why?" Solomon asked. "That seems totally crazy."

I opened my mouth to answer, but realized I didn't have one.

I thought of Mr. Barrett. Whatever he was, he hadn't always been like that. He'd been a kid once, and full of magic like all children are. Somewhere along the line he got broken, twisted. And started hurting people.

"Because I want to believe that people have a choice," I said, struggling not to whisper. "Whether to become monsters. I want to believe that if you give them a chance, they'll choose not to continue hurting people." I paused. "Maybe you're right. Maybe it is totally crazy. Do you want to come?"

"Where you go I go," he said.

Which was lucky, because if he had said no, I might not have been able to do it on my own.

We went.

I wish I could say that I walked in there knowing exactly what to say, how to make them see the light, how to get them to do the right thing. But that's not the way it was. I was scared, and awkward, and didn't know what the hell to do.

Justin's house smelled like steamed dumplings, and his mom was supernice to us and I felt really awful handing him the photo I'd developed with my eyes shut, channeling (*the other side*) whatever gave me the ability to see things that weren't there, but were still real.

He stared at it for a long time, and then handed it back to me. Looked from me to Solomon and then back again. "How did you get this?"

So he *could* see it. So they *were* visible to the person who was in them.

"Never mind how," I said.

His Induction had been pretty mild, compared to the swastikas and arson of some of his teammates. He'd put a dirty magazine into the backpack of Rory Lowell, a Jehovah's Witness classmate of ours so strait-laced that back in first grade he had to go to the principal's office whenever we celebrated someone's birthday.

The photo didn't show what happened when the

magazine was discovered. If a parent found it and flipped out, or if Rory found it and recognized it for the bullying tactic that it was, if he got scared and upset. Or if he was superhappy about this forbidden fruit landing in his lap. It just showed a slightly blurry Justin sneaking it into Rory's backpack.

"Are you going to show my mom?"

My heart broke, at that. At the sadness in his voice. He wasn't scared of the cops or the teachers. He just didn't want to disappoint his mom.

"I'm not going to show anyone," I said, and did not add, *because no one but you and I can see this photo.* "But I want to stop the Induction Ceremonies, and I want your help."

He nodded. He listened.

"Sheffield is the one who should go down for this," I said. "He's the mastermind. But he only has the power that you give him. If everybody got together, you could stop this before it gets any worse. Before people get hurt, or go to jail."

He nodded, but slowly. He wasn't agreeing to anything. Not yet.

Thinking about Sheffield as the mastermind, it occurred to me for the first time to wonder what Mr. Barrett's place might be in all of this—the destruction planned by the football team he coached. If he knew about it; if he was involved.

"Thanks, Ash. For not telling my mom."

"No problem," I said. "Just please don't mention this to anyone, okay? Not yet."

"And stay tuned," Solomon said, standing up. "We'll call you soon, with how we're proceeding. What we need from you."

"Yeah," Justin said, and stood up too, and shook our hands very awkwardly. "Sure."

"One down, twenty-nine to go," I said to Solomon, when we were back in the car.

"You're amazing," he said.

"I learned it from watching you," I said.

In the rearview mirror, I looked at how he stared out the window. His face seemed to lose focus, and I wondered what he was seeing. From my car speakers, Ms. Jackson told us about the Hudson Police Department's plans for an increased presence at the annual Halloween dance, *in light of recent destructive acts.*

SIXTY

SOLOMON

We went back to dockside. Because we had nowhere else to go, and no idea what to do when we got there. I felt sick and scared and helpless. We knew something terrible was going to happen, and our power to do a damn thing about it felt so limited.

Ms. Jackson was droning pleasantly from the little radio, talking about the Darkside Police Department's plans for an increased presence at the Unmasking Day celebration, and then she cut out.

Citizens of Darkside came a familiar voice—boyish, almost cheerful-sounding. But it stopped the blood in my veins, made me tug hard at Maraud's reins, stopping her so short she snarled.

"Sorry, girl," I said, and kissed the top of her head.

The Shield said, *Please forgive this interruption. My followers have temporarily jammed the signal for several radio stations, to permit me this opportunity to speak to you directly.*

All up and down the block, people were hearing him. Some looked angry. Some looked excited. Happy. Proud.

At this moment, I am addressing the Refugee Princess.

Ash flinched. She was well-disguised, but suddenly I felt like we were both exposed. Visible to anyone.

Are you listening, Princess? I think you are. I know you found me. I felt you watching. Come to me, now, alone, and I shall trade your freedom for that of your two friends. No harm has befallen them. By morning, I cannot promise this will still hold true.

"Monster," I hissed.

People of Darkside. Tonight—finally—the truth will be revealed. The thing Queen Carmen has tried to keep hidden for so long. The proof that her time is over. I call on her to abdicate now, and set a date for free and fair elections.

Some people on our block cheered. Others looked like they were about to cry.

Do so now, or I cannot guarantee your safety and that of your beloved othersiders. Once they know the truth, there is no telling what the people of this city may do to you. And to all the monsters that live among us.

"We have to go," Ash said, her mouth inches from my ear.

"Please," I said. "Wait. Don't do this. Not without—"

She told me where to find the movie theater. She did not listen to my additional attempts to talk her out of this mission, or respond to any of them.

SIXTY-ONE

ASH

I wish I could say that I snapped my fingers and used my magic and made everything okay. Punished the guilty; brought peace and justice to the people who'd been hurt. Brought the whole sick Induction Ceremony scheme tumbling down. But that's not what happened. There was no grand gesture. There were only a lot of little gestures.

After Justin, I called Tom, got his address, asked when would be a good time for me to come by and show him the photos.

Ravi didn't pick up when I called, so I slid into his direct messages on Twitter and asked him the same questions.

I knew where Will lived, and I went there directly.

Some agreed. Some cried. Some told me to fuck right

off. Some swore they'd do whatever they could to help.

Regardless of the ultimate outcome, I knew something now. I could see things. I could use photography to make other people see things. That was my ability. My magic.

Solomon sat in on every meeting, but he rarely spoke a word. In some cases I figured it helped, having him there. A big strong guy, in case they felt like getting angry over what I was saying to them. In others I felt like it hurt me more than it helped—set them on edge, made them scared, silent.

I wish I could say that I had this conversation thirty times, once for each boy on the team. But lots of them never responded to my calls, or the hundred different forms of digital messages I sent their way.

Blair looked me dead in the eyes and shrugged and said, "Bros before hos." What I saw behind those eyes gave me the shivers, and they didn't go away for a long, long time.

Sheffield had broken him. Snapped something important. The boy he had been was gone.

That's what Mr. Barrett almost did to Solomon, I thought, and the shivers deepened. *Something broke in my best friend, but something survived too. Something stronger.*

On my way out of his house, however, I saw Blair's little sister sitting on the front lawn smashing toys together. Four, maybe five years old. She smiled at me when I came down the walk, but then she got distracted.

By a glowing blue fairy, the size of a sparrow, flying slowly through the air. The little girl laughed and reached for it, but it didn't stop, so she yelled, and it turned and did a slow figure-eight in the air before continuing on its way. That seemed to satisfy her, and she returned her attention to the toys in front of her.

I stopped, watched it go, turned to look at the little girl and tried to keep the shock off my face. "You saw that?" I asked.

She shrugged, like, *Duh.*

Shivers overtook me. A cold day had just gotten a lot colder.

What if Solomon's monsters weren't in his head—hadn't infected me as I followed him down the rabbit hole of his trauma? What if what I was seeing was just a different reality, no more or less valid than the one without monsters?

Children know that monsters are real. We forget, when we get older. When we decide we are grown-ups. We block out the monsters. Turn our backs on all that magic.

But maybe not everyone does. Maybe some people never leave that reality behind.

Maybe it wasn't trauma that made Solomon see the world as full of magic and monsters. Maybe it wasn't his sickness. Maybe that's just who he was. Special. Gifted.

Artists, writers, musicians—photographers—they all had to be able to tap into something *(the other side)* that wasn't there, some other better world, and grab hold of things, and bring them back so the rest of the world can feel the magic too. Diane Arbus did it, at great personal cost. The world was better for having her photographs in it, even if that struggle ended up killing her.

With a shiver, I realized: *It takes a very special kind of crazy to change the world.*

Solomon was already in the car. When I got in, I didn't ask him if he'd seen the blue fairy, or relay my conversation with the girl.

I looked at my list. So many dumb, gullible boys, so many petty, little crimes. Those football players weren't blameless, but Sheffield was the twisted brain behind it all.

Sheffield was the one I needed to focus on.

But by then it was late. And my head was spinning. And we were hungry. So we headed for my house.

"Shit," Solomon said. Because both my parents were sitting on the porch.

That afternoon, I'd told him that I'd told them. Seeing them, seeing how he stiffened in his seat, I grabbed his hand and held it tight. "Do you want to go?"

They stood up, came toward the car.

"No," he said, but he sounded like a man going to the guillotine.

Before he'd taken a step outside of the car, my mother had him in a hug. My father put a hand on his shoulder.

"We are so, so sorry for what happened," he said. "And *I* am so sorry for how I've treated you."

In the kitchen, over coffee, once most of the crying was over, my father said, "I want to call a meeting, of the school board. We spoke with a lawyer—strictly confidential, and without giving your name, Solomon—and she thinks that could be a good place to start. At the very least, that man should not be allowed to continue to coach or teach anyone. But before I move forward, I want to make sure: Are you okay with this? We want to be really careful not to do anything that might hurt or further traumatize you."

Solomon stared into his coffee cup. "Let me think about it?" he said, but I could hear the doubt in his voice. And the fear—the power Mr. Barrett still had over him. And my coffee turned to toxic sludge in my stomach.

I texted Sheffield: *Can I come over?*

Almost immediately, he wrote back: *My mom's got people over.* And then: *Meet up at the old movie theater?* I sent an *OK*.

Solomon and I looked out the window. A massive stingray flew high overhead, flapping her wings leisurely. A pair of storm giants lumbered past. Children ran by in monster masks. We watched them go. I wished I was one of them.

SIXTY-TWO

SOLOMON

"Here," Ash said.

The abandoned Darkside Cinema Palace really did blend in with its surroundings. The whole block had been painted blue. In that run-down district, a line of buildings with boarded-up windows and "Destroy All Monsters" graffiti was barely noticeable.

"You're sure," I said.

"Of course not."

In the distance we could see the bridge, lit up so bright it felt like a brand-new constellation. Twilight was bleeding into evening. Snowflakes began to patter down around us. I tied Maraud to a paddock a couple blocks away, and took a deep, deep breath. Ash and I walked forward hand in hand.

Children ran past us in giant papier-mâché masks: megalosaurs, gorillas, fish men. Unmasking Day street vendors sold them in plain white, and then you bought the paints so you could decorate them yourself.

A woman at a pushcart was steaming dumplings to sell; the air was rich with the doughy warm meat smell of them.

The building was busy, for being so obviously out of service. The wide front doors were propped open. People came and went. Posters out front promised "The Truth Will Be Revealed." Journalists stood on the steps and scribbled.

Ultramarine armbands were everywhere.

"Welcome," someone said to us, as we approached. She handed us each a flyer. "The Revelation is upon us. Thank you for being with us for this historic event."

I nodded. Ash sank deeper into her hood. We got through the front door, no problem, but I knew our luck would not last much longer. Security would be tighter, the closer we got to the Shield.

"Announcement is in less than an hour," someone said.

"What are we going to do?" I asked Ash. I'd tried to ask her a couple times, on the way over. I didn't think she was ignoring me. I think she was just as out of ideas as I was.

"This way to the assembly hall," someone else said,

and we followed the slow-moving crowd.

"We need to look around," Ash said. "See if we can find where they're keeping them."

"This is ridiculous," I said. "We have no weapons, and two magical abilities of extremely limited usefulness in a combat situation."

"Don't forget about my one move," she said, grabbing me by the wrist and elbow.

I rolled my eyes.

"The weird weather's getting weirder out there," Ms. Jackson said, on the radio in my pocket, and the sound of her voice was comforting. "Snow reported in some places. Thunder and lightning coming in from the west. Storm giants seen all over Darkside. Dress warm, everyone heading to Unmasking Day. Rely on body heat if you need to. Hold tight to one another. It's going to be a bumpy night."

SIXTY-THREE

ASH

"Snow reported in some places," Ms. Jackson said, from my car's speakers. "Thunder and lightning coming in from the west. Dress warm, everyone out trick-or-treating, or heading to the Halloween dance in Hudson tonight."

We still had an hour before I was supposed to meet with Sheffield. And two hours before his team was set to burn the whole town down.

Every time I slowed for a stop sign, I snuck a peek at Solomon. He seemed . . . fine. Normal. Sane. But there were always times between episodes when everything was fine. And times when he seemed fine, but was completely losing it on the inside.

I should have been planning. Figuring out what to

say to Sheffield. I had no photograph to lay in front of him. He himself hadn't done anything wrong. Not yet. His portrait wouldn't help me, when I got there. I could only use my words, and I didn't know what they would be.

So, yeah. I should have been scheming. But Solomon was beside me, wide-eyed and smiling, in a rare moment when he could maybe receive it if I said something he didn't want to hear.

And maybe it made me a bad person, but I realized—I would let Sheffield burn down everything I knew, if it meant saving Solomon.

"Hey," I said, faking nonchalance poorly. "Did I ever tell you I was on medication?"

"No," he said, and frowned. "For what?"

"For depression."

"Oh," he said. "I didn't realize it was so bad." He paused. "What kind of friend am I?"

"The best kind," I said. "It's just that I never want to talk about stuff like this with you."

"Why? Because I'm so much crazier than you?"

I didn't know how to answer.

He smiled. "Has it helped? The medicine?"

"A lot," I said. "I'm not cured. But I want to get out of bed in the morning. I feel like I can do things."

"Are you going to tell me I should take medication?"

I sighed. "I don't know, Solomon. Everybody's

different. But I think you need help, one way or another."

He frowned into his hands in his lap.

I said, "I used to think it would . . . change me. *Break me.* Turn me into someone else. A zombie, or something. But it's mostly just made me a lot less miserable. Just . . . think about it, okay?"

He grinned. "Is that an order, Princess?"

"Yes, my loyal subject."

"You know you saved my ass," he said. "By telling Child Protective Services where I was."

"How so?"

"They would have turned my case over to the cops by the end of that day, if they hadn't gotten information on my whereabouts. As far as the cops could tell, I didn't have an open CPS case when they arrested me. Otherwise they wouldn't have let me go so easily."

"How do you know all this?"

"I called them," Solomon said. "Spoke with a case worker."

"Are you serious? That's amazing!"

He shrugged, then nodded.

"Are you going to go in and talk to them?"

"Maybe," he said.

My phone rang. Somehow we'd ended up under the Rip Van Winkle Bridge. I pulled over to answer it.

"Ash," Connor said, and his voice had a hitch in it.

"Hey!" I said. "Everything okay?"

"No," he said. "Absolutely nothing is okay. I need your help. Can you come over to my house?"

I looked at Solomon. Watched the happy leak out of his face. My mouth would not make words.

"I'm getting my stuff," Connor said. "I bought a train ticket to Poughkeepsie, to stay with my aunt. But I don't want to go back to my house alone. I'm sorry. I really need your help, Ash."

"Of course," I said. "I'm on my way."

Overhead, the bridge was lit up so bright it felt like a brand-new constellation. Snowflakes began to patter down around us. I put the car in drive, and took a deep, deep breath.

SIXTY-FOUR

SOLOMON

We made a circuit of the theater, and found that security was far too tight for anything we might have tried. No dozing guard at the door to the backstage; no unattended uniforms we could suit up into and pretend we were a couple of the bad guys.

"I can try to destabilize them," I said, when we reached the last possible access point that could have gotten us behind the scenes—and found five armed men and women standing in front of it. "You could show me something horrific, and then when they're incapacitated by the emotions I project, we can rush in."

"Too risky. We have no idea if it will work," Ash said.

And still, somewhere behind one of those doors, up or down a staircase, Niv and Connor were being held.

"The only way out is through," Ash said, and headed into the theater, so swiftly all I could do was follow.

The seats had been removed. People were packed together—thousands of them, easily. At the front, before a massive movie screen, a bonfire blazed. A smaller version of the Great Fire that would be burning across town, at Darkside Park, at the official Unmasking Day celebration, with half of the city in attendance.

Bright light lit up the back of the screen: a loading bay door that opened onto the alley behind the theater. A good potential escape route . . . except getting to it would involve fighting through a crowd full of people who hated us.

A priest appeared beside the bonfire, and blew through a parasaurolophus crest, signaling the start of the Unmasking Day ritual. A cheer went through the crowd.

We threaded our way through the press of people. A wandering holy man in burgundy robes, with chalk and ash and pigment streaked across his face, handed us each a mask, and waved incense smoke at us, and talked us through the familiar prayers for filling the mask with the parts of our selves we did not love. Bad memories, bad attitudes, weaknesses and sins and anger. It all went into the mask, which would be thrown into the flames at the end of the ceremony and destroyed.

That was the theory, anyway. I didn't imagine my

own bad parts would be so easily burned away.

Ash and I put on our masks. Children ran past us, little make-believe monsters.

"We pray," said the holy man, and he led us in the Song of Burning.

And then the Shield appeared, and the crowd went wild. A sweet-faced old woman standing beside me had tears in her eyes, she was so happy. Nausea overtook me.

"Citizens of Darkside!" the Shield called. "Today is the day when we finally reveal the truth. The day we *all* take off our masks."

SIXTY-FIVE

ASH

Connor's street was full of children in masks. Little make-believe monsters. *There's a real monster on this street,* I wanted to shout.

But that wouldn't stop him. I had to trust that my mom and dad would be able to do something about Mr. Barrett. Stop him somehow. I had to hope.

I parked the car down the block, where Connor was waiting for us. Solomon waved to his stepbrother, through the windshield.

"I'm sorry," he said, when I unbuckled my seat belt. "I just can't."

"Don't be sorry," I said. "Every great escape needs a getaway driver."

"But I can't drive."

"Well, then, every great escape needs somebody to sit in the car and wait."

"You're stupid," Solomon said, grinning. "Just call me if things get scary, okay? I'll kick down the door if I have to. Punch his face off."

I didn't doubt that Solomon could do so. He was taller and stronger than Mr. Barrett. But in Solomon's mind the man would forever be the biggest, most frightening monster in a world that was full of them.

"Hey," Connor said, when I got out. And then he hugged me so hard I wanted to cry for him.

"Is he . . . ?"

"His car is in the driveway. Could be out for his afternoon run . . . could be taking a nap. So . . . we'll need to be superquiet just in case, I guess."

I took his hand, and we started walking. There were still forty-five minutes, before I was supposed to meet up with Sheffield. Provided we got in and out without incident or confrontation, that wouldn't be a problem.

Connor said, "I feel dumb, asking for your help."

"Don't be stupid."

"It's not that I think he'd hurt me. Although I guess I really have no idea what he is and isn't capable of, if I never . . ."

I didn't answer. Connor didn't need my advice, my wisdom. All he needed was someone to listen.

"I'm just afraid if I see him, I'll—I don't know, lose it."

"I get that," I said.

I could see the treehouse looming in the backyard. Early twilight; it held nothing but darkness inside.

We slipped into the house silently, and made our way upstairs. Connor went to work, sloppily stuffing shirts and pants into a duffel bag.

I stood in the hallway. Watched Mr. Barrett's bedroom door. Prayed it wouldn't open.

And then, it did.

And there he was. Struggling into his fancy clothes, for the Halloween dance. Bleary-eyed, like maybe he hadn't slept so well, but otherwise the same. Strong, broad, scary shoulders. Muscled arms. He could hurt us, if he wanted to.

"Ash," he said, and a shiver went through me. And nausea. And rage.

You broke him.

"What's the matter?" he said. "Why are you standing in the dark?"

The next breath would not come.

"Hey," he said, and reached out his hand, and touched my forearm—

And he wasn't trying to hurt me—he had no reason to, he had no idea how much I hated him—and my brain knew that, but my body—

Reacted. Tapped into something *(the other side)*, some

skill from somewhere else entirely *(the other Ash)*, and my arms moved fast as lightning, grabbing his wrist with one hand and his elbow with the other and *twisting*, bending his arm a way it should never go, bringing this big strong man to his knees with a yelp of pain and surprise.

"Hell of a move," he grunt-laughed.

"Don't fucking talk to me," I said. Whispering; praying Connor did not come out of his room.

Now he wince-laughed. "What happened, Ash?"

I didn't mean to say anything. I knew the smart thing was to get the hell out of there without risking a confrontation. Let the wheels of justice handle Mr. Barrett.

But part of me didn't trust those wheels. And even if anything came of my parents' attempts to hold him accountable, it would arrive in the form of legal papers, a phone call. Something that would give him plenty of time to put on a brave face, lie his way through it.

I wanted to see the fear flicker in his eyes.

"I know," I hissed. "What you did to Solomon."

"Solomon has a serious mental illness," he said, shaking his head in false sadness. "And you're not helping him if you indulge these persecution fantasies—"

"I saw you," I said. "The day I fell from your treehouse. I saw you *sexually assault* him."

His face went blank for just a fraction of a second. His eyes twitched. If any fear flickered there, it was only for a split second. And then—he laughed.

"And you've known all this time? Or, let me guess, you've suddenly regained your memories?" He laughed again, and I stopped myself from twisting his wrist and elbow and breaking his arm. "I don't doubt that *you* believe what you're saying. You're worried about your friend, and your brain has manufactured a narrative that—"

"It's not manufactured," I said. "And there will be a reckoning."

More laughter; more barely stifled urge to shatter his bones. "Oh, my dear. You have been watching too many movies. Nobody who knows me would ever believe whatever story you've concocted," he said. "And *everyone* in this town knows me."

I opened my mouth, but no words came. Nausea closed up my throat. I'd been an idiot, to believe I could break him with a weapon as flimsy as the truth. He had confidence, arrogance, a mighty armor made of toxic masculinity.

I felt sick; I felt helpless. I'd imagined I could destroy him, but I'd misjudged where his power came from. How deep his sickness ran.

He let me stand there, sputtering for something to

say. Enjoying the sight of how angry I was, how impotent.

And then, a door creaked open, behind me.

"Hey, Dad," Connor said.

Mr. Barrett's jaw dropped. This time, I saw the fear in his eyes. Real fear: raw and thick. I could smell it. The scent of guilt, of shame.

"You told him that we know," Connor said to me.

Mr. Barrett took a step forward. "Connor, you understand this is nonsense," he said, but I could hear his confidence deflating fast.

"You said no one would believe me," I interrupted his pleading. "But Connor does. Connor knows. Everything."

Mr. Barrett's eyes went wider than I'd ever seen them. His face tightened, then crumpled. I could see the struggle in his face over how to respond—to trivialize, to threaten, to humiliate, to beg. I saw him realize it would do no good. Connor *believed*.

His walls fell down. His armor melted away. All the metaphors failed him. Confidence, arrogance, toxic masculinity—none of it could shield him from the pain of having his son understand exactly what a monster he was.

Connor didn't say anything. He didn't need to. His eyes did all the talking, and what smoldered there was raw hate. Contempt. Revulsion. Mr. Barrett took a step back, as if physically feeling the force of his son's disgust.

Connor saw him for what he really was—and for the first time, so did Mr. Barrett. The mirror his son held up to him, the pure power of his loathing, showed Mr. Barrett the monster he'd spent so long pretending he wasn't. I could see it hit home. Saw his eyes fill up with tears.

"Who else?" Connor asked.

Mr. Barrett didn't budge, or speak. So much passed between their eyes in that instant. How the balance of power between father and son had been forever shifted. How Mr. Barrett's monstrous actions had cost him the most important thing in his life.

"Who else did you hurt like that?" Connor was shouting now.

"Sheffield?" I asked. "What you did to Solomon, did you do it to him too?"

Mr. Barrett stammered, "Connor, I—I—" But he was all out of words.

"You're a fucking monster," Connor said. He shouldered his duffel bag, and headed for the steps.

"Ash," Mr. Barrett said, his mouth slack, his face shattered.

It was what I'd prayed for. The unbreakable monster, broken. But whatever pride or victory or happiness I had hoped to feel was dwarfed by Connor's pain.

I followed him down the stairs, and out into the cool dark.

"Are you okay?" I asked, once we were a block away.

"Ash, I will *never* be okay." Connor waved to where Solomon sat on the hood of my car. "Let's go talk to Sheffield. See if we can stop some arson."

SIXTY-SIX

SOLOMON

Standing before the movie screen, the Shield continued to work the crowd. "Why do you think Queen Carmen refuses to help us?"

Shouts; inarticulate rage.

"Why does she sit back and hide, while othersiders abuse and exploit us? While they destroy our society, and harm our loved ones? Why does she refuse to stop them?"

People shouted back answers. Most of them were ugly.

"That is the truth I have come to reveal," he said.

Cheers. Pleas.

"I know you're here, Ash," the Shield said.

Ash and I exchanged glances, mask to mask. Frightened eye to frightened eye.

"You can't," I told her.

"I have to," she said.

I turned back to the stage. Watched the crowd. They were so worked up, so angry—they'd have torn us to shreds at the slightest word from the Shield.

"Come out, Princess. For too long, you have hidden your face from your people."

At a wave from the Shield, his people brought out two figures in chains.

"Niv," I whispered, recognizing him first, and then, "Connor."

He was so little. And so scared. His clothes were filthy.

"Come out, Ash, or I will break these two in front of everyone."

"You'll come with me," Ash said, grabbing my hand again. "Okay? We'll try your idea—I'll trigger something in you, something that will incapacitate them, and we'll get Niv and Connor and get the hell out of here."

"Okay," I said, feeling extremely not okay. There would be no getting the hell out of there. Not alive. Not with so many angry people all around us.

I felt her hands grow sweaty. So did mine. We started walking toward the front of the big hall.

The crowd slowed us down, and by the time we got halfway there it had become impenetrable.

Ash took off her mask, carried it under her arm.

Someone gasped. No one else seemed to notice.

"Make way for your princess," I said loudly.

The gasps spread. People turned, stared, cried out. Some shook fists. Some dropped to their knees.

I heard the rumor ripple through the crowd, watched a path open up for us. I heard the click of camera shutters, and wondered where mine was. When had I lost it, in the whole wild ride of the past couple of days?

A big guy stepped into our path. Tears in his eyes.

"No. I can't let you do it, Princess," he said.

"Step aside, brother," she said, and touched his arm. And then she winked, and smiled. And he nodded. Stepped aside.

I watched it happen, how effortlessly she won over the crowd. Her fearlessness impressed even these people who a moment before had been perfectly okay with tearing down her mother's government.

Courage does that. It transforms people. With a shiver, I realized: *It takes a very special kind of crazy to change the world.*

The Shield saw the change happen too. I could see him growing more furious, the closer we got to the front of the park.

"Seize her," he said.

Connor saw me. He called out my name. Niv looked barely conscious.

A pair of Destroyers took hold of Ash, and I tried to fight, but three of them were on me and they wrestled me to the ground. My face was pressed into the filthy scuffed carpet, and I could barely see the scene as it unfolded. As they forced Ash to her knees. Turned her around so her back was to the Shield, her face out to the crowd.

"No!" I cried.

She was going to be broken. Maybe murdered. They all were.

I had to do something. I shut my eyes, reached out for the Shield. Took hold of my anger, my fear. Tried to magnify it. I fumbled with the rush of my emotions, sprayed hatred in his general direction, felt a few drops of it land, a stream, a trickle, strengthening, connecting . . . I saw his twisted smile widen—

But no. Hate was what had gotten us into this problem. Hate had only made him stronger, meaner, more dangerous.

"Now I will reveal the truth," the Shield said, and took a gun from his nearest soldier's hand. I looked around the inside of my mind for a weapon, and found it.

Of course.

I had to dig deep. Burrow down into myself, as far as I could.

Fear was obvious.

Rage was easy.

But love . . . love was hard.

What did I love? I loved Ash. I loved Radha, and
Connor. I loved Maraud. I loved Cass, and the *Clarion*. I
loved my city, and the way the sunset lit the riversea up,
and the taste of roasted chestnuts from the street vendors in Raptor Heights. I loved Niv, in a very weird and
conflicted kind of way.

Fear and anger felt so strong, I'd come to rely on
them. So I'd never noticed before how full of love I was.
How it filled up my spine with a shivering so strong it
made my whole body shake.

It was him, I knew it. The Solomon on the other
side. The one who had been hurt so badly but was still
so full of love. I felt it leaking into me. I let it fill me up.

"The Refugee Princess is a monster," the Shield
shouted, and took the safety off his gun. Pressed it to
the back of her head. Screams resounded through the
crowd. So did cheers. Ash's face was fearless, defiant.

Love. I focused on that, and not the horror before
me. Love filled me up, and overflowed. My spine was
electric, alive, a conduit for lightning. It had always been
there; I'd just been too blind to see it. Too focused on my
anger, and my fear. My teeth chattered with the surging
energy in my backbone. It poured through my bones,
down my arms, out my fingertips. I felt the feeling leak

into the soldiers who held me; felt their grips weaken. And I saw it reach the Shield. Saw his smile tighten, vanish. His mouth opened in a silent cry. Tears began to flow down his face. He shut his eyes, and accepted it. Embraced it. For just a split second.

He smiled. Had he felt love at all, in the years since the Night of Red Diamonds took his mother away from him? But he felt it now. And he let himself feel it.

Time slowed down, for me and him. That's the only explanation I can come up with. Because I watched everything unfold with crystal, perfect clarity, even though so many things were happening at once that there's no way a normal human mind could have observed them all.

Beyond the reach of my aura of projected love, the Shield's soldiers had raised their guns. They saw how he and I were locked in a trance together; they thought—correctly—that I was enchanting him; they were ready to kill me to save their leader. Ash's eyes were on me, wide with terror. Convinced she was about to watch me die.

All hell had broken loose in the crowd, and people had run screaming from the spray of gunfire they believed to be imminent.

But the men with guns had stopped. Frozen. Their fingers hovered in midair, millimeters from the triggers.

The ground trembled. Trembled again. In that moment a roar split the air. Like an elephant's trumpet and a tiger's snarl, tapering off into a wolf's howl. A shriek not of anger but of power, of confidence. An animal who was not afraid of anything on Earth.

People screamed. Pointed. The Shield stood motionless, his head turned in the direction of the roar. All his anger and rage and violence held back for a few slim seconds by the love that bound me to him.

The Earth shook. Like distant thunderclaps, one after another—*boom! Boom! Boom! Boom!* It shook the teeth in my gums. There was a sound of ripping.

Time sped back up.

A white blur tore through the old movie screen with one clawed foot. Something massive. Something with eyes like storms and teeth like nightmares. Something most citizens of Darkside spent their whole lives praying to get a glimpse of. It stomped through the rip and roared again.

Queen Carmen's white Tyrannosaurus rex.

I thought, *It worked, Ash. You did it. You reached her.*

Soldiers and peasants and prosperous merchants all fell to their knees and pressed their foreheads to the ground. Like thousands of dominoes falling in quick succession. The tyrannosaur stood fifty feet from me, and I realized—she wasn't albino at all. She did have pigment: a marbling of purple along her spine, fractal spirals tapering down her sides. Queen Carmen looked unstoppable in the saddle.

Inches from where my hands were pressed against the ground, a foot as wide as a tree trunk smashed into the floor. The tyrannosaur came to a stop, tail whipping around for balance. All the men and women with guns ran away screaming.

Only the Shield and Ash and Connor and Niv and I remained, frozen in place, and only for an instant more. Fear and awe overwhelmed me, at the presence of this magnificent monster. Fear and awe crowded out every other emotion, including love. Released from my crippling bond, the Shield turned to flee.

Of course he did not get far. Effortlessly, without even moving her body, the tyrannosaur lowered her muscular neck and opened wide her terrible mouth and picked him up with her terrible teeth. She tossed him up into the air, a cat playing with a mouse, and caught him in her jaws. And bit down once, hard, snuffing him out.

With a lightning-fast whipcrack motion, she jerked her head around and flung the body into the bonfire. And roared. A long and earsplitting sound every citizen who was there that day will hear in dreams for the rest of their lives. Will tell their grandchildren about. The sound of power, of ferocity. Of a mother protecting her baby. Of order and balance restored.

SIXTY-SEVEN

ASH

We were late.

I broke laws, getting there. Driving through yellow lights that were really already red. Speeding. Praying Sheffield would still be waiting. That he hadn't gone to strike a match and set the school, the woods—and likely half the town—ablaze.

"Calm down," Connor said, uncomfortable with my very minor transgressions.

"You texted him?"

"He hasn't responded."

"It doesn't matter," Solomon said. "Whether he's there or not. He'll have someone else start the fire for him."

Neither Connor nor I had anything to say to that,

because it was probably true.

He was still there, when we got to the empty movie theater parking lot. Sitting in his car with the door open, listening to music.

"What can I do for you three fine upstanding citizens?" he asked, when we got out and walked up to him, and I could tell by the hostility in his face that he knew. What we were up to. The conversations we'd had with his teammates. The photos we'd showed them.

"Call it off," Connor said. "The fire."

"Whatever do you mean?" he said.

Solomon muttered something under his breath, and wandered away.

"You know what we mean," I said.

Sheffield's smug smile started the shivering up in my spine. It triggered rage, but something else.

Vision.

I could see things. The pain under Sheffield's bravado. Big and jagged, like a spider made of black broken glass.

It was her, I knew. The Ash on the other side. Her magic. Leaking into me.

I could see the future. Sheffield's future. He'd go to an Ivy League school; enter the corporate world and keep on manipulating people into doing terrible things for him. He'd become one of the wicked men who run the world.

Like Mr. Barrett.

But I could see another future. A different one. Where he broke the cycle, confronted it, and grew from it, and moved on. Where he made the world better, instead of worse. Where he acted out of love instead of hurt and manipulation.

"I know what he did to you," I said.

"What who—"

"Mr. Barrett," I said.

Sheffield's eyes went wide. He looked from me to Connor and back again. Took a step back.

"No," he whispered. "I don't know what you're—"

"We know, Sheffield."

But I hadn't known. Not really. I'd taken a shot in the dark, praying I was wrong. If Connor was as surprised as me, he hid it way better.

"How—?" he whispered. Even in the dim light we could see his face redden. Darken.

Connor and I stood there, not saying anything. There was nothing we could have said.

Tears came, fast and copious. He tried to say something, but what came out weren't words.

"Please," he said eventually. "He told me no one could know. Please don't tell anyone."

I said, "That's not what this is about."

Confusion filled his eyes, along with all that pain.

Mr. Barrett was what he was. A monster, past saving.

Sheffield was still becoming.

"You're better than him," I said. "You can still choose. You can decide not to hurt people."

"I—" But then Sheffield gasped. As if startled by the sight of something. Connor and I turned around, to look in the direction he was facing.

All Connor saw was an empty parking lot, with Solomon strolling through it. But what I saw was Solomon leading his big mauve allosaurus along, throwing sticks for her to go fetch.

I saw Maraud, and Sheffield saw her too. I know he did.

His hand flew to his mouth.

"Oh god!" he cried. Between sobs, he choked out, "What the fuck is that? What did you do to me?"

"Nothing," Connor said, but that wasn't true.

We'd snapped something. Broken through the barriers he hadn't finished building.

As we grow up, we forge armor for ourselves. Defenses, against the reality of monsters and fantasy. In his shame, Sheffield's had given way. He could see all the horror and wonder that the world truly held.

The allosaurus turned in his direction. Their eyes locked. Then she looked away, utterly uninterested in him or his fear.

Connor walked toward him, and Sheffield staggered backward.

"Shhh," Connor said, and opened his arms. He folded Sheffield into an awkward embrace.

They stood that way a long time. Stiff limbs settling, relaxing. Talking in low voices. I couldn't hear what they said, and didn't want to. I imagined a whole secret language guys use, when they're alone together and in pain.

Finally Sheffield nodded, at something Connor said, and took out his phone. Sent a quick text. There was a big wet smear on his sleeve, where he'd been wiping his face.

And just like that, it was over.

"I gotta go," he said, and we let him. He walked backward, all the way to his car. Never taking his eyes off the dinosaur. After he was gone we stood around, barely talking. Solomon sauntered over, allosaurus and all.

"Let me drive you to Poughkeepsie," I said to Connor. "I'm way cooler than the train."

He nodded. "I kind of want to go to the dance. Just to stick my head in. Is that crazy?"

I was about to conjure up an excuse, for Solomon's sake—Mr. Barrett would probably be there—when my best friend shocked me by putting his hand on his little brother's shoulder.

"Of course," Solomon said to Connor.

A vast night sky stretched above the high school parking lot. Stars shivered, feeling so far away that they might as well have not been real. The scene outside was alive, electric. I took photos. No monsters, no darkness. I could control what I saw through my lens now.

Outside the lens was a different story. A unicorn sharpened her horn against a wall. A gaggle of six-inch-tall goblin boys catcalled a very fit eight-foot-tall golem boy, whose cheeks blushed red clay.

Inside, the sound of the crowd sucked me and Connor up. It made him smile, to be among the people he loved, and that made me smile. Mr. Barrett never showed.

I looked from football player to football player, compared their faces to the photographs I'd taken of them. And how they'd looked when I confronted them. The goofy or sullen or happy or sad human beings that they were.

At the end of the day, a photo says very little. Even the most brilliant images in photographic history could only say, *This happened. This person existed. This incident occurred. This thing was once real.*

That's the Truth. The thing I learned from the other Ash.

Seeing the future doesn't mean anything. We have so many futures. The one we end up with depends on who we are. What we *do*.

I stood up. My fingers tingled. The final pieces of my project clicked into place.

Photographs were not enough. Photographs could

only go so far, say so much. Who we are is bigger than what can be captured in an image of us.

Later, I drove fast, all the way to Poughkeepsie, even though I knew that I was cutting short the little time Connor and Solomon and I had together. I drove even faster on the way back. In spite of my vision being blurred by my tears.

I had writing to do.

Things happened fast.

I wrote an essay to accompany my project, and built a website for it. I ran it by Cass, who edited my sentences and challenged me to go deeper in what I wrote. About the photography, she had nothing to suggest. Just nodded a lot, flipping through the prints, lips pressed tightly together in a very slight smile. One that carried pride, and happiness, and something else—something I had seen in myself and never imagined I could inspire in another person: the complex pleasure of artistic experience, the telltale tingle down the spine. When she handed them back to me, she said only: "You did it, Ash."

I wrote:

Football players. I hate them, and I'm scared of them.

They are big, they are strong, they are powerful.

I see them coming down the high school hallway and

*I flinch. Every letterman jacket and team-color cap
makes me think of date rape, gay bashing, drunk driving. Every bad thing society expects a boy to be, they
become.*

That's how it seemed to me, anyway.

*But I knew that wasn't the truth. Not the whole
truth, anyway. Because they are people, whatever else
they might be. I embarked on this photo essay because I
wanted to understand. . . .*

Under each image, I wrote a short paragraph.

I published it on a Tuesday, and I tagged a bunch of
my favorite photographers and photography blogs into
the posts I did on social media. I slid into the direct
messages of editors and influencers, asking them to take
a look at what I had done. What I had made.

Some people liked it. It got some retweets. Not a
ton. By the end of the day I was ready to accept that I
would not be going viral, blowing up. I was fine with
that. That had never been my goal.

*We live in a small town. Everybody is up in every-
body else's business. When I started photographing
these boys, I already knew things about all of them.
Good things—who volunteered at the local mosque,
who had stood up to a racist bully in seventh grade—
and bad things. Who had hit a friend of mine, when*

they were dating. Who told offensive jokes, because he liked to see people squirm.

But I didn't do this because I wanted to tell anyone's secrets. I did it because I wanted to find a deeper truth, about who they are. A truth with a capital T.

I wanted to understand them. I wanted to be less scared, of the things they do. The crimes people commit. The way we participate in their misdeeds by turning a blind eye. And I wanted to hold them accountable for the damage that they do.

I'd been writing about them, but I'd also been writing about Mr. Barrett. About how we're all complicit in their crimes. How we give up our power. Turn a blind eye. Decide not to fight back against the monsters in our world, because they seem too powerful to destroy.

I didn't write about the Induction Ceremonies. I didn't include a photograph of Sheffield. That wasn't what the project was about.

I wrote:

These boys aren't monsters.

I wrote:

I'm still scared. But maybe a little less so.

Six days later I got a call from the California Institute of the Arts—which, nbd, is only the number three top-ranked photography school in the country. They said they had seen my project. They wanted to know where I was going to college. They wanted me to apply.

I called up Cass immediately afterward. And asked, "You wouldn't happen to know anyone from the California Institute of the Arts, would you?"

I heard her suck in cigarette smoke. "I know lots of people in lots of places."

"You didn't maybe make a call to one of them? Send them a link to my site?"

I heard her blow out smoke. "You made something great, Ash. That's your gift, as an artist. My gift as an artist is the ability to make sure that people who make something great can get recognized for it. And get the support they need, to keep on making great things."

I had so much to say, but all I managed was "Thanks, Cass."

My spine shook, with a thousand magnificent, possible futures.

SIXTY-EIGHT

SOLOMON

A pair of dire wolves waited patiently at the entrance to the Queen Ananka the Second Hospital Recovery Pavilion, as big as horses and just as uninterested in anything the humans around them were doing.

"Ma'am!" someone called, hurrying behind us.

I'd been about to take a picture of the dire wolves, but Cass snapped her fingers at me to keep me moving.

"Ma'am, you can't be back here!" said a nurse, when he finally caught up with us. For all her years, my boss could move pretty fast.

"Nonsense," Cass said, not slowing down.

"Ma'am, I'm going to have to call sec—"

"But we're visiting our friend," she said, stopping in front of a shallow pool marked "Physical Therapy," where a young man sat with no shirt on. "Aren't we?"

"Um," Niv said, so startled to see her that he didn't know what to say, and didn't see me at all. "Yes?" Because who ever said no to Cass?

"You see," Cass said, and turned to watch the penitent nurse until he scurried away.

"Solomon!" Niv said, and stood up. Water poured off him, and he winced.

"Oh, Niv," I said, seeing the bruises that covered his body.

"Sit back down," said the young woman healer at the side of the circular pool.

Niv sighed gratefully, as he slid back into the warm water. It flowed against gravity, following the healer's skilled fingers. Glowing slightly, where it came into contact with his wounds.

"Don't be scared," Cass called, to the hallway where Radha and Connor had been hiding from the stern nurse standing guard. Radha came in cautiously, but Connor ran right for the pool and cannonballed in fully clothed, then hugged Niv so hard that the poor man screamed.

He'd been beaten pretty badly by his captors. Three bones broken. Stitches required. Dehydration; malnutrition. Psychological scars as yet unassessed. But he'd kept Connor safe from the worst of it.

"What are you all doing here?" Niv asked, reaching out his hand. I took it, and sat down on the cold tile.

Connor splashed me, and I splashed him back.

"This is a huge story," Cass said. "The boy who risked everything to save his princess? Who learned of a plot against her and hid her away, incurring a charge of treason and becoming Darkside's Most Wanted for several days? You're a star, Niv. For at least a couple more days, until some other story rises to the top of the news cycle."

"Oookay." He looked adorable when he blushed. "You're not going to take photographs of me with no clothes on, are you?"

"Not right now," I said.

Niv smiled, and it was like nothing in the world was wrong. When he smiled, I didn't see all the bruises and blotches across the light brown skin of his face. He was so beautiful.

"I'm so sorry this happened."

He squeezed my hand. "What, this? Doesn't hurt a bit." He laughed, and the laugh became a cough.

"Are you two almost done?" Cass asked, picking up a copy of the *Post* that had been lying around. "We have *actual* questions for you, Niv."

"Give us a second, will ya?" I said, and Cass laughed, raising the paper to give us some privacy. Clucking her tongue at the poor quality of their writing.

The photos were good, though.

The crowd surging forward to throw their masks

into the bonfire, burning away their sins and crimes along with the body of the Shield. A flock of people kneeling before their queen, as tightly packed as the petals of a chrysanthemum. Queen Carmen's enigmatic smile. Ash's quiet regal grace. Laughing faces, with a white tyrannosaur towering over them. A single anonymous figure, seen from the back, tossing an ultramarine armband into the flames.

The queen's words, spoken to the crowd. Revealing the truth the Shield had promised:

For too long, I have kept my daughter's truth a secret. The fact is, she's an othersider, and that is nothing to be ashamed of. We've let hate and fear control our city for far too long. The time is past, when othersiders must keep themselves secret.

I leaned forward, rested my head on his knee. He stroked my hair gently.

"I hear it's rough out there," he said. "Street fights."

"It's bad," I said. "But things are already starting to change for the better."

And they would continue, with Ash set to begin her formal training—in diplomacy, the intricacies of how city government functioned, in martial arts, in how to master her ability. Whatever Queen Carmen couldn't or wouldn't do, Ash would eventually accomplish. I was confident of that.

Niv shut his eyes. He looked exhausted. He needed rest. His body was working overtime. Connor mirrored his actions, his hero worship so obvious it made me grin.

"I should go," I said.

"Ash wants you on her security detail with me," he said, eyes still closed. "I want you there too."

"That sounds wonderful, but I already have a job. Staff photographer for the *Clarion*."

Niv laughed. "Yeah, I figured. But I had to try, right?" He opened his eyes. Looked straight into mine. "Where are we going to go for our first date, Solomon?"

Now it was my turn to laugh. "Good question," I said. "Let's think about it. We have a while to figure it out. You'll be stuck in this tub for more than a minute."

"I always wanted to ride on your allosaurus," he said.

"Don't be inappropriate," I said.

"I didn't mean it like—" Then he splashed water at me. Then I kissed him on the forehead. Then I kissed him on the lips.

"Shall we begin?" Cass asked, uncapping a pen.

SIXTY-NINE

ASH

The last time I ever saw Solomon in the flesh was a month after I posted my photo project online.

I found him down by the river. For a week I'd been looking for him, in a haphazard and unstructured kind of way. Stopping by the train tracks or looking under the Rip Van Winkle Bridge whenever I could. I'd been too busy to mount a proper search—my application to the California Institute of the Arts; fielding anger and appreciation from the football players, some of whom were loving and some of whom were hating the fact that tons of people online had seen and commented on their faces.

Solomon sat on the rocks, his guitar on his lap. Winter was well on its way by then. He wore a lot of layers.

"Hey, mister," I said.

"Ash," he said. He smiled, but he looked sad.

I hugged him, and he pressed his face into my neck. "You doing okay?"

He shrugged. So, no.

I'd meant to tell him the latest about Mr. Barrett. That my father had succeeded in convening a meeting of the school board, to talk about getting him dismissed. That he'd already spoken with two people on the board, friends of his, and convinced them of the truth of what he was saying. So he wasn't going in there alone. So something might happen.

But also, nothing might happen. Mr. Barrett had a lot of friends. He could brush it off, deny the allegations, bring a suit against my father for slander. We could be the ones whose lives got ruined.

I didn't say any of that. I sat down on the rocks beside him and grabbed his arm in both hands and squeezed.

"Thanks, Ash. Some days are better than others."

"You're still seeing the therapist they assigned over at CPS?"

"Yeah. She's nice. I don't think she really gets me, but she doesn't put up with any of my bullshit and I appreciate that."

"That's amazing."

We were in touch, sometimes. Messages, voice mails. Whenever his phone was on and charged, which wasn't often. I knew he was trying his hardest to get help. Some days he was more successful than others.

Solomon looked at his mittened hands. "I just . . . will I always feel like this?"

"No," I said. "You absolutely won't."

"Lots of survivors of sexual assault spend their whole lives dealing with the aftermath."

"That doesn't mean you'll always be . . . whatever you're feeling now."

Solomon shrugged.

"Look at you and Sheffield. Mr. Barrett hurt you both, but look how differently you responded to it. He started hurting others. You didn't. And he was able to choose to stop. We are not our trauma. We are not our brain chemistry. That's part of who we are, but we're so much more than that."

Six weeks later Solomon turned eighteen, and then he left town. I could see it, then, even though it hadn't happened yet. Who knows how. A vision of the future; a gift from the Ash on the other side. He would leave. Forever.

"I mean, look at Helen Keller," I said, feeling like my throat was starting to close up. "Everyone just assumed that with all her challenges, she'd never do anything with her life. Even the people who loved her just wanted to keep her in the house like a shameful secret. But she got the help she needed, to figure out how to live and thrive with her disabilities."

"Don't you use Helen Keller against me," he said, his face opening up into a big beautiful grin.

"I read that book you gave me," I said. "Her autobiography."

"Amazing, right?"

"So amazing." Tears sprang to my eyes, as much from the memory of Helen's story as from the realization that was settling into my stomach. That I was losing my best friend in the world. "She died knowing she hadn't accomplished everything she wanted to accomplish, making all the changes she wanted to make in the world. But she died happy, because she knew she did everything in her power to make those things happen."

For a while I would get messages from him, on social media platforms. For a while he would send postcards—from Montana, from Saskatchewan.

Then he wouldn't.

Sitting there, watching the sun slip away, I could feel the loss of him even though he wasn't yet lost. I couldn't control what I saw. I got the outline, but not the details. Did he become a hugely successful rock star? Did he find a boy he loved, who loved him back, and then build an incredible life together? Solomon strummed a chord, which came out muffled with his mittens on.

I'd been reading a lot, about people with severe

mental illnesses. Their memoirs, their essays. Books and articles by the people who loved them. I knew what weird, twisted paths their lives took. How often they ended up in jail, or dead in a ditch after a knife fight, or a cabin in the woods with no contact at all with the outside world.

But those weren't the only stories. People got treatment, found jobs, built families. Created great art. Made the world a better place.

His life would be full of pain, but also beauty and love. So would mine. So was everyone's.

Solomon could be happy, in a life I couldn't imagine. One where I played no part, not because he didn't love me, but because life would take us down two different roads.

He would be okay. So would I.

He held his guitar closer. Strummed three chords. A shiver went through me. The telltale tingle.

"Play me a song," I said.

He smiled, and started to play. I shut my eyes and saw, as clearly as when I looked through the lens, the story he was telling. Great clouds and bubbles and spreading ink stains of emotion. The eerie power of what he was making, and how his emotions could transfer to me. How he could make me feel what he felt. Music was magic, and he summoned it up from somewhere *(the other side)* I could not imagine.

"You're going to do great things," I said.

"So will you," he said. "You fucking lunatic. I pity the fools you go up against."

At the exact same time, we both said, "It takes a certain kind of crazy to change the world." Then we laughed together. Then we fell silent.

A long serpentine neck rose up out of the water, capped with the beautiful, terrifying head of a water dragon. Blue metal scales glistened in the weak winter sunlight.

"Pretty," Solomon said, pointing.

"It really is," I said.

What a gift that sight was. Solomon had taught me how to see a whole other world, but it had nothing to do with our trauma or our brain chemistry. The things he felt—he could make other people feel them too. That was his gift. His magic. It would serve him well in his life as a musician. As an artist. Like me.

I still got glimpses of her, that other Ash. Sometimes she showed me things. Futures, that might or might not be mine. Sometimes she told me things, when I was on the border between waking life and dreams.

We're all a little bit magic.

The world tries very hard to break us.

Sometimes it succeeds.

We can be broken and still survive.

"This place gets the best sunsets," I said, pointing

across the river. The sky above the Catskill Mountains was painted in broad, messy strokes of mauve and orange and blue gray.

"It does," he said, and reached out his hand. I took it, and I held it. High overhead, the lights of the bridge came on. Ms. Jackson spoke softly through the open windows of my car. She played old songs we loved. New ones we hated, and would one day discover to our great surprise that we loved.

"It's okay," I said, and it was not a lie. "We're okay."

Solomon nodded.

I wanted certainty. Clarity. The belief that everything would be fine. That we'd be strong enough to survive whatever the future hit us with.

But I knew I couldn't have any of those things. I knew nothing in life was promised. Nothing was truly ours. Everything would be taken from us. All we really ever have is the moment we are in—and in that moment, we had each other.

SEVENTY

SOLOMON

A month passed, before I could see Ash again. She was busy, of course. Meetings and trainings and lessons and long-delayed quality time with her mother. Which was mostly spent arguing, according to the stories Niv was not supposed to be telling me.

High overhead, the lights of the bridge came on. Ash sat beside the riversea. Soldiers on ankylosauruses were stationed all around her, and they tried to block me and Maraud when we rode up, but Ash barked "Let them through" and the line parted for us.

They had put me on her schedule between meditation time and history reading. She'd missed out on all her basic education from the age of twelve on, so there was a lot of general stuff to catch up on—at the same time as she was learning the very specific family business.

The meditation was supposed to help her control her ability. Give her the kind of clarity and insight to see what she needed to see. And to tune out all the stressful stuff that cluttered her royal mind.

It didn't seem to be working.

She opened her eyes when I climbed down from Maraud, and frowned. "I hate meditation," she said.

"I hate broccoli," I said. "But I've got to eat it."

"I missed you," she said, standing up. The hug I got was intense. "I'm sorry I haven't been able to see you sooner."

"How have you been?" I looked into her eyes when I asked, but she looked away.

"It's so much, Solomon. I thought I understood, before, how complex this city was. How hard my mother's work is. But what I knew—what the public knows—that's just the tip of the iceberg. Our intelligence reports stuff to us every day that would make you cry. Or scream. Or run away to live in a cabin somewhere superfar from the nearest human being."

"We're the worst," I said.

"For real."

I took pictures. One where Ash was looking off into the distance. One where she was picking absentmindedly at a scuffed spot on the regal black sweater/cape/

robe/gown that she wore. One where she was stroking Maraud's neck. One where she was smiling at me, rolling her eyes.

"Speaking of complex," I said. "What's going to happen to Commissioner Bahrr?"

"I don't know," Ash said. "And even if I did, you know I can't tell someone who works for a newspaper."

"I'd keep the secret," I said, but I sensed that this was a distraction. Getting me to take it personally, so I wouldn't pursue the conversation about the police commissioner. She was clearly learning a lot in her training.

"He should be in jail," I said.

"Not my call to make," Ash said. "But my mother knows everything now. She'll be keeping him on a much tighter chain from now on."

"I hope that's true," I said.

"I'm not happy, Solomon. I thought I would be."

"I know," I said, and reached for her, but she had turned away.

"I thought it would be easy to fix things. I thought all I had to do was be brave and be strong and smart and do the right thing. . . ."

"Me too," I said.

Maraud screeched, and dove into the water. Came up a few seconds later with a jeweled eel in her jaws, spewing rubies.

I could see it in Ash's face. Her light was dimmed.

She'd been damaged by her experience, and she might not ever heal.

"I'll help you," I said. "I don't know how much help I can be, but I'll do whatever I can. And there's a lot of other people who will help too."

She smiled. Then her eyes narrowed, looking at me, and the smile went away from her face.

"What?" I said, laughing. "What did you see?"

"Nothing," she said, and turned away. So I knew it was something.

"Something about me?" I asked.

"About us," she said.

"I don't want to know," I told her.

"Good," she said. "It's stupid."

"This place gets the best sunsets," I said, pointing out over the riversea. The sky was painted in broad messy strokes of mauve and orange and blue gray. Ms. Jackson spoke softly from the radio around Maraud's neck. New things to be afraid of, and to feel hopeful about.

"It does," Ash said, and reached out her hand. I took it, and I held it.

I wanted certainty. Clarity. The belief that everything would be fine. That we'd be strong enough to survive whatever the future hit us with.

But life doesn't give us those things. Anything could happen. New threats, sudden sicknesses, a slow change into someone new and different. Violent political uprisings. Irreconcilable interpersonal differences. *Kaiju* accidentally stomping half the city.

"We can do this," I said.

Ash smiled, and then she said, "We can do this."

Nothing is promised. Nothing is truly ours. All we ever really have is the moment we're in—and in that moment, we had each other.

ACKNOWLEDGMENTS

This book goes out to all the kids like me who had the normal trauma of high school made way worse by mental illness, who didn't know how to get help or were afraid of what that would mean. You are magnificent. No matter what the world might say is wrong with you, know that you can and will have an incredible life full of joy and wonder and love and pain, just like everyone else.

Destroy All Monsters owes an awful lot to:

My magnificent agent, Seth Fishman, who always knows exactly when and how to calm me down or hype me up or set me straight.

My genius editor, Kristen Pettit, whose sense for story and voice and humor and the most efficient way to break hearts is unfailing.

Sensitivity reader Jen Larsen, whose wisdom and insight dramatically improved this narrative. Writers, take heed: Sensitivity readers make everyone better. Even when we're writing #ownvoices fiction rooted in our own experiences, that's still our own experience. Everyone is different, and getting other perspectives will only make your story stronger.

Bradley Silver of White Rabbit Tattoo, who put a big beautiful allosaurus on my body to celebrate this book. Amber Kline, for vital insights and amazing stories and a lifetime of so much laughter.

The Get Along G'Aang—Juancy Rodriguez, Kathy Rodriguez, Kalyani-Aindri Sanchez, and Patricia Thomas—the bestest group chat on earth, bringing me so much laughter on the days when we need it most. My best friend, Walead Esmail-Rath, and Erica, and Lola Bee; bright lights in a dark world. My extended family at Picture the Homeless: hundreds of incredible humans, including Jean Rice, Nikita Price, Mo George, Francine Walker, Arvernetta Henry, Darlene Bryant, Rogers, Chyna, Doc, DeBorah Dickerson, Tyletha Samuels, Darlene Bryant . . . and of course Lynn Lewis. Y'all's power and pride give me hope that even when we're fighting monsters as big and scary as capitalism and racism, we can still destroy them all.

My family—Deborah Miller, Sarah Talent, Hudson Michael Talent, Eric Talent, Flavia Aleida Castillo, Jose

Rodriguez, Tia Yani, Mama Tola, Maria Alejandra and Maria Fernanda, Bready & Dabriel & Carla & Zaiel and the Blackwells—Emilia & Michael & Leilani & Marie . . . and my husband, Juancy Rodriguez, the guiding light behind all the good parts. Only the mistakes have been mine.

In the process of promoting and touring for *The Art of Starving*, I was grateful to count on the support and hustle (and air mattresses) of Blair Overstreet, Matt Dunn, James Tracy, Juliette Torrez, Jessica Hilt, Esther Wang, Jonathan Fortin, and Michelle Matos.

I'm just generally a hardcore fanboy, and this book is shaped by some of my deepest passions. I had my mind blown by Sam Kieth's *The Maxx* in its incarnation as an MTV animated series, and there's a lot of its DNA in this strange hybrid creation. Pretty much everything I create has been influenced by my profound love for the *Avatar: The Last Airbender* universe, but *Destroy All Monsters* owes a particular debt to season one of *Legend of Korra*. Ash's gift is partially an homage to the character of Cass Neary in Elizabeth Hand's masterful *Generation Loss*, which is why there's a character named after her here. My love for Jewelle Gomez's *The Gilda Stories* also inspired a character name. If you like this book, and don't know those things, I hope you'll check them out. They're all way better.